J.A. w .S.

The Journey,
The Approach,
The Work
to Success

JOSHUA   ALBERT   WALTER
EDWARDS   THOMPKINS   BARRETT

DEDICATION

I dedicate this book to my friend and inspiration, the Holy Spirit. My Family, my TCI Church Family, my Real Estate Family and all the people who have encourage the greatness in me.
-**J**oshua Edwards

To Albert 5th and Naomi, may the guiding principles within these pages illuminate your paths as brightly as you illuminate my life.
-**A**lbert Thompkins

Dedicated to all those who have impacted my life in some way, whether positively, or negatively. You shaped who I am, and propelled me to chase after success.
–**W**alter Barrett

CONTENTS

ACKNOWLEDGMENTS

I would like to honor the Holy Spirit. He has preserved me and encourages me to keep going and to keep living. His love is everything to me.

I acknowledge my Wife Elvetta and our sons Josiah and Lemuel. I thank God for them and their love for me.

I thank God for Apostle Gladstone Hazel who in my time of distress check in with me and encourage me spiritually.

-Joshua Edwards

PREFACE

Welcome to J.A.W.S. Not the movie, but the movement. J.A.W.S. is not some large, oversized, dangerous predator in the ocean that attacks boats and swimmers, but rather, a massive, living, moving body of thoughts, ideas, principles, and concepts that attacks stagnancy, mediocrity, and status quos.

J.A.W.S. is, in actuality, an acronym that was first formed during the time of our joint book launch. On March 28th, 2019, Joshua Edwards, Albert Thompkins, and Walter Barrett, three male friends who were united in their passion for writing, public speaking, and transforming lives, came together to plan the greatest book launch that the Virgin Islands had ever seen. Dubbed 'The Three-Man Book Launch,' the event was meant to be an introduction of three new books into the world. However, it would turn out to be the birth of an entirely new movement.

As the three of us met more frequently on the days leading up to the launch, it was Albert who found himself mulling over how we could combine our voices to speak even more loudly as we launched. Amazingly, he stopped us in our tracks one morning and shouted out, "JAWS!" Joshua and I wanted to know what the Eureka moment was, at which point, Albert turned our attention to the most amazing, simple thing. The first letter in each of our names spelt out the ward, JAW. Joshua, Albert, Walter. The same JAW that is used to crush. To grab hold. To control the amplification of the mouth and the words that are uttered from the lips. Later on, we would learn that JAW was more than just an acronym for our names. No, that word was pregnant with so much more, not only for us as authors, but for everyone that we would later endeavor to reach with our life-changing message.

While celebrating the revelation of JAW, we managed to go even further, deciding there and then that our next book would be a joint effort. We decided that we wanted to use the same acronym J.A.W., and create something meaningful from it that we could write about. We wanted to help people who were as hungry for success as we were. We would write a book about how to be successful, but we wanted to include JAW in the title. What we came up with were the words, Journey, Approach, and Work. Our book would later be called, 'J.A.W.S. – The Journey, the Approach, the Work to Success'.

The launch of our individual books was a success. The world was introduced to Joshua's book, *Arise and Shine: It's Time to Declare Yourself Blessed*, Albert's book, *The Potter's Power: Understanding the Destiny You Didn't Choose,* and Walter's book, *Paul: Persecutor, Preacher, Prisoner.* At the launch, a word was spoken over our lives by Joshua's mother, Prophetess Dorylin Edwards. She said that we would be successful, as a trio. That whatever we put our hands to would succeed. We were also told that there was another book launch coming, one that would see us presenting to the world a book that we had co-authored. It was more of a confirmation for us, as her words echoed a decision we had made among ourselves during our journey, our approach, and our work, to bring something great to the world.

This book is a testimony to its very name. It speaks of the journey each author had to embark upon, the approach they took in their writing, and the work they had to put in for their project to be a success.

Joshua – The Journey

What an experience! J.A.W.S., a book, and movement that will change and empower lives was being planned and executed; yet, so many things happened along my journey that delayed me from manifesting. My wife was pregnant; COVID-19 was on the rise, and personal challenges with taking care of a growing family were plentiful. One of the major things is that our second born baby boy came one week before the COVID-19 lockdown in March 2020. The experience was very challenging for me because my baby boy had to stay in the hospital one week after birth, with a challenge of fluids in his lungs. Just before he came out of the womb the umbilical cord was around his neck. Thank God for life. He came out healthy and strong; this caused a bit of a delay in my writing in 2020. Many days I was too tired to even stay up to focus and write my chapters of J.A.W.S. It was the encouraging and inspirational power of my wife that got me up and going again. "Success will demand that you get up even when there are no feelings of excitement. You just have to remember your commitment to something greater and bigger than you and your current challenges. I got my part completed at the end of 2020 and now the full manuscript is completed. J.A.W.S. is ready to shine the light on what it means to be a successful individual.

Albert – The Approach

Since childhood, one of my aspirations has been to

become an author. While my first book came together relatively smoothly, when God placed the concept of the JAWS book in my heart, it was a formidable challenge. As depicted within these pages, my Journey was a tumultuous one, marked by unforeseen twists and turns. Initially, the creative process flowed effortlessly, with words pouring onto the page with ease. However, fate dealt a cruel blow with the sudden illness and subsequent passing of my mother, plunging me into a downward spiral of grief and creative stagnation. Despite Joshua and Walter completing their sections of the book, I found myself grappling with a lack of inspiration, causing significant delays. It was a period of personal reflection and a reassessment of my Approach that ultimately propelled me forward. Thanks to the immense prayers and unwavering support from my wonderful wife, Shanique, I found renewed inspiration and encouragement, reigniting the flames of my creativity. As you delve into the depths of this book, understand that these words are not merely ink on paper, they represent a Journey of transformation that has profoundly impacted my life. Through perseverance and a shift in Approach, I overcame obstacles to bring this Work to fruition. My hope and prayer are that this book serves as a source of empowerment, igniting positive change and fostering success in your own life.

Walter – The Work
Who really likes to work, anyway? Getting up every day, heading out the door, leaving loved ones behind to face a day filled with the unknown. Work is hard, but necessary. Work reaps rewards. Whether it's a salary, an accolade, or a feeling of self-actualization and

achievement, work is important. It took a lot of work to get this book done. In fact, it took a lot just for me to get my part complete. There were times I had to lock myself away from the noise, the people, the places, and the distractions, just to ensure that I put in the work that was necessary for this book to be a success. And I could not depend on Joshua and Albert alone doing their part, or doing their part well, if the overall goal was for the book to be a success. I had a responsibility to push past the pressures of my own life and accomplish the task that was set before me. Many times, I would attempt to write and my mind would go blank. As a husband and father of three children, I often felt inadequate, less than enough, even undeserving of the family that I had been given. There were forces working around me that were trying to make me abandon the mission. *What's the sense in working so hard, when there is hardly anything to show for it in the end? Why kill yourself writing what no one is going to read anyway?*

What made the difference for me, was ensuring that although forces were working against me on the outside, I was settled on the inside. I had to believe that there was a plan and a purpose for every word in this book, and that once I committed myself to putting in the work, it would bear its fruit in the end. It would be a blessing to others. It would be a success, and it would teach others how they, too, could work their way to success.

They say that nothing good ever comes easily. What I know for certain is that when you work hard at something, the reward at the end of your labor is cherished so much more, because you know just how much effort was put into that thing. You know what you gave up, what you endured, and what you overcame, to work your way to the end. That is a reward that no one can take away from you.

As you read this book, it is my hope that you become inspired. Inspired to write that book, to get that degree, to take that trip. Whatever you've been procrastinating about, whatever you've been leaving undone because the climb looks too laborious, I encourage you to at least start the journey. When it gets overwhelming, don't give up. Explore another approach. And don't be afraid to work hard, because the work you put in today will literally determine the world you create tomorrow.

Let's go!!

BOOK ONE:

THE JOURNEY

By Joshua Edwards

AWAKE
It's time to Focus for the Journey of Success

1. AWAKE TO YOUR IDENTITY

"Unless you know who you are, you will always be vulnerable to what people say." – Dr. Phil McCraw

You were born to be a success! The moment you came into this life, a fight was provoked and is being carried out by multiple forces. Family, friends of family, and people who you don't even know shaped you into who they believe you should be. Your true identity is then left to really fight against all the false, and misfit identities that the world tries to shape you into. Therefore, you must focus on discovering who you are fashioned and designed to be in this life. Success is not something you achieve; it is who you are or who you become in the process of achieving. Everything you achieve in life is the fruit of success, and you are triumphant. You must be careful not to wrongfully label yourself based on another person's achievements or failures. You are a champion. You are a winner. You are strong and very creative. You are disciplined, dedicated, and diligent. Going on the journey of Success simply means taking a journey of being yourself consistently, while, enjoying the benefits and fruits produced along the way. Beware, sometimes you might get lost along the way. Losing your way on the journey happens when, 1) You take up an attitude of people pleasing, 2) You try to be exactly like someone else and, 3) You are led astray by false hopes and dreams. It's time to awake from false identities and live out who you are to enjoy the journey of success. I will share a few identities that you should wake up from, and identities that you should awaken to for you to have a meaningful successful journey. Failure to awaken can cost you negatively on the Journey of success.

Awaken from Pride

Pride is very destructive. Pride will allow you to reach a high point in your journey of being successful and then cause you to self-destruct; it won't matter which area of life it is, whether business, politics, media, entertainment, or spirituality. Once you develop a heart of pride it will prohibit you from enjoying long-lasting success. Going on a journey requires the help of multiple people. It requires you to be able to rely on their gifts and talents that are different from yours. As an individual on the road to success, pride is an inner infection that will cause your team and support staff to turn away from you. It is very difficult for some people, companies, and even organizations to realize that the image they have created is responsible for their lack of growth and success. Your image reflects who you are; once pride is seen in that image success can become hard to maintain. "IF your pride is bigger than your Heart and your ego is bigger than your head, grow up or you will be alone for life." – Quoting.com.

Awake to Humility

Humility is to a man like gas is to the engine of a vehicle. A man must find his humility to be prepared and walk in safety while on the journey of success. Humility will equip anyone with, 1) Wisdom, 2)

Understanding, and 3) Bringing honor into their life and business. According to Success Magazine, Patty Onderko; November 4th, 2015, follow these 6 things and you will be humbler: 1) Ask for Feedback, 2) Confront your prejudices, 3) Start with a question, 4) Really Listen, 5) Accept setbacks, and 6) Discover awe. Once you awake to humility you will find it easy to grow on your journey of success. Humility is the key that you can use to unlock and harness the knowledge, wisdom, resources and wealth of people who under normal circumstances are considered hard to relate to or receive from. Once you continue to grow in humility you will be ready to face anything the journey of success throws at you.

Awaken from Laziness

Laziness is a cancer that has robbed many people of the potential of being successful and enjoying the fruit of success. It is my belief that laziness is a virus that attaches itself to your emotions and is transmitted to every cell in your body. Once this happens it causes you to become sluggish and paralyze any desire for upward and progressive movement. What causes a person to be lazy? Do you know? A person is affected by laziness when they fail to be diligent with their business, dreams, passions, and goals or what belongs to them. Laziness comes to take you off of your journey. Laziness comes with the mindset that someone else will do it. It comes with the mindset that you are entitled to have someone else work hard while you relax or just sit idle. Laziness comes on a person to make them inactive, passive, dormant, slow, and ineffective, having a dullness of mind and heart towards their business or the area that they would like to be successful in. Laziness moves with procrastination which causes a person to put important things off for another time. In the world of business, it's all about taking risks and being in the right place at the right time. What will happen if you fail to be active in your business, on your job, in your marriage? What will happen if you continue to be sluggish towards life? Ask yourself, what is causing me to be lazy? What thoughts am I thinking when it is time to work? Sometimes people are lazy because they are not yet motivated or inspired to move. Most times it takes a personal passion that is huge to move them to success. Below are eight things that lazy people fail to do:

- Fail to plan.
- Fail to do the hard and important stuff first.
- Fail to say no when needed.
- Fail to build and invest in themselves.
- Fail to surround themselves with successful people.
- Fail to study and practice their craft or skills.
- Fail to be accountable for their actions.
- Fail to believe in themselves.

If you are going to be ready for the journey you must fight laziness in all areas of life. Seek to turn all the above into the opposite and be successful. You can do it. You will!

Awake to Discipline, Diligence, and a Proactive Attitude!

Most people fail to be successful because they have not awakened to a life of discipline, diligence, and proactiveness. Do you know that only the diligent ones will rule? Do you know that laziness leads to force or slavish labor? The road to success will not always be smooth. In fact, there will be things on the way to prevent you from achieving success. However, it will not always be rough either. One thing you must have if you are going to start and finish your journey of success is a disciplined mind. A disciplined mind is very focused and keeps its eyes on the goal. Discipline is not a one-time hit. Discipline is a lifestyle and requires you to develop it daily. If you are an individual wired for success you must discipline yourself to, 1) Develop and grow, 2) Renew your mind from negative and destructive mindsets, 3) Plan and prepare for each day of your life, and 4) Cultivate and grow covenant relationships. A disciplined person will be diligent and live from a proactive mindset. Examine your life right now. Ask yourself, am I disciplined? Am I diligent (attentive always) to the gifts, assignments, and dreams, entrusted to me? Remember, to be ready for the journey you must know and learn to understand who you are. You must begin to remove any false identity or labels placed on you. Therefore, you must be proactive in discovering your true self and be diligent in developing yourself to rule well in the realm of success. Do you know the areas of your life that must be developed? It would be wise to list them out and work on creating a growth/development plan. If you don't wake up now and be diligent consistently, your life will become like a garden infested with weeds. It is time to tend to your life. Get ready to go on the journey of success and produce exceptional fruit.

Awaken from Fear

"Too many of us are not living our dreams because we are living our fears." – Les Brown

Fear is a major infection that has hampered the identity of many persons in life since the first set of people moved about the earth. Remember, "God hath not given you a spirit of fear; but of Power, Love and a sound mind (2 Timothy 1:7 KJV)." Fear is an enemy you will have to face on the journey of success. Fear is responsible for keeping you away from your true identity. It focuses on making you inactive, and it works to make you delay or sabotage your destiny. Fear puts you in bondage and keeps you locked away from your true self and gifts. Aristotle says it best, "He who has overcome his fears will truly be free." You will never be free to be and do all you can if fear is influencing you the wrong way. Fear is responsible for keeping you in the clutches of procrastination. Why are you afraid to start? Look at what Dale Carnegie said, "Inaction breeds doubt and fear. Action breeds confidence and courage. If you want to conquer fear, do not sit at home and think about it. Go out and get busy." Your life was never intended to be stagnant and inactive or bogged down with doubt and fear. The longer you fail to move towards your goals and dreams because of fear, your life will slowly regress into failure and eventually die. Don't let fear kill your purpose of success. You were born to overcome and be a success, that is who you are.

Awake to Courage, and Boldness

"It takes courage to grow up and become who you really are." – E. E. Cummings.

"Having Courage and showing courage means we face our fears." – Maya Angelou.

Have you ever wondered why some people make it through tough times and others don't? The answer is, that one chose to take courage and the other failed to walk in courage. If you are going to make it from the start to the finish you must walk in courage. All kinds of circumstances and people are going to come against you. Situations are going to tell you, "turn back you can't be successful in this arena, you don't have the skills, money, or even the connections to make it happen." People are going to tell you, "You are not cut out for this. That can't work here. You are over your head with this one." Be careful not to allow people or situations to make you afraid. Stand in the face of everything and everyone, and go forward to your purpose, dreams, and goals. Having courage is the internal strength, grace, and mental fortitude that pushes a person past every fear to the point of overcoming and succeeding. Set your heart and face with boldness and determine that nothing is going to stop you from being who you are. You are a ball of success. You are a Fire that cannot be extinguished. You are a light that shines so brightly that others are inspired to be successful because of your courage and boldness. If you are going to be free, you will have to walk in boldness. Boldness speaks of one who will face fear or anything head on. You will tackle all situations with the courage that you will come out victorious. Boldness will drive you to be courageous. Success requires you to identify yourself as a bold and courageous person. Step out of timidity and walk into a spirit of boldness to face the challenges of being successful. Remember, "Freedom lies in being Bold."- Robert Frost. Go and get your daily success. The Journey and the process begins the moment you step out as a bold and courageous person.

2. ARISE AND GO
It's Time to Take the Journey to Success

The Genesis of your Success Journey

Your Journey of Success begins when the passion to fulfil your dreams, ideas, purpose, and assignments in life is greater than the pain of starting and getting to the finish line.

Genesis Adebayo, says it best, "… Journey to success…

Prepare

Position

Partner"

Success can fit everyone. Everyone can put on success. However, not everyone is ready to commit to their journey of success. Not everyone is ready to forsake the meaningless for the meaningful. Knowing the difference can be challenging; especially when the meaningless is dear to your heart. However, before you start your journey you must make a sold-out commitment to the vision and dreams that burn within you. Commit to not allowing anyone or anything to stop or hinder you from starting your journey of success. Success requires that you prepare every single day for the next day, week, month, and year. Start now. How do you prepare for success? How do you make sure that you have all the right tools for your journey? Should you wait until you have all the tools to start?

Your preparation for success commences in your mind and heart. The atmosphere of your mind will determine if you are ready to take the lifetime journey of success. The atmosphere of the mind is revealed as attitudes. This atmosphere surrounds you, and everyone who comes into your presence will know you by your attitude. Your preparations begin with your attitude. Your attitude is broken down into three significant areas: 1) Thoughts, 2) Words, and 3) Actions. These areas must be taken seriously if one desires to take the journey of being successful in one's daily life. Fulfilling your destiny depends on how strong you develop in your attitude.

Your attitude is the voice of your character. People will decide if they will help you along your journey based on your attitude. Thoughts are the building blocks of words. A man who keeps his word will be seen and known as a man of great action. He/she will be known for their integrity. On your journey, your words will justify you or condemn you. What you tell yourself daily will be the launching pad or the sinking sand from which you excel greatly or fail horribly. Let your words only tell of your vision and what you will do to live it daily. If you understand words, you will begin to speak only your vision, your goals, and your plan of action in the form of declarations, affirmations, and confessions. Your journey will have difficulties. You shouldn't conform to the difficulties, for they are only there to test your ability and commitment to your vision, goals, and plan of action; what you do is address the difficulties with solutions and the assurance that you will overcome any obstacle that presents itself on your journey of success. Success begins with you and ends with you. The journey of your success begins when you take the first step and continue walking towards your vision. Remember, success has the same foundation for everyone. If you are going to be successful, compromising the foundations of success will not be tolerated in the journey. If you plan to go on this expedition, you must build your success on the following foundational principles:

- Discipline
- Consistency
- Service to others
- Focus
- Clear vision, goals, and plan of action
- Know yourself.
- Know your God-given purpose.
- Be accountable to mentors and learn from them.
- Seek and understand knowledge while you develop your gift and craft.
- Good work ethics
-

Great foundations are the footage by which all great structures stand the test of difficult times. You are building a success structure so that others can come and enjoy the legacy that you will pass on.

Mindsets of Success vs. Mindset of Failure

A mindset is the union or the merging of emotions, knowledge, and desires that a person or a place is programed to operate by. Mindsets are what determine the trajectory of individuals, marriages, families, communities, governments, and a nation's ultimate success or failure. If the mindset is wrong, then the holder of the mindset will function wrongly. What mindset are you operating from? Do you know your mindset will determine the quality and kind of success journey you have? Whatever you perceive you will receive. Whatever you desire the most will find you eventually. Most times because of the wrong information that we live by our good desires are crippled and prevented from flourishing. We must seek to correct our mind if we ever expect to enjoy the pure and fruitful success that can be harvested on our daily walk of life. Everything rises and falls on mindsets. For example, let us look at the Mindset of the ants. The ants are programmed to work and store food in the summer, and while it is winter, the colony will have food to eat. The collective mindset of ants is: 1) A mindset of teamwork – they will work together to carry food that is twice the size of one ant and 2) A mindset of preparation – they will prepare in summer for winter. If you can master these two mindsets, your journey to success will be made easier.

The Journey to success requires you to prepare every single day. It requires you to study today for tomorrow. It requires you to be ready now for later. Most times we want to get ready at the last minute. What kind of mindset will have you scrambling to get ready at the wrong time or just before a moment of manifesting the fruit of your success? The enemy of a prepared mindset is a slothful, lazy, and sluggard mindset. These types of mindsets will rob you of your vision, goals, purpose, and plan of action. Lazy mindsets speak up and say, "I am too tired to finish this now." A sluggard mindset will say, "I will finish it in my own time, and I will take as long as I want." This mindset of sluggishness will make you miss opportunities and cause you to always be late. Since the desire is to bear the fruits of success daily on the journey, one must be mindful of the type of mindset that governs their lifestyle. You must seek to unearth any mindset that is responsible for fruitlessness and hindering you on your journey to success. Following is a list of other mindsets that will aid you and that can be a danger to you on the journey of success.

Good Mindsets to have	Bad Mindsets to get rid of
Diligent Mindset - (Elevates you to a position of Ruler-ship. This mindset seeks out to finish what it starts. It is this mindset that gives you strength to endure.)	**Wasteful Mindset** – This mindset causes individuals to misuse time, resources, gifts, talents and have nothing to show for what they had.
A Mindset of Service – (Helps to connect you to the right people that can help you)	**Unthankful Mindset** – This mind refuses to show gratitude thereby
Creative Mindset – (Sets you up to be in a position to develop new things, new ways of doing things, and helps you solve problems)	**Entitlement mindset** – This mindset makes you feel and behave like everyone owes you something. This mind pushes you to expect others to always be at your call.
Bold Mindset – (enables you to move fearless and gives you an eye for healthy calculated risks)	**Fearful Mindset** – This mind keeps you from pursuing your dreams, visions and passions because of a wrong perception of that which is to be pursued.
A Mindset to Work – (One with this mind will see things that needs to be done and do it. The have an eye for details and they go the extra mile plus more. Success requires this mindset.	**Procrastination Mindset** – This mindset makes you believe that you have time and it can be done another day. This prevents persons from given their best in the journey of success. This mindset can also be rooted in a fearful mindset. Procrastination hampers your growth and destroys your cha
Generous giving Mindset – This mindset empowers individuals and corporations to release portions of what they make or receive to help build and support others. The success of this mind is to see others have in abundance. This mindset will keep you from withholding information.	**Prideful Mindset** – This mindset propels a person to see themselves as higher, better and more valuable than others. This mindset causes a person to over-step healthy boundaries, by doing so it sets them up for failure.
Mindset of Integrity – This mind will protect you from rotten behaviors as you journey in success. Integrity is the ability to do what is right even if it cost you greatly.	**Leach Mindset** – This mindset takes and never desires to give back. In the realm of success it appears that this person is successful but on the inside they are empty, stagnant and stick. The person affected by this mindset comes under a poverty mindset also.
Wise and Understanding Mindset - This mindset will help you to know what to do, how to do it, and why you are doing it. This mindset brings you into realms of knowledge and understanding	**Poverty Mindset** - This is a wicked mind that comes to cause individuals to walk in lack, insufficiency, mismanagement, disorder, confusion and greed. It enables the person to become crippled in life. Get free be activating an abundance Mindset

As you take a closer look at these mindsets, ask yourself; "Am I creating a positive and healthy mindset, or am I entertaining negativity and a destructive mindset?" It is important to know the type of mind you have. This will help you determine the level of development and empowerment needed to be effective on the journey to success. Every Mindset, good or bad will help to shape and determine what kind of life you experience daily. According to Proverbs 23:7, "As a man thinks in his heart, so is he." The pattern of thinking you are programmed to will determine who you become daily. In the journey of having daily success, you must pay attention to your thoughts; failure to mind your thoughts can lead to disappointment. I encourage you with Romans 12:1-2, that you must renew your mind, and you will know the perfect will of God for your life. This renewal will help you to remove old and negative mindsets. If you are going to renew your mind from the old mindset, follow the steps below:

Step One: Admit and Confess

Admit that you need to change your old lifestyle. Making this confession of change that is desired must be in the area you want and need to change. Doing this will weaken the old mindsets that are influencing and giving power to the old behaviors and cycles of failure.

Step two: Think About What You're Thinking

It is very easy to allow the wrong thoughts to dominate and run wild in our minds. However, there must come a time when you will focus on what is being fed to your mind daily. You must analyze, scrutinize, and determine if you will allow or disallow any thought to stay in your mind. Do this by asking yourself some questions.

1) Will this thought enhance me?
2) Will this thought bring me success, or will it lead me to failure?
3) What actions will this thought lead me to? Is it positive actions or negative actions?
4) Will this thought bring glory to God?
5) Will this thought help to build my character?

If the thought is not good for you, address the thought by simply saying, "I reject you and prohibit you from having access to my mind, will, and emotions." After you repeat that statement, you will then move to replace the thought with what you will accept. For example: I choose to only accept positive thoughts that will enhance and lead me to success." You must engage your mind daily otherwise it will be engaged for you by other forces which could lead you into a life of failure and unfruitfulness. The journey of success requires your mind to be free from all negative and destructive thought patterns. You must examine every thought and decide if it will lead to fruitfulness.

Step Three: Meditation

Meditation is a powerful key that can help to transform your life. Daily we are meditating on the wrong things; doing this can cause us to struggle on the journey to success. **Meditation is the vehicle that the**

subconscious mind uses to determine what to act upon, pursue, eliminate, and prevent from happening in a person's life. Meditation is like engraving a program that will determine the pathway of your life. Whatever you meditate on consistently will be given permission and granted access to manifest in your life. The question is, what are you meditating on daily? Is it:

- Fear of failure?
- Worry about where the money will come from to pay outstanding bills?
- Negative beliefs about your life and success?
- If you will ever be able to make lots of money, or even save and invest money?

Or, do you meditate on positive things like:

- Your vision.
- Your purpose.
- Your goals and plans.
- What you desire for your life and family
- The success of your marriage
- The success of building wealth.
- The success of every year of your life.

Start now and replace every negative mindset with your daily meditation. Remember anything that you give to the heart through the subconscious mind will become the law in your life.

Step Four: The Power of Self-Directed and Inflicted Words

It is said that words are extremely powerful. Much research has been done on the power and effect words have on people and objects. Words carry spirit, life or death. The words that you speak will free you to excel or put an embargo over your success and restrict you from walking and living in fruitfulness. If you are going to change your mindset from negative to positive, you will have to passionately speak like the examples below:

- I am diligent. I desire to finish my English exam strong. I will put in the work required.
- I refuse to procrastinate. Procrastination will prevent me from enjoying the success waiting for me. I choose to act now with wisdom and clarity. I will complete everything on time.
- Today I seek to give cheerfully. I will be intentional about my desire to give abundantly.
- I am passionate about living my vision, dreams, and desires. I move towards my vision with excitement and a sense of urgency, knowing I must leave a strong legacy.

On this journey of success, you must release positive spirit-filled words that will create the right kind of atmosphere for you to grow, act, and transform into a person of great success.

Step Five: Develop a Lifestyle of Transforming Actions

Enjoying the right kind of mind and life requires you to be a person of consistent, healthy life changing actions. A person that is going the wrong way will end up in a ditch. The stuck person will end up losing out on life's treasures. However, a person driven by divine vision will end up living a life saturated with daily fruitfulness. Movement tied to a vision and plan is very crucial to your success. It is said that "actions speak louder than words." Every accomplishment will be established through the power of your previous actions. No action no fruit. A fruitless person is an aimless person. An aimless person will end up missing the mark of daily success. It is important to be a person of vision with daily actions. Be careful not to allow stagnation and lack of motivation to be found in you. Daily review your vision as you go on the journey. Build a life that is made from consistently acting upon vision, purpose, and destiny. The life you build today will be the life you live tomorrow. It starts with life-transforming actions.

The mindset or set of principles and beliefs that you hold dearly in your heart will determine the quality of your success and the length and dimension to which you will grow and be fruitful.

The End from the Start; Have you Seen it?

Have you seen the end of your vision as yet? In your mind's eye, do you have a picture of how you desire to see the end product of your goals? The truth of the matter is you will not be able to start or finish your journey of success if you don't have an idea or picture in your mind of where you are going. Start today by seeing yourself running across a finish line. See the name of what you want to accomplish being held in the hands of your friend, family member, or even significant other. It is time to vividly see yourself crossing the finish line of success in that area that you desire to be fruitful in. Once you have that vision, imprint it on your mind and take the journey. Seeing the end will give you hope, endurance, and faith to continue moving towards that vision. Don't ever forget to meditate on your vision. Remember the journey requires you to start with the end in mind; once you do you will finish.

3. HEART FOCUS

The Key to Getting the Most Out of the Journey!

The Process of the Journey

The quality of your life will depend heavily on whether you went through the process to enjoy the fruit of your success. Have you ever wondered why so many people want to get things quickly? They want to get to the top now; not desiring to put the work into the process of being on the top. Anything or anyone that omits the process will end up feeble and useless to themselves and others. The process of success helps individuals develop the strength, resistance, skills, and endurance necessary to bear the fruits of their daily success. The process of success is not for the people who like their current state of being fearful, lazy, inconsistent, unorganized, and prideful. If you struggle within yourself to be self-disciplined, and you desire to change, then the journey is for you. Every person in life will go through a process of success. The purpose of the seed is to die while the plant bursts out to grow and bear fruits with more seeds. The process for the plant starts the moment a seed is buried in the soil and dies. The Tree continues to grow as it submits to the process, and at the appointed time it will bear fruit, once all went well during the process. Your process should help you to become your best and most exceptional self. There are some tools that you will need to reach the fullness of your success with the evidence of continuous and long-lasting fruit. These tools are listed below:

Self-Discipline

Self-discipline is the art of leading and restraining oneself to fulfill personal assignments and goals. Once you develop the muscle of self-disciple you will reach your destiny by manifesting vision. Vision is birthed through self-disciplined and consistent people. Self-discipline demands that everything around you that is hindering your success needs to be cut off or left alone. Self-discipline is most of the time hard because it requires us to leave our comfort zone and die to self-gratifying desires that could hinder our success. For example: spending less time on the phone, refusing to spend money on unnecessary hairstyles, giving up unhealthy relationships, walking away from the wrong jobs and businesses. Anything that is connected to you that will threaten you from becoming your optimum self, will need to be cut off. This is where the pain of the process comes in. Success demands that you pay the price; the price is paid in the journey of your process; not someone else's process. The caterpillar has to pay the price of being confined in a cocoon for some time. The caterpillar then has to pay the price of pushing itself out to build strength in the wings, and only then can it experience life as a butterfly. Failure to pay the price can cause you to become ineffective with no value. Discipline yourself on the journey of success and you will emerge as a whole individual ready to bear much fruit consistently.

A Heart and Mind to Study and Research

Success requires that you build your knowledge base so that your gifts and skills will have fuel to work with. Do you know, lack of knowledge will cause your gift to be a danger to you and others? A person who lacks knowledge will fade away on the journey of success. That person will become irrelevant, valueless, and eventually obsolete. Seek to know about yourself, and the field that you desire to be successful in. Develop your gifts, talents, and skills. Challenge yourself to learn and apply something new every day. Challenge yourself to research the top 10 successful persons and put into practice the principles they live by. If you are not growing in the process then you are losing traction to advance and expand and you will end up stagnant, stuck, and a candidate for lifetime failure. **Study to act daily and meditate to transform consistently and your life will never be the same on this journey of success**.

Quality Morning and Afternoon Time with Yourself and the Creator

Are you one to get up late and rush out of the house to start the day? Are you one to get up early but sleep pulls you back into the bed? Are you one to get up early, but, that time is not spent with your Creator? The early morning riser who meditates on his Creator and listens for instructions will be well equipped to tackle the day ahead and be fruitful. They who sit and map out their day will experience great clarity and peace; however, those who fail to practice the principle of rising early to focus on God and their day will not experience that clarity and peace. Seek to take hold of your day and command how it should flow. Successful people rise early and map their day.

Also, there is something powerful about reflecting at the end of each day. This practice will help you to be still as you analyze and critique all that occurred. This will allow you to make corrections and prepare for the following day. Persons who fail to evaluate their life and actions will end up making the same mistakes which could hinder the fruitfulness that should come from their daily success. **Do you know a person can look successful and still be a failure? The only thing that matters is - are you bearing fruit?** A tree that has healthy leaves but has a problem with bearing fruit is indicative of an unhealthy root system. Your foundation is everything. Develop your foundation. Seek to correct any wrong mindsets you might have about the process of success. Take time to grow. Remember, haste creates waste. People might not see your foundation, but it will be revealed in your ability to bear fruit after the test of time.

Mentors and Counselors

Are you one of them that doesn't want anyone in your business? Well, not everyone should be allowed to know your business. However, you must seek out mentors, coaches, and counselors if you are going to navigate the dangers that are waiting to destroy you before you make it big. Many people began the journey of success and failed because they were not accountable to anyone. They had no one to give them wisdom and insights about situations. They had no one to guide them and nurture their potential as they walked the road to success. If you are going to be successful in your process, find your divine mentors, coaches, and counselors. As you grow and develop, they will change. As you become strong in one area of life, other areas will need the attention of divine mentorship. This tool will help to iron out any hidden faults or weaknesses that you might not be aware of. Mentorship has its rewards and the benefits are countless.

Patience

On the journey of being successful you will have to be patient as you go through your process. Patience helps to ground you and develop in you a viewpoint of gratitude and appreciation for what you are pursuing. Lack of patience can cause you great hurt when it comes to the journey of success. Acquiring anything too soon can put you into great problems. Patience prepares you and brings you to a place of maturity required to handle the fruit of your success. Patience gives you power to control great wealth, and resources, by bringing your emotions into control. Patience is the biggest regulator that keeps us from becoming obsessed with material stuff. Walk with patience and you will not lose your fruit before its time.

Humility

The journey to success can be one of great wealth, riches, and great power; if you take humility with you on the journey of success. Once you have humility, you will not lord over others, and you will not look down on them. A heart of humility seeks and desires to serve people with its gifts and resources. This is the key to great and long-lasting fruitfulness. Humility lifts you up and establishes you forever in the realm of fruitfulness. However, pride will allow you to get very high, only to cause you to fall extremely hard and lose everything. Let your process be filled with humility. Anyone with consistent humility will rule over great wealth as they gain mastery in their process of success. Remember, as you humble yourself you will be lifted into success by the creator of all.

Wisdom and Understanding

"Wisdom is the principal thing; therefore, get wisdom: and with all thy getting get understanding." – Proverbs 4:7

Wisdom and understanding should be your best friends on your journey to success. Wisdom will show you what to do and how to do it. Understanding will tell you why you are doing it and help you to apply the knowledge you have received in the right way. Many people go on their journey and ignore the cry of wisdom and understanding. They operate foolishly and miss the mark of success. Wisdom desires to make a clear pathway for you and understanding desires to make you rooted and grounded in the truth. The truth is found in the pathway designed just for you by the Creator. Without understanding you will miss out on your new seasons, and without understanding you will misapply strategies and end up mishandling the wisdom given to you. No understanding means you will be full of solutions but not know how to use them properly and effectively for the good of yourself and others.

As you pay the price to reach your destiny, by taking the journey of success, remember to take these tools and other tools that will benefit you while you endure the process. Trust your process, join and stay connected with your process, grow and pass the tests in your process and you will enjoy a life of unlimited fruitfulness.

Pitfalls to be Aware of on the Journey to Success

"The road to success is always under construction"
- Larry Wall

The journey of success is not a smooth one. It requires you to pay attention as you move along the way of life. Have you ever realized that some people become extremely successful and then they fail or lose footage? I call it falling for the traps of success. Many things will try to steal your success or prevent you from enjoying it. These things appeal to our natural desires. They always appeal to your weaknesses. Once you choose to walk the journey of success a decision will have to be made by you to stay focused. Many pitfalls can hinder your progress and fruitfulness on the journey to success. They are mentioned below:

Being Dependent on Approval

Seeking wisdom and advice is all good. However, there comes a time when you will have to make some decisions on your own. Constantly seeking the approval of people before you move forward could become a major stumbling block to your continued success. This pitfall pushes you to become fearful of making any moves without first checking in with that person or persons. Remember, that person will not always be there. If you are going to take this road of success, you must grow up quickly and make key decisions by yourself, for your growth and development. Persons who fall prey to this trap tend to not truly know what they want to do. They listen to everyone's ideas about what they should do or be, and in the process, they fail to hear their own heart about what they should be doing. Be careful of becoming too dependent or co-dependent on everything related to your success. Believe in yourself, trust in your abilities, and walk in your gifting. Yes, listen to advice, however, the decision is yours to make.

Dwelling in your Comfort Zone

This pitfall prevents many individuals from realizing their full potential and ability. It causes people to fall prey to the comfort of previous accomplishments and successes. Every goal achieved is now the enemy of the next goal. We as individuals love to settle too long in comfort. Do you know that if a person stays too long in their comfort zone, failure will begin to stop them from tackling the hard things to experience new and exciting achievements? This journey requires you to always be on the edge of creating new platforms and amazing pathways to success. Seek to live outside of your comfort zone even if it costs you. At the end of it all your life will produce great and rewarding fruits.

Overwhelming Anxiety

Anxiety is very dangerous. It prevents its victims from seeing clearly. It's a sign that the individual is no longer in control, and they fear the outcome of their journey. Anxiety causes some people to do two things. 1.) Be stuck and unable to make decisions, and 2.) Cause individuals to make hasty decisions that create major problems along their journey. Beware of anxiety. Be anxious for nothing. Let your requests, desires, and hearts visions be made in prayer unto God your Father. Doing this will give you the strength to overcome the pitfall of anxiety.

Prideful Heart

This pitfall is generally close to the top of your success journey, even though it can manifest itself anywhere in your journey of success. Pride opens the door for you to disregard others. A prideful person will go as far as seeing themselves better than everyone around them. If they are not better, it causes them to become bitter and resentful. Pride sets you up for massive failure on your journey of success. If you are going to be successful with fruits, then you must live a life of humility straight through your journey of success. Persons with pride will lie, steal, kill, and do anything just to be seen as the best or to maintain a position of superiority. Of course, this is the extreme side of pride. Let your life be saturated with humility and you will shine.

It is important to know that everyone will experience a prideful heart at some point in their lives. Also, know that this is not the only pitfall. You will also experience sexual temptations, money challenges, integrity challenges, and much more. Just know that you must desire to live a life led by principles and values. The journey will not be the same for everyone. However, everyone can use exceptional principles to overcome challenges on their journey to success. Remember that only you will determine how exceptional you will be on your journey. Everyone else will just be assistance and support. Choose to go hard so that others will reap the benefit of your success. Be known as a person who creates a positive legacy to be followed and lived. Let your success journey be one that others can take note of and glean from.

Blind Spots

"Blind Spots are like rowing a boat that's full of holes, but you can't find the holes." – Unknown.

Life is full of people who have sight but no vision. Blind spots are very real, and many leaders, pastors, and even well-known persons end up failing in life because of these major pitfalls that show up as invisible enemies. It is said that "Every leader has three to four blind spots." (Bill Hybels) A blind spot is an issue or weakness that a person has. They are completely oblivious of it. Blind spots are dangerous pitfalls because they become invisible enemies on our journey to success. Taking the journey of success will bring you face to face with your greatest challenge and struggle, which is YOU! You are the only person who can hinder your progress on the journey; because of this, you are going to need someone or a number of trusted persons in your life who can identify your weak points, blind spots, and major challenges and give you counsel on how to navigate them. The great book, the Bible says, "Where no counsel is, the people fall: but in the multitude of counselors there is safety." (Proverbs 11:14) Do you know why people fall and end up dropping off the journey of their success? Many people have the attitude; I don't need anyone to be successful. Others feel they don't need anyone instructing them on what to do. Another group of people suffer from pride and a high-minded attitude, which believes that they are better than everyone else. This attitude prevents the bearer of it from receiving wise help and counsel. The best way to overcome blind spots is to consistently allow someone to reveal them to you. Once this is being done the onus is on the individual to become aware consciously and create a plan to fix the blind spot.

Examples of Blind spots are:

1) Going it alone (fearful of asking for help)
2) Being insensitive of your behavior towards others
3) Having an "I Know" attitude (valuing being right above everything else)
4) Avoiding the difficult conversations (avoiding conflict)
5) Blaming others or circumstances (playing the victim; refusing responsibilities)
6) Treating commitments casually (not honoring the other person's time, energy, and resources)
7) Conspiring against others (driven by a personal agenda)
8) Withholding emotional commitment (emotional blackmail)

9) Not taking a stand (lack of commitment to a position)
10) Tolerating "good enough" (low standards for performance)

These blind spots will prevent you from being successful if they are not remedied. Looking at these blind spots in a greater light will give an appreciation of why you need to cure them.

Going it Alone – Fearful of Asking for Help

Success can be a very lonely journey. However, it does not mean you must take the journey alone. Understanding this blind spot is very critical to your ability to overcome it. A series of questions can be asked: Why do I want to do it by myself? Why am I afraid of trusting people to help me? Why am I afraid of what people think about me, and what I desire to do? Am I afraid of being rejected? These questions will deal with the person's sense of identity and self-worth. Many people go the journey alone because of past hurts, disappointments, rejections, and fear of living the bad experiences over again. Others go alone because they are unable to relate and work well with others. The fear of what people think keeps these types of people from finding the help and connections they need to be extremely successful on their journey. Success requires you to be open to war daily. Only by taking on the war of life will you learn the lessons needed to grow and master your journey of success. If you choose to go alone, chances are you will end up experiencing more pain than if you had trusted the process of walking with others.

Being Insensitive of your Behavior Towards Others

This blind spot has caused many talented and gifted people to be ignored and shy away from others because they are unaware of how they treat the people around them. According to John Maxwell, "People don't care how much you know until they know how much you care." You can have the world of knowledge; if you don't know how to relate to and care for others you will push them away. This is the cause of many talented people falling deep into failure. They fail to see how they treat the very people who hold the help that they need. Insensitive people most times struggle with self-centeredness and selfishness. Others are insensitive because their hearts are unable to feel and be aware of the needs and concerns of the very people who are wired to help them on their journey. To have success you will have to battle with yourself daily. Most times you don't even know that you are the one sabotaging you.

Having an "I Know" Attitude (Valuing Being Right Above Everything Else)

Are you someone who knows it all? Do you appear to always know? When someone is sharing information with you: do you tell them, I already know that? Well, beware, this is a dangerous place to be in. What happens is you turn away people from being free to share information with you because you always appear to know it all. The key here is to listen even if you heard the information before. Chances are you will learn something new if you remain humble, teachable, and receptive to receiving information from good sources. Doing this will open you up to knowledge that will aid you on your journey to success. The blind spot of knowing it all has robbed many persons of valuable information, all because you fail to listen and receive information. The more you don't know while having the desire to know, will catapult you to a place of always receiving top of the line knowledge and wisdom. Success loves when you are eager to learn and grow.

Avoiding the Difficult Conversations (Avoiding Conflict)

Conflict is the portal prepared to take you to the better and greater you. Most individuals don't find the other side to their better self because they avoid conflict. Avoidance of difficulty is a major blind spot for some. It prevents them from being successful. The moment a difficult conversation, situation or conflict presents itself, they run away, hide, or go missing in action. Avoiding difficult conversations is a sign that you are not ready for success. It's a sign that you are unwilling to deal with the hard things. Maybe because of fear and not wanting to handle anything that requires you to be tough and bold. Without conflict, your journey will be shallow, and your success will not be proven. The quicker you deal with conflict the more ready you will be to handle the challenges, barriers, and difficult times on your journey of success. Remember, conflict is just announcing that you are being prepared and it is now time to become the greater you. Within every conflict is the code and blueprint for your next level of success. Pay attention and step into conflict with confidence knowing you can learn from it, grow through it, and solve it.

Blaming Others or Circumstances (Playing the Victim; Refusing Responsibilities)

Blaming others is a serious challenge and blind spot that prevents individuals from learning and growing into the great purpose God has created for them. Blaming others implies that you are not responsible for your own life. Walking in the habit of blaming others for your challenges and mishaps in life shows that you are not willing to take control of your life and what takes place in it. A person who blames others is simply saying: if you would have done this, become this, or given me this; I would have been better off and further along in life. The problem with this idea and belief is, that the individual is held hostage to the belief that other people are responsible for their success, achievements, and journey in life. Individuals with this blind spot and mindset become victims of their belief systems; causing them to refuse to take responsibility for their change, development, growth, and accomplishments of dreams and goals. The truth is, According to Robin Sharma, "Blaming others is nothing more than excusing yourself." If you are doing this, you must decide to get back in the driver's seat of your life and take the courage and strength to make things right for your own life. Decide to open yourself to see and understand more about yourself as it relates to blaming others. Once you overcome this your life will be opened to rivers of success. Go after your success NOW!

"Everything you do is based on the choices you make. It's not your parents, your past relationships, your job, the economy, the weather, an argument, or your age that is to blame. You and only you are responsible for every decision and choice you make." – Wayne Dyer.

Treating Commitments Casually (Not Honoring the Other Person's Time, Energy, Resources)

Success is never a one man show. Being the fullness of who you are requires the skill of relationships and committing to the fruitfulness of each one. Commitment begins with you. Commitment is a personal issue and will never be seen in relationships, businesses, and any other area of life unless it is first seen in the individual's relationship with themselves. Google Dictionary states commitment is "the state or quality of being dedicated to a cause, activity," it is also, your ability to be sold into fulfilling your responsibility to your dreams, goals, decisions, family, and purpose in life. Whatever or whoever you commit to, it is important that you follow through on your word.

Many people don't realize that lack of commitment is the reason for their failure or success.

"Commitment unlocks the doors of imagination, allows vision, and gives us the right stuff to turn our dreams into reality." –James Womack

One day of commitment to all your goals and dreams is enough power, energy, and wisdom to push you and your generations forward for one month. Imagine if you are committed every single day of your life to your vision, dreams, goals, and purpose. Your results will be limitless and explosive. Don't allow your lack of commitment to continue to be a blind spot in your life. Lack of commitment will block you from success, fruitfulness, and significance in your life. When you refuse to commit to your journey of success everything that is wired to be yours will be close to you and you will not be able to benefit. Commitment is a connector and revealer. Everyone you commit to will at some point open up to you and reveal their heart to you. Every dream, purpose, and goal you commit to will eventually give way for you to enjoy its manifestation. Whenever you commit to someone or something you become one with that person or thing, giving you the ability to know and understand what is required to be successful with the person or the object (vision, dream, and goals). A life void of commitment will never be able to handle tough, rough, and challenging situations. They will bail on their journey of success every time something bad or daunting happens. Commitment says, I am going to hold on until I see the manifestation, even when I have the manifestation of what I committed to. Commitment is the heartbeat of love and success. It's the very essence of what keeps things going even after the emotions, the hype, and the glamour have faded away. Without commitment, you will fail. You will give up and you will not be able to see the fullness of your vision and goals as a reality. Andy Andrews said, "When confronted with a challenge, the committed heart will search for a solution. The undecided heart searches for an escape." Let your commitment help you through the journey of success. Day by day, week by week. Decide to commit every single time. Decide to give it your all or nothing. Decide to fight for your dreams, goals, and passions, because "commitment is what transforms a promise into reality," stated Abraham Lincoln. It's to defend your success. It is your birthright; your divine gift from your Creator. Decide to go hard after it, cultivate it, and transform the world with it.

Conspiring Against Others (Driven by a Personal Agenda)

There is a type of person who will go to extreme links and heights to make sure that others don't make it. They heap dirt on persons to sabotage their character; thereby causing shame to the person and tarnishing their names in the minds of others. This bind spot is created by insecurity, jealousy, fear, and the need to be in the spotlight above others. Persons who are selfish and whose sole agenda in life is to get to the top, most times are plagued with the idea that anyone who is ahead of them should be brought down.

As you take the journey it is very important to understand and know who you are around. People will be attracted to what you can do and what you can give them. These kinds of people will make you feel like you are obligated to help; you are not. Don't let anyone blackmail you into doing what you are not wired or called to do on your journey of success. People will go to extremes and plant negatives like, "He is not fit for that promotion; be careful of giving it to him." Others will say, "He is not qualified, give it to someone else." These success killers know you can do the job, yet they conspire against you to see you fail. Don't become alarmed or lose sight of your vision, goals, and purpose. Your fruits, consistency, diligence, and humility will be your defense and help against the wrong done to you. Remember, success is not a straight pathway. For some, they have to jump over pointy wires, scale mountains, cross high seas, and create doors in walls to pass through. The key is to keep moving and see every challenge as an opportunity to become the new you, develop, and grow. See the negative persons as manure; created to help you grow. See every false statement as an opportunity to grow through the dirt and unfair treatment. It is only then you will be able to see your true value and strength.

The blind spots of others that rub you the wrong way on the journey of success are being used to shape you and prepare you for being successful daily.

Emotional Blackmail (Withholding of Emotional Commitment)

Emotion is energy in action. To be emotionless on the journey of success is to lack the internal energy that is required to make things happen and complete them. Emotions should not be the determining factor of whether you should start or finish. This is a major blind spot for many, and their emotions have caused them to experience up days and down days. Success is not a destination; success is your identity. You are successful! You are successful! You are successful!

So why do some people still achieve their goals, even when they don't feel like doing anything and others don't achieve anything? The key is one group allows their emotions to be the influencer of who they become, and what they do; the other group of people allows discipline to be the influencer of who they become and what they produce. Emotions can be used against you internally and externally. You must become emotionally mature and strong. Emotions are created to be our servants; they are the energy that rolls off your every thought whether it is your conscious or subconscious thinking. Emotions can be used to blackmail you if you or the individual being used by the negative emotions don't realize.

The emotionally stable, mature, and wise will overcome every emotional weakness. There might be a slip sometimes, but it will not be anything major to hinder them. You will overcome this blind spot in yourself by practising the following:

- Pay attention to how you feel and why you feel that way. Write everything down.
- Speak and respond to your emotions with reason, creative power, compassion, and direction.
- Always practice creating and cultivating the emotions you desire through meditation and thought implants.
- Ask persons to evaluate your emotions
- Use discipline to lead your emotions even when it's not in agreement.
- Connect with a friend or emotional growth coach and practice emotional sharing and

emotional adjusting. (Emotional sharing is stating how you feel and why to a trusted person without any judgment; this helps to create healthy expression and clarity and Emotional adjusting is asking yourself what can you do to change the way you feel right now and restore your emotional power over your feelings)

How do you overcome emotional blind spots in people? The fact is: that you must be an observer and not a reactor to other people's behaviors on the journey of your success. Observing people will put you in a better position to help them become aware of their challenges. You will also become aware of your emotional challenges. Reacting negatively will cause you to become emotional, leading to unhealthy responses. Success loves it when you help another person to be their best self. An observer of emotional blind spots is one who constantly seeks feedback from others. They overcome the blind spots of different persons by asking questions and not taking the reactions of others personally on their journey to success. Blind spots in others will create challenges for many individuals on their journey, who have not mastered the art of emotional maturity. An active way to overcome emotional blind spots in others is to host emotional development training that will help individuals become aware of their emotional blind spots, showing them how to fix them. It is important to have an open growth mindset as you communicate with individuals on the journey to success. Remember, your emotions are just the energy and presence of your thoughts in reaction mode. Keep your thoughts focused as you go on the journey of being successful. You will obtain success once you embrace the journey and keep your eyes on the goal. You are wired to succeed and be successful every single day; nothing will hinder you from success, once you be an observer of yourself and others' emotions. A ship needs more than one person to sail the ocean on its journey. Therefore, go and connect with people emotionally in a healthy way, your success depends on it.

Low Standards

"Success will not lower its standards to accommodate you, rather you raise your standards to achieve it." – Mr. Vybs Live

Many persons are blind to the slow and detrimental character of low standards that they adopted in their lives. Standards are the principles, rules, and values that people live by. The journey of success is a road that is travelled by many who have lowered their standards to cut corners and make it faster in life. The issue with this behavior creates flaws in the foundation of individuals. These flaws could include cheating, stealing, bribes, and victimization, and entitlement mindsets. Many people don't see what they are doing as low in standard and this affects their level of success and the lives of the people around them. Success is open to everyone and provides a clear pathway to obtain their goals; however, many people have created look-alikes and shortcuts that have caused them to hurt their character, lives, and family. Compromising situations are presented when we believe that integrity is no longer the only way to have genuine success; creating danger zones for you and everyone connected to you.

Today, decide to raise your standards to that of excellence, integrity, honesty, loyalty, and accountability. Once you do, your life will attract the right people, opportunities, and situations and propel you to becoming a person of success. Decide to seek knowledge to know when you are flying low in standards and lift the bar as soon as you are aware. You are born to succeed.

Lack of Commitment

"Most people who fail in their dream fail not from lack of ability but from lack of commitment." – Zig Ziglar

Commitment is the state of being completely focused and dedicated to a relationship, vision, goal, or task. Commitment is the glue that prevents you from being distracted. One who is not committed will fail to be successful. Commitment requires self-discipline, self-denial, and delayed gratification. Many talented people who take the journey of success in their dreams fail because they allow the enemies of commitment to steal their purpose and destiny of success and significance. The enemies of commitment are:

- Laziness
- Fear
- Sluggishness
- Selfishness
- Procrastination
- Unfaithfulness

- Distraction

What is taking you away from being committed to your goals, vision and assignment? Are you afraid of commitment? If you are blind to the fact that you might not be as committed, you will lose momentum and persons less talented and gifted will surpass you, because they are more dedicated to their goals. It's time to allow yourself to be sold out on your journey to success. Let yourself become focused, diligent, and determined to accomplish everything you set your desire on. "Most people fail, not because of lack of desire, but, because of lack of commitment." – (Vince Lombardi) Lack of commitment is a dangerous trait and blind spot to have. Do you know how to overcome a lack of commitment? Following are a few nuggets you can practice daily:

- **Have a vision and dream big**: Meditate on your goals and dreams daily for about 15 to 30 minutes. Doing this will bring to reality your goals and dreams.

- **Cultivate a big "WHY"**: This is the food and nourishment for your commitment. It must grow daily and be stronger than any challenges, minor or major setbacks that may come your way. Your WHY helps you to stay focused no matter what.

- **Find and submit to an accountability coach or mentor:** Following this process will put you on the cutting edge. They will be there to encourage, coach, and remind you of why you started and need to finish.

Your coach and mentor's goal is to keep you on track with your commitments.

- **Prioritize and stick to the order. Be tough:** Most times it is the easy or comfortable things on the priority list that get done; leaving the more difficult tasks undone. I challenge you: **Do two hard, one easy and two hard**. Follow this order and keep it moving. Stick with it and you will see success.

- **Make a decision to work daily on your action steps:** Working on your action steps daily will move you toward your goals and dreams much quicker. Every time you complete a goal your mind is strengthened and you build trust in yourself and your abilities. Deciding and following through on your set actions is life to your success journey.

Fight to be committed daily; one year of commitment will advance you by 10 years if you decide to go all the way. Commitment will be a double-edged sword for you, it will remove distractions and protect you from failures. Decide to cultivate your muscle of commitment and deal with any blind spots concerning your commitment. The time to commit to your journey is now! Not tomorrow!

4. LEADING THE ONE

The Key Ingredient to Being Successful Daily:
Self-Leadership

Leadership begins with the individual; as a leader leads others he must first lead himself. According to Lao Tzu, "Mastering others is strength. Mastering yourself is true power." On the journey of success, you will have to influence people to buy into your vision, goals and dreams. John Maxwell says, "Leadership is influence, nothing more, nothing less." The key to being successful is that you must seek to know and understand what it takes to influence yourself first. The journey of success will require you to become extremely self-aware, confident, responsible and diligent in pursuing your vision and goals. Experiencing the journey will increase your leadership skills, the same will happen for others on the journey. As you are more aware of your gifts, and value, your ability to lead yourself will increase. Do you have what it takes to lead yourself to be successful? Are you aware of what it will cost you? Well, according to Bryant, Kazan 2012, self-leadership is, "having a developed sense of who you are, what you can do, where you are going coupled with the ability to influence your communication, emotions and behavior on the way to getting there." Every single person is wired to be a leader of their actions and must take responsibility for themselves. Not everyone takes on the responsibility. Therefore, not everyone is successful.

My friend, success is not a fly by night. Success is not something you can do today and quit tomorrow.

Success is not a one size fits all. Sure, the principles and characters are the same; however, everyone's success is tailored to their identity, purpose, wiring, vision, goals and destiny. Your life is a story of success from birth to the day you die. The journey between birth and death is called living intentionally. Successful people lead themselves even when it is difficult. They make tough decisions; they select delayed gratification to enjoy the benefits of their sacrifice later in life. On the journey of success, only those who are strong in will and action to direct themselves will eat the fruit of their discipline and diligence; others will only wish they were more self-governed.

The journey of leading oneself is in your ability to do the following consistently:

1) Create a personal vision and mission for your life and legacy.
2) To focus on creating an action plan with small to large goals accompanied by a set timeline.
3) Commit and follow through daily on the plan of action.
4) Get up early.
5) Be organized.
6) Study your craft and research to be better and excellent.
7) Make new friends and cultivate the current ones.
8) Be grateful daily.
9) Renew your mind daily for success.
10) Being focused on your life, family and purpose.
11) Mind your own business.

12) Practice discipline, diligence, consistency and commitment as you move towards your end goal in life.

There are many other areas that a person will have to lead themselves daily. What are some of the things you must lead yourself to do? Is it writing a book, developing yourself, leading your home, or is it producing excellent work on the job? Well, take some time and write down the areas you need to lead yourself personally and professionally. Also, write down the areas you must lead yourself into effectively doing. Once you complete them, credibility in your self-efforts will affect others positively.

Leading the one is going to take cultivating some areas once you are ready to go on the journey. Leading the one is a fight with yourself and a fight that you must win to ever have the successful chance of leading others on their own journey. The areas one must be developed in are:

- Self- Awareness
- Self-Confidence
- Self- Discipline
- Diligence
- Mental Toughness
- Self-Efficacy
- Self-Management
- Self-Motivation

These areas are paramount to completing your journey in such a way that others will have a positive reference to look back on and acknowledge your life's accomplishments and legacy.

Let's look at them.

Self-Awareness

To be unaware is to be in the dark. Lack of self-awareness is a dangerous place to be in for a long period of time. To not know yourself keeps you ignorant of who you are and what you are capable of doing; hence, self-awareness is being able to know and understand who you are, and what your strengths, weaknesses, abilities, and core values are. Self-awareness is understanding what gets you going, what keeps you going, and what things pose a danger to your momentum. The more you grow in self-awareness, the greater your self-leadership and management can be. You can't influence in the dark. You need the light to shine on the matter or person that you desire to influence; in this case, it is you. Shine the light on yourself and get to know who you are.

Seek to know your why, desire, purpose for living, and your dreams and life mission. A life without awareness of purpose is a life preparing to crash. Your journey of being successful requires you to grow in self-awareness. Take the time to build a relationship with yourself. Build trust, respect, love, appreciation, character, and integrity. It's time to get you moving in the right direction; you have what it takes to win.

Self-Management

On your journey of success self-management is like taking a daily bath. One must learn to manage who they are and their own expectations. Self-management is one's ability to handle work and day to day activities to be productive at the end of the day. Management of self is bringing yourself to do the work required of you in all areas of life; home, marriage, family, business, job, relationships and anything else that concerns you. Learning to manage your life well will put you on top of your game.

The journey requires you to manage your priorities, activities, marriage, family, goals, dreams and much more. Being skilled in allocating time for everything in your life boils down to one question, what is important to me and what will it take for me to have and cultivate it? Self-management is about applying self-control and mastery in your life to work towards your daily goals and life's purpose. Without self-management you will revert to a child, but it's children and babies who need to be managed 100% of the time. Adults have gained levels of self-management and must show themselves responsible for their output and accomplishments.

- What will it take for you to manage yourself?
- Do you find that you rely on others to handle your affairs and constantly make decisions for you?
- Are you afraid of responsibility?

- Do you know what it takes to govern your affairs?
- Do you prefer to be managed by others or yourself?
- What kind of mindset do you have regarding self-management?

Questions are important! On your journey to success, will you need someone to hold your hand and take you there? Or are you able to move towards your desired end goal by yourself, with some accountability partners to check in now and again to help you stay on the path? You and only you can answer the question. It's time to manage you and others will gladly help you when you need the help. Get a hold of the person you desire to be, put in the daily work, and manage your performance and productivity. You can do it. You have with it takes.

Self-Motivation

Motivation is the energy derived from external or internal forces to get people moving towards their goals.

Motivation is the ability to induce energy in order to create movement in an intended direction. There are internal and external motivations; having both of them is important, yet having the right one for the journey is even more important to gain rewards and lasting joy. It is awesome when we can be motivated by others to get moving and accomplish our goals and dreams. Life will not always provide motivation. People will not always be there to motivate you. Most times the same people we look to for motivation are the source of demotivation. It is important to know your why and cultivate it. Your why is your internal motivation that gets you up in the morning and keeps you going. It must have great importance to you. Your why is the key to turning you on. If you rely on the "whys" of other people you will be at the mercy of their feelings and thoughts towards you. Get in touch with your creator and let him give you His "why". You are wired to succeed. Failure is a learning ground and must be seen as such. You did not fail when you made a mistake; you just actioned the wrong information in your life. All you must do is change the applied information and the outcome will change. Let your life be a true motivation to others and let your why be a burning light of fire to motivate you to be successful. You have what it takes to persuade yourself. I believe in you. Find reasons to be inspired. Your destiny depends on it. Your daily experience will be the legacy nuggets of future generations to come.

Self-Discipline

Self-Discipline is the art of cutting one's self away from anything or anyone that will take them away from their desired goal and purpose in life. This cutting away can be temporal or permanent; the idea of cutting out the wrong mindset to attain and cultivate the right one for exceptional action is the work of discipline.

Theodore Roosevelt once said, "The one quality which sets one man apart from another-the key which lifts one to every aspiration while others are caught up in the mire of mediocrity- is not talent, formal education, or intellectual brightness – it is self-discipline. With self-discipline all things are possible. Without it, even the simplest goal can seem like an impossible dream." Life is wired to reward the ones who persevere through self-discipline and accomplish what they set out to do. Your level of success is determined by how great your self-discipline is. No discipline = no success. Some discipline = some success with low levels of excellence. High discipline = great success with high levels of excellence. You see, discipline helps to develop a sharp focus in your life. Discipline compounds all efforts and turns all who walk with her into great successful people. Discipline is a painful process, yet over time it gets easier. The higher in life you go the more you will have to cut off things and people to become who you are designed to be. Discipline will help you accomplish this difficult ordeal. Self-discipline will get you to the finish line even after all motivation is gone. Self-discipline is not a one-night stand character you can have today and leave tomorrow. Every day you must engage her, and she will promote you beyond your wildest dreams. Remember the words of Jim Rohn, "Discipline is the bridge between goals and accomplishments." You are going on the journey of success, don't leave home without discipline. If you do, it will cost you a lifetime of regrets and shame. This is why Dwayne Johnson stated so lovely, "all successes begin with self-discipline. It starts with you." You must become one with discipline if you are going to see what you desire in life. "I could only achieve success in my life through self-discipline, and I applied it until my wish and my will became one." - Nikola Tesla

Self-discipline applied daily unlocks great strength and grace to get you to where you are going. You will be glad if you marry discipline and love her daily even when things are tough. Success is designed for those who are willing to put in the work and keep putting in the work until their purpose is completed and all goals and dreams are attained. Be wise and cultivate discipline now. Your generations will praise you and stand on the legacy you created.

Diligence

According to vocabulary.com, 'diligent' comes from the Latin word diligere, which means, 'to value highly, take delight in,' but in English, it has always meant, 'careful and hard-working.' Therefore, we can say one who is diligent within their life span will have high regard and value for their work, goals, and dreams to the point of great delight, that pushes the individual to be wise, careful and hardworking in order to bring about the desired fruit. In this case, it will be exceptional success in whatever area of life you are journeying in. Within self-leadership a diligent person will always bear rule over themselves and others. Their life will be fruitful in all areas attended to.

1) *A diligent person will find the strength to overcome and the wisdom to handle every situation that comes against their desired goal.*

You see, the journey to success is made with bumps, rough roads, high hills and many roadblocks that sometimes seem impossible to get through. The diligent one by their preparation and tenacity will garner the fruit of their labor. Against all odds strength will come, creative ways to overcome challenges and divine solutions to major setbacks will flood the minds and hearts of the one who chooses to be diligent in accomplishing their goals in life. Diligent people study their craft and set their focus on whatever they are aiming to achieve. Lazy, idle and slack people waste time, procrastinate and fail to prioritize their life and time around their purpose, goals, assignments and destiny. Diligent people overcome and gain wisdom as they focus on the prize and move towards it with precise care and attention given to obtaining the goals at hand. Seek to be diligent. Pay the price daily and the benefits will make you smile on your journey of success.

2) **"To be idle is short of death and to be diligent is a way of life; foolish people are idle, wise people are diligent." – Buddha**

Idleness is the state of a person that lacks vision, drive and the why in their life. They lack the internal discipline to lead themselves to victory over internal and external distractions. The product of an idle person is the death of their purpose, gifts and any chance of influencing the world for good. On the other hand, the way of the diligent person leads to life and goodness. It is important to develop the skill of diligently moving towards your God-given purpose and goals in life. It is foolish to foster the mindset of sitting idly, believing that life will somehow hand you your desired goal or desires. Wisdom will inspire you to create a plan with a sustainable way of action to help you along your journey to success. Choose to be wise and walk in diligence.

3) *"Seest thou a man diligent in his business? He shall stand before kings; he shall not stand before mean men." – Proverbs*

Diligent people have a way of attracting individuals who can advance them further and pay for their skills or services offered. Diligence releases a sweet smell, and persons who have value and appreciation for it will open doors for you in your life. You will attract the kind of people that you are. The diligent can stand before kings because kings are diligent. Slothful people will stand before mean and debasing men because they are also mean and shameful. On your journey of success, it is important to understand that you are the one responsible for your success or failure; your character will determine who you will be in fellowship with and who you will connect to. Your diligence or slothfulness is like a magnet and you will eat the fruit of whichever one you are. Your life is important. Decide to be diligent on your journey of success. Every minute of diligence will compound into years of great success for you and your generations to come.

4) *"Leisure is the time for doing something useful. This leisure the diligent person will obtain the lazy one never." – Benjamin Franklin*

It is a very troubling problem when you hear someone say, I don't have the time, or I am too busy right now. Anything you are doing that is not useful to your purpose, vision, goals and destiny is a waste of precious time. The key to being a success is in the mastering of prioritizing your activities within the amount of time you have, which is 24 hours. Everyone has the same 24 hours, yet not everyone gets the same results or uses their time in the same manner. I have seen people struggle with time wasting, allowing the voice of laziness in their hearts to talk them out of being diligent in attending to their goals. The question you must ask is: What do I do with my free or down time? How much time do I waste doing nothing but surfing the net and looking at other people's social media? If you were to track your activities and the amount of time spent on each, you would be able to tell where your energy and focus are going. It is time to refocus and decide to use your time in useful and meaningful activities that will add value to your life, family, and future generations and cause you to be a blessing to others. NOW is the time to be intentional, and move towards your true goals and desires. Cast off every challenge, situation and circumstance into the hands of your Maker. Be thankful and watch how things turn around.

5) *To be as diligent as an ant is the key and underlying current to unlimited success.*

Ants are very disciplined, consistent and self-driven. They are motivated by one factor which is to prepare in the summer for winter. My wife, Elvetta Edwards will always say, "Preparation is the key to mastering your stepping stone." To be successful in life preparation is key, and it must not be done haphazardly. Careful thought and consideration must be given to what is needed to be successful. The ants work together to make it very possible for them to be ready for winter. As you take your journey, it is important to have a well thought out plan and have an idea of who your helpers are going to be on your journey of being a success.

As you move towards your journey of success remember you must mind your success and think in terms of a farmer, investor and one who just started a company. In all these areas the key factor to success is time. You must put in the time, and water your seeds with good habits. Be steadfast in your diligence and your success will blossom, yield great increase and bring in great profits, once you stay the course and work to the end.

Self-Confidence

Leadership begins with confidence. Leading your own self is futile if there is no self-confidence. Confidence is the internal strength, belief and trust in yourself to accomplish a specific task, or role even when there is great difficulty, setbacks or opposition from others. Successful people develop confidence in themselves. You must operate with boldness and you will have what it takes to make it happen regardless of the process or time it takes. The journey of success requires you to develop in the areas of:

- Self-Acceptance
- Self-Love
- Self-Trust

- Self- Dependence
- Self-Control
- Self-Development

Self-Acceptance

The truth is if you don't accept who you are and what you are capable of you will lack the confidence to pursue your goals and dreams. Self-Rejection is a major player in people not being confident in themselves and what they are capable of doing. When one person rejects you that is ok, you can bounce back. However, when you reject yourself, you are pining away and losing all sense of life and purpose. With the light of confidence and desire for yourself, success will spring alive and everything within you will come alive. To reject yourself is to reject your vision, purpose and destiny; it means you have also rejected all the people you were wired to inspire, empower, and help along your journey of success. When you reject yourself, it means you have an identity crisis. "Self-acceptance is pure power," stated Amy Leigh Mercree.

The more you accept yourself, the more power you will be aware of to lead yourself into greatness; the confidence that will spring from you will be unbelievable. "Once you accept the fact that you're not perfect, then you develop some confidence." – Roslynn Carter – Confidence is key, and it is needed on your journey of being a big success. Choose to allow your true self to shine. Believe and trust in yourself to accomplish anything that is given to you and everything that you are wired to do. "You'll never know who you are unless you shed who you pretend to be." – Vironika Jugaleva.

Self-Love

See a man who genuinely loves himself; that is the man who beams with confidence to tackle anything in life. Love that is made perfect becomes a barrier to fear. The presence of fear means the absence of self-love. If you don't love yourself and others, you will not be a success. Without love for yourself and others, success will be very hard to experience. The more you love and value yourself, confidence will spring from the core of your heart and propel you to keep moving towards your desired dreams and goals. Now is the time to dig deep within and appreciate who you are and the value you bring to the world. Be bold and lead yourself with massive love.

Self-Trust

Trust is a key ingredient to being successful with others and most of all with you. Self-leadership is futile if you can't trust yourself. Are you able to keep your word to you? Are you one that goes back on your promises to you, concerning your goals and deadlines? You see, the more we miss the mark of fulfilling promises that we make to ourselves, the more our subconscious will begin to not take our desires, goals and plans seriously. Mistrust of oneself is a problematic place to be. When you don't trust someone, you shy away from connecting and growing with them. Imagine not trusting yourself; you will be bombarded with thoughts and actions that make you doubt yourself and believe that you can't be trusted to accomplish big and important things. You will also experience self-rejection. This is a major hindrance for many people on their road to success. Their journey is compromised because of a lack of trust. If you desire to be a major success, trust yourself to make it happen. Trust yourself to shine and know that you will make it tremendously.

If you struggle with a lack of self-trust, say to yourself: "I forgive me for not being true to my own words, goals and desires. Today, I choose to walk in self-trust and believe that I have what it takes to honor my word to myself and others. I refuse to reject myself. I choose to accept myself and believe and trust in who I am. Remember if you are going to be confident in yourself you must develop self-trust.

Self-Dependence

I believe that we can depend on ourselves to stick to our goals no matter the challenges, trials and setbacks. Self-dependence says that I can rely on my willpower to drive me to get the job done. You can rely on you to be disciplined to accomplish your goals. When someone says you are undependable, they are saying that you are not consistent in your ability to be trusted and to be partnered with to get important things done. In building self-confidence, you must believe and know you can be dependable. When you consistently do what you have planned for yourself it builds great momentum, self-value, worth and a great sense of appreciation for yourself. Open your mouth and say: "I depend on myself to be committed to self-growth, development and the journey of success. I am excited to be me; I get the work done." Refuse to be unstable in your pursuit of success. The one who is not dependable is deemed to be double-minded and ends up falling off the pathway. Choose to depend on your gifts, talents and abilities by developing, growing and using them daily to assist you in your journey of success. You will not regret it, ever.

Self-dependence is golden and will take you far in life. Choose to succeed. Choose to be confident.

Self-Control

One of the keys to turning on self-confidence in your life is self-control. The question is: who has control of you? Is it fear, doubt, unbelief, procrastination and embarrassment? You as a student on the journey of mastering success must take full control of your mind, heart and actions. Take control of your emotions. Take control of your thoughts. Tell yourself that you will not be a slave to fear and doubt. You must grab all of your dreams, passions and destiny and move forward into triumphant victory. A man of self-control has the power to experience great success through his ability to discipline and rule himself. Choose to be confident in who you are, and your success will shine forth as the sun and light up your dark areas like the stars. Choose to win. Choose to dominate your life and be a success.

Self-Development

If you desire to grow and walk in self-confidence you must self-develop. Self-development is the process of taking oneself into constant improvement, growth and learning new skills. Self-development is looking at you and saying, since I desire to lead, I must develop in leadership. It says since I desire to be confident, I must develop in my gifts and abilities. Self-development says that you are serious about your success journey. It communicates that you desire to advance in your goal to lead the one; by doing so, you prepare to lead others into their success as well. Self-development requires you to be fully focused and aware of where you want to go in life and in what areas you want to be exceptional and excellent. As you develop and grow your life will take on importance and be more valuable to others.

Self-Efficacy

Self-efficacy is the key to confidence and self-leadership. The ability to believe in yourself and in your capabilities to accomplish anything you start or the ability to function well in any situation. You must believe that you have what it takes to succeed. You must believe that you have what it takes to win in life. The journey to success requires a great deal of self-belief. As you go about life many things will come your way; many situations will unfold right in your pathway. Do you know how to handle tough situations? Do you believe you can achieve this? Are you able to organize a strategy to overcome and keep moving towards your specific goals and dreams? Do you have the fortitude to pick yourself up from a major setback and still believe you have what it takes to win and win strong?

You see a person's self-efficacy is the key to their journey being meaningful and impactful. Success is attracted to the one who knows and believes in their identity and gifts to accomplish major things. Self-efficacy is the bedrock and wiring of the individual. Your belief in yourself has the same effect on you as the blood has a major effect on the life of the individual. Self-efficacy is the blood of self-leadership; without it, self-leadership will be a daunting task. Anyone who does not believe and trust in their capability to succeed will fall prey to the following:

- Negative thinking
- Unhealthy feelings and emotions
- Self-doubt
- Lack of energy
- Procrastination
- Lack of focus
- Lack of organization
- Low self-esteem
- Jealous attitudes towards anyone that succeeds.
- Unable to be productive and successful.
- Fearful of taking risks and stepping up to challenges.
- Lack confidence in oneself.

Understanding self-efficacy is like understanding how to use a standard vehicle; if it's used wrong it will cause serious life risk. Having efficacy is important to your ability to survive in the world and advance through everything that tries to pull you down. Choose to develop your heart and mind, your personality and your purpose. Persons who are rich in efficacy can handle tough times and situations.

The beginning of self-efficacy takes its place in early childhood. This process of development takes place when the child starts learning to deal with a wide range of experiences, tasks and situations; here is where self-belief or belief in self-abilities are formed. Self-efficacy continues to develop throughout our lives as we acquire new skills and take on new and more challenging responsibilities. How we view ourselves in handling these skills, responsibilities and situations will determine our level of self-efficacy. People with a high level of self-efficacy:

- See problems as opportunities to grow and gain something new.
- Can bounce back from setbacks and continue moving towards goals.
- Are committed to goals and assignments, are strong and tend to stick to finishing what they started.
- Are high in self-confidence and have a healthy social life and relationships.
- Enjoy a challenge. They see it as a learning and growth opportunity.

You must choose to be around people who think like you, hold the same or similar goals and aspirations, and are going in the same direction. Why is this important? People who don't hold your DNA or the same understanding to success will be a threat to your journey. These people will drain you, cause you to be delayed, set back and taken off your pathway to success. Be mindful of who you connect to in terms of successful partnership. You will interact with all kinds of people but you will have to choose the right ones to bring into your cycle of success. Choose wisely. Choose based on their level of discipline, diligence and way of thinking towards life and challenges. Not everyone can be trusted within your cycle of success and this attitude requires you to be secure in yourself and your abilities.

As we continue to look at Self-leadership, it is important that you understand success requires you to battle with every negative habit you have cultivated. Once you have overcome negative habits, leading you to all that you desire will be a success. Doing this will qualify you to lead others into their journey of success. Develop your willpower and take action daily. Don't let anything take you away from your journey.

The Heart of Self-Leadership

Leading the one requires a strong demand for creative wisdom and understanding. I say this is the heart of self-leadership. Leading yourself to become continuously successful will require you to have a range of skills, knowledge, and the ability to apply the knowledge. Many persons are full of information yet lack the wisdom and understanding to put the knowledge to work. They are unaware of times and seasons. Success in life requires a heart which I call, "Wisdom and Understanding." When you understand and apply wisdom you will advance and excel. You will be able to handle yourself and the personalities of others while journeying to success. Foolishness, lack of knowledge and understanding are enemies of your self-leadership. A foolish person becomes a heavy and unpleasant burden to all that encounter him or her. Lack of knowledge exposes you to danger on the road to success. What you don't know has the capacity to destroy or prevent you from having major success and gaining mega opportunities. Knowledge is gained power. Wisdom is applied and utilized power. Wisdom is the ability to put to action what you know in the best possible way that will bring great results. One who lacks understanding will be a danger to self and others. Understanding is the ability to judge rightly with the knowledge you have; knowing the best possible way to utilize what you know and have.

Leadership requires focus and vision. Self-leadership then is the focus on carrying out your vision solely to be your true self, empowering your family, helping others and leaving a legacy for your children and generations to walk in and take note of. Leadership is always about changing lives; even if it is self-leadership and that is the heart of it all, service.

Will Power: The Key to Continued Action

The will of a person is the internal desire and intentions. Will power is the active and burning force to make an intention happen. We know that many persons have the motivation which is the desire to move; yet they lack the willpower to start and complete the action. What holds your "WILL" hostage? What is hampering your "WILL" from being a reality? What are the reasons for your inactivity? To free your "WILL", you must know what has it captive. As humans, willpower is so potent that a sick person who has the will to be better will get better. A person who is on their death bed will be made well just by the "WILL" to stay alive. Don't let anything destroy your will. Say to you, "I have the mind and "Will" to work and be fruitful." Prepare your Will to function. A person that has no will to do is like a lifeless shell that has been abandoned. Get up and prepare for action.

How to Build your "WILL POWER"

Will power responds to faith and doubt. If you believe in yourself and what you can do, your will power becomes inspired to function for the benefit of making you accomplish your goals and assignments. If you doubt and lack belief in your abilities to function then your will power fights against you in order to keep you from accomplishing that which you really want to achieve. This is why you get headaches when you start to do a particular task, or goal. The will is the power and life of the mind. Whatever you feed your mind is what your mind will give life to. Feed your mind with positivity; thoughts of being a winner, a success, a champion, and an overcomer. The actions of thinking, visualizing, speaking and doing are how you feed your willpower.

The Food of Right Thoughts

Right thinking is good and healthy food for the will power of an individual. Do you desire to succeed in life? Do you have a vision for yourself? Do you have big dreams? Right thoughts towards yourself and your dreams will be the food that helps your mind, will, and emotions to move you in that direction. We understand that thoughts are substance and every substance you see came from a manifested thought. Choose your thoughts wisely, cultivate them skillfully and manifest them joyfully. According to James Allen, "As a man thinks so is he", if you desire to be great and successful, carve out some time for right thinking, creative thinking and analytical thinking. Your life will never be the same. Choose a time, place and space and stick to it. Don't be distracted. Your life of success and generational legacy depends on it. Below are some of the thoughts you should be thinking:

- I have what it takes to win; I enjoy winning tough challenges.
- Today I will make progress, I enjoy being productive.
- Life is full of excitement.
- I must win, I desire to win, I have the will to win, today I won.
- Everything good is happening for me and others around me; I expect goodness.

These are some thoughts you can think of while you are going about your business. Always do mind checks. Ask yourself, what am I thinking? What am I feeling? What decisions am I making? If the answer is not in alignment with your goals, dreams and vision for yourself or your family, proceed to change. If it is good, continue. Whatever you desire to be and do inject by way of your thoughts. Protect and empower your will with your thoughts. I have found the principles and words from the Bible as good thought food.

The Food of Right Speaking

There is tremendous power in speaking. Words carry life and death. They are the very force that has everything moving in your life for good or bad. Right words are like medicine. Daily inject health and words of life and you will find your will increasing in power. Cindy Trimm states, "Whatever you release from your mouth you give that thing permission to exist." The question is "What do you want to exist in your life today and tomorrow?" write them down and speak them out for the next 90 days. Your journey of success will be justified by your words or condemned by your words. Have you ever heard the following words?

- Nothing good ever happens to me.
- I have bad luck.
- I could never keep money.
- I could never get anything right.
- Everybody is against me
- Life is hard.

These words are a danger to your will, success, and journey in life on a whole. It is important to be careful what you say while you are experiencing challenging times. Words add fuel to positive or negative experiences. Words can also extinguish fires and start them. If you are experiencing something that you wish not to experience on your journey of success, learn from it and speak the opposite to it. Below in the diagram are some alternatives to negative experiences and words:

Negative Statements	Positive Statements to counteract	Negative Experience	Positive Statement to counteract
I can't	I will work at it	Today was bad	Today was a learning experience
That will never happen for me	I believe that it will happen for me	I did not get the job	Even thou I did not get the job, I enjoyed the interview.
I am a loser	I am born to win	I could never keep a relationship	I have learnt about myself from my past relationships
I don't look good	I am fearfully and wonderfully made, I am attractive.	I could never get along with co-workers	Daily I will say something nice to my co-workers
I have bad luck	Today I am expecting Favor	No one loves me	I am experiencing genuine love from everyone I meet today

It is important to watch your words and handle your experiences properly. Everything faced in life is a key to unlock doors of success or failure. Failures are ends and successes are beginnings. If you believe you are failing, there is nowhere in life to go for you; if you believe you are succeeding in life there are opportunities opening for you daily. It's your perspective on everything. Mistakes are learning opportunities. They hold the keys to your success. Learn from them.

The Food of Visualizing

The ability to see beyond the current is the function of the heart and imagination. Seeing in pictures what you desire is food to your will power. The more you live in the place you desire to be by vision is the more your will power will be activated to make it happen. Who do you want to be? What do you want to have? Where do you want to go? What experiences do you desire? Open your imagination and look at them in your mind. See it as your desire, and your will power will activate a plan of action in your mind and push you to that desired goal. You have to envision it in your mind and speak it with your mouth, your feet will move towards it by your daily actions. No vision, no direction. Begin to see your future and your mind will help you get there.

The Food of Action

Action is the fruit of your thoughts, visions, and words. Action is given birth by your will, once the mind and heart has come into agreement with your desire. This is a process that can take seconds or years. This is why you must develop and grow yourself daily through discipline and diligence. Action is the key to manifestation and fruitfulness. Without action, your dreams and desires will not take feet and wings.

Action should be intentional and planned. Every day you should intend to take 2 to 3 steps towards your goals, dreams and desires. Doing this will assure your will that you are serious about this endeavor and that it is a major priority. Spasmodic actions will force the will to believe that you are not serious, and chances are you will stop moving towards those goals. The bible says, faith without works (corresponding action) is lifeless. Today, decide to take action and move towards your goals. Declare, "I am taking action daily."

Remember as you feed your will, what is required for you to succeed will move along nicely and smoothly in the journey, without problems.

Your will is the biggest area you will need to develop to lead you to success. Without your will, you become a liability to yourself and others. You will digress to having to have others make decisions and major choices for you. Choose to grow in self-leadership and your journey to success will be amazing and rewarding.

The Order and Structure of Success

Success is different for everybody. However, a few essential elements are universally required, such as setting goals, harboring dreams and desires, possessing a compelling reason, and demonstrating discipline, diligence, motivation, and will power. These components are just the beginning, there are so many more factors involved. The key factor in developing order and structure so you can last a life time in success is having a stable and fortified routine. Routine is to your success what your internal body functions is to your life. Without routine you will become unstable, flimsy, and some day aimless. Routine gives you focus, clarity and direction.

Many successful persons have different routines. However, most of them rise early before the crowd and before the sun. Getting up early puts you ahead in your journey of success. Your success lies in what you are able to do consistently on a daily basis. What you do today will be the foundation of what you do and accomplish tomorrow. Lazy people do nothing and accomplish nothing. Some persons rise late and go to bed late. That is their routine. If you want to become successful and move out of a failure province you must heed the words of John C. Maxwell, "You'll never change your life until you change something you do daily. The secret to your success is found in your daily routine." Routine is the blood of success, without it your successful life will dry up. Your future is full of possibilities and awesome things waiting to be manifested, however, "the secret of your future is hidden in your daily routine." – Mike Murdock

If you want to be successful next year your, daily routine this year will unlock next year's success. What you do today will advance you tomorrow and what you do this week will advance you next week. It is the power of compound effect. You might be saying you have not been able to create a routine; well, now is the time. Now is the "time to tidy up your life. Time to start again." – David Nicholis

Start today with a million-dollar, billion-dollar routine that will change your life forever. You can do it. You have what it takes to make it happen. Plan and take action in your day and your day will give you good fruits. Each step will build you for success. Each step will create the pathway for others to follow and learn from. Don't give up. Don't settle for less. Go far and do your best. Create your routine, work your routine, adjust your routine and your life will become a routine of daily success and greatness.

In connection with the remainder of this book, I leave with you the importance of order and structure. Your life will not go anywhere if you don't plan and action it. As you plan your life take note of the people that are wired to help you. They are called destiny helpers. Destiny helpers are important to your daily routine; without them your life will feel hard and sometime aimless. They are people wired to connect you to other opportunities, and people that hold important nuggets to your success. Your approach in life will determine whether you meet these destiny helpers. Your routine and your actions will attract them or repel them. Do your best and pay attention while you learn on the journey of success. Success is who you are. Failure will also be you if you choose not to pay attention.

Go and be successful!

BOOK TWO

THE APPROACH

by **A**lbert Thompkins

1.   The Approach to Success

"It is our attitude at the beginning of a difficult task which, more than anything else, will affect its successful outcome." ~ William James

In life there are times when you face various situations, challenges, and difficulties. You face obstacles that can distort the direction you are trying to go in. It can be frustrating, intimidating, and sometimes the reason you are not where you want to be. But then you must look within yourself to see how you can accomplish the goal you set out. Because really there are only two options in life: Do it or Don't do it. That's it. No matter how you try to sugarcoat it, that is the conclusion of the matter. At the end of the day, you will have to answer the question, did you complete or not. Did you get it done or nah? Were you able to finish, persevere, or do that which you know in your heart you truly desired to do? And if the answer is no, then the next question is why not? And even though I don't know you or your circumstances, I already know the answer to why not. No matter the reason you state, the answer will be that your approach did not work. Period.

You can come up with all sorts of explanations as to why you failed. But the answer will always be that the approach was off. It's amazing because there is always a path to success. But will you choose the right path? Now, I don't want you to second guess yourself. We all have failed. Failure is one of key components to success. However, it is how you view failure. The failure just tells you that you had the wrong approach.

If you just change your approach, success will be inevitable.

So how do you choose or create the right approach? We will review in Chapter 3. As we begin this portion of the journey, it is important to understand that you have to take an honest look at yourself first. You must look at your pride, perspective, and your potential. If you address the 3P's, you will be able to find or create the new approach that you need to overcome. When failure comes it just births a platform for you to seek a different way or look within to innovate something new. And I want you to see challenges as an opportunity. Look at problems as a chance to grow and change. I don't want to get ahead of myself, but your failure is the privilege to do something that you have never done before. Now, back to the 3 P's. I will expand at length in Chapter 3, but the 3 P's are the foundation to having a new approach to life. Pride, Perspective, and Potential.

P #1 - Pride

Pride, while often touted as a virtue, can swiftly transform into a formidable barrier on the path to success. It's natural to take pride in oneself, in our work, or in our background. However, when pride swells to the point where it obstructs growth and change, it becomes a perilous obstacle. Have you encountered individuals so entrenched in their pride that they resist any semblance of transformation? How are they faring? Often, they find themselves immobilized, stagnating in life's journey. Their dreams remain elusive, obscured by the veil of unwavering pride.

It's imperative to recognize that excessive pride is a master of deception. It whispers falsehoods, convincing us that change is unnecessary, that adjustments are superfluous, and that acknowledging our true circumstances is inconsequential. Moreover, pride can infiltrate the minutiae of our existence, clinging stubbornly to inconsequential matters. While upholding foundational principles is commendable, stubbornly clinging to insignificant details driven by pride can impede progress.

Consider, for instance, the fleeting thoughts or judgments we adamantly hold onto out of pride. What if, by relinquishing these trivial notions, we could revolutionize our approach and inch closer to our long-standing aspirations? What small, pride-induced habits or beliefs are hindering your progress? Perhaps it's time to reassess and shed these burdensome shackles.

In addition to hindering progress, pride blinds us to the possibility of error. It obstructs our ability to acknowledge when we may be on the wrong side of an issue, trapping us in a cycle of stubbornness and stagnation. Embracing humility and openness to different perspectives is the antidote to this blinding pride.

In essence, pride, when left unchecked, can morph from a source of empowerment into a formidable impediment to growth and progress. In other words, pride prevents you from addressing the 2nd P, which is perspective.

P #2 - Perspective

How you look at things can lead you to a new approach. Perspective is interesting because how you view a thing can impact your success. The reality is you can only see what you can see. And you are usually drawn to things that you feel best suit you. You usually gravitate to optics that are favorable to your outlook. We tend to avoid things that are counter-intuitive. It's part of our survival mode. However, what many fail to realize is that every so often we must perform maintenance on ourselves. For instance, your vehicle has periodic maintenance to ensure it operates at peak performance. Every 3,000 miles you should get your oil changed, you have to refill the fluids, and change the air filter. Why? Because overtime the filter gets clogged by debris and it cannot operate as it should. This happens to us as humans as well. There are times when our perspective gets messy because life can get messy and that can be an indication that it's time to adjust our perspective or vision and see things from a different viewpoint. And this is really the basis of a new approach. There are instances when we can alter how we see ourselves. We have to look introspectively and unearth our potential, which is the 3rd P.

P #3 - Potential

What is your true value? What is the accurate assessment of what is budding-up inside of you? When will you pour out that which is lying dormant in you? How do you measure up to what you know is lurking within? It may be in embryonic form, but you know it's there. As you go through these chapters I challenge you to do a self-inventory (there is a self-inventory later in this chapter) to determine what you are actually capable of. I know you have accomplished in the past, but what about now? Do you have more inside of you than what you originally thought? You may need to up your skill set. Or you have to stop the voices of the past that told you lies about your capabilities and capacity. Additionally, you may need to cease doing things that occupy space for things you are better at. Are you living or acting or believing below your potential?

I know looking within yourself can be frightening, but it is absolutely essential if you are going to get a new approach to life. Your new approach can be discovered if you address your pride, your perspective, and your potential at which point you can actualize what you always dreamed to be. Even that dream you had when you were a kid. Remember that? When you were young and had this urge to be something special when you grew up. Well, it's not too late. If you swallow your pride, modify your perspective, and reassess your potential I know you can get there.

As stated in the previous chapters the first component of success is the Journey. Despite our current culture of spontaneous satisfaction, instant gratification and immediate results there is a process to getting into the place we call success. In addition, we must consider how we view or perceive the journey because what you desire to accomplish may be closer than what you realize, but you may not recognize it.

Let me begin addressing the Approach to success by telling a story. It's the story of A Pilot, His Instruments, and His Approach:

"There once was this pilot who was flying into a small Caribbean airport in the middle of summer. It's important to note that the instruments on the plane were a bit antiquated. They were the kind that all the instrument procedures were non-precision. They were so imprecise, in fact, that many pilots invented their own techniques for landing "blind." Needless to say, the pilot was flying with less than ideal tools to help him. And today is the day that the pilot and his instruments will be tested.

On the plane's approach to the airport, the pilot received an alert by the onboard instruments to climb immediately to avoid hitting another plane that was very close to him. So the pilot climbed as instructed. While doing so he sees the offending aircraft below him and decides to continue the approach. On a 3-mile straight in the final approach to the runway, the pilot spots a wall of torrential rain rapidly approaching the field. Judging from his instruments it looks as if the rain is far enough away that he can beat it to the airport. However, about 100 ft. off the runway the rain hits the plane and the pilot's view goes completely white-out, and he can't see anything out of his windshield. Immediately, the pilot starts a go-around maneuver, and he gets the plane as low as 20 ft. before it finally starts climbing. Upon exiting the rain, and at about 500 ft., the pilot is finally able to see again, and at that very moment he gets ANOTHER alert of a helicopter that is right in front of him! This time Air Traffic Control instructs the pilot to descend to safety!

Takeaways from the story:

1) When flying, you depend on your instruments to determine how you approach.

Your approach is only as good as the instruments that inform it, which then determines your success. And in life our major instrument is our soul. I will expand on this extensively in the following chapter. But for now, just understand that it all comes down to what's in your soul. Who you are in your most inner being is ultimately where your navigational technology to success is located.

2) Approach is like a lens

On a camera a lens is the material that transmits light to form an image or the material used to form an image for viewing. Therefore, your Approach is like a lens in that it is the material that allows you to form an image of circumstances, situations, and opportunities that could lead either to success or failure. It is the essence that forms the image of how you view life. But what happens when your lens is compromised, obstructed, or dirty? Can you view properly? Now imagine that corrupted lens is your approach. Are you able to view circumstances, situations, and opportunities in the best way? Is your image of your life distorted? Do you need lens cleansing? Does your approach need an upgrade, a complete change, or overhaul? What is preventing your lens from working properly? Or are you so accustomed to seeing things a certain way that you don't realize it is skewed to hinder your success. Are you aloof to how your lens on life is but others can see it? Is your lens cracked, damaged, or otherwise awry to your own detriment? I don't pose these questions to chastise or frighten you, but rather to give you pause for your consideration of where you are in your approach to life.

We must all self-reflect and analyze if the lens or approach we currently utilize is allowing us to view life in the best light. Like a camera lens, depending on how the lens is affixed will determine the picture we are capturing. The same can be said about our approach. There are times we must look at ourselves to determine if we are hurting ourselves on how we approach life. It's one thing to see that our current lens is not conveying the best light. But it's another thing to be oblivious to it. If you are constantly having the same issues that hinder you from achieving a certain goal, then we must look to self.

Let's say you lived in a certain city or town for a few years, but you seem to not have success due to circumstances, situations, and challenges. Then you hear of an opportunity in another city, town or country, and you move there. However, as you venture through that new area the same issues that arose in your previous location continue in this new place; something is wrong. If the environment has changed and the same stumbling blocks seem to occur and things still don't turn out to be successful, we must then consider ourselves. This may come across as harsh but sometimes it takes a little push to get to the place of change. And sometimes all the change you need is a change of the lens of your outlook. If you change your approach, you may be amazed that you are closer than you think.

Like the above story of the pilot, it took someone on the outside to help him see his proximity to his destination. The outside person had a different lens than he had. Not only could the other person see where the pilot was, they also had a view of what the pilot was working with. There are times in life you need someone to show you that your lens is not working correctly. Will you allow me to point out your lens to you? Can I show you another approach that might help you?

3) Approach is the axis of vision - You must have vision for your approach

To further illustrate the point of the significance of your approach, examining it as your axis of vision can be beneficial. The definition of axis is that it "forms part of the basis of a space or is used to position and locate an area or plain." Meaning, an approach to life is how you will locate your current location and also assist in determining where you land. The place within success that you aspire to be is based on how your axis is situated. In other words, how you will bring yourself to and unload in the land of success is totally on your approach. Your axis of how you envision life will cause you to arrive in a place of success and the condition you will be within that space. This is so because everything revolves around the axis of an object, like the earth rotates on its axis. How you approach life (your axis of vision) will determine the way things will rotate around you. It's all about the angle in which you place it upon. In other words, your approach will dictate how you arrange situations, circumstances or problems in life. It's all how you view it.

Going back to the above pilot story, he needed assistance from his instruments to determine the axis of the earth as he was approaching to land. In addition, he also had to figure out, given the circumstances, what was the best approach. His natural perspective was not enough to ensure a safe grounding. This tells us sometimes how we view things at first glance, may not be the best option. We may have to circle around situations, circumstances or problems a few times to resolve the best course of action. As with any axis, as things turn you will see things modify. That is good news because what you are currently looking at can change. Things will not always be the same. The truth is the only constant in life is change. It is our past experiences that sometimes corrupt how we view our current circumstance.

However, if we give it a little time, as the rotation of life continues, we will get a new perspective. This is why you cannot judge situations, circumstances or problems too soon. As you adjust your axis, giving things greater importance as you move forward, you can better conclude on a more perfect way to proceed. But be patient with yourself and with life. As the pilot keeps trying different times to land, you can try different approaches to success.

4) All kinds of things/items/deterrents try to hinder your approach

The last and final take-away from the pilot story is we must be mindful of the influences of your approach. In the story there were three distinct things that were attempting to impede his successful land: another plane, rain, and another vessel. It is interesting to examine each because it informs of the hazards we must also be aware of.

First, as the pilot was attempting his first approach to safely ground the plane, there was another plane in very close proximity. And the thing is, the pilot did not even realize how close the other plane was. It wasn't until he distanced himself that he could see the danger. This is a great example for us to be mindful of the people that are close to us. They may be too close in that they could negatively influence your approach to life. This may include, but not limited to, loved ones, friends, co-workers, partners, and the like. Furthermore, how you were brought up, nourished, and educated can be a major source of contradiction to one's approach. Just because you were raised a certain way, does not mean it will work for you in this current time in your life. Have you ever learned a certain behavior growing up that you realize now may not be the best way to act? Yes, we appreciate our parents and grandparents, uncles and aunts who tried to raise us the best way they knew. But some family traits are best forgotten. Traits such as anger, malice, disrespect, sarcasm, unruly behavior, and the list goes on and on. If you noticed any of these, now is a great time to recognize it and change it. Many times in life we must grow out of the mental conditions that nurtured us so that we can embrace enhanced methods of processing life. Most likely it's not those far off that stymie our growth, it's those close to us. Be very aware of your circle.

This brings up the topic of nature versus nurture. On the one hand, some of us are hardwired to think, behave, and to perceive in a definitive way. Then there are others that were cultivated in a very specific way. And as we mature, we have to recognize if how we are currently living life is serving our success. If not, what do you do? Do you continue on the same path and expect things to change on their own accord? Do you ignore the signs indicating you are not making any progress? Do you neglect the aching in your heart to cry out for change? Or do you have an honest look within and change?

The question to consider is, how do you alter what was put in you? How do you modify what is innate to who you are? Is it possible to change a tiger's stripes? But I believe this is the essence of this book. Because these are people, customs, and manners that you may truly love and hold dear to your heart. But if what you are, is hindering you and you have a stronger desire for something greater, then you must be willing to allow the old ways to die and experience a rebirth to the new you. This is why we wrote this book. To provide a source of information and inspiration for you to manifest into who you want to be. But first begin by acknowledging where you are and then making the hard decisions to break away and shift to a new you.

To apply the story to our lives, you must ponder how to deal with others who interfere with your approach, your way of life, which is your path to success. What would you do if someone was blocking you? How do you deal with a person who is intentionally or perhaps unwittingly obstructing your entryway to success? Let's observe what the pilot did in the story. According to the tale, when the pilot was informed another plane was so close that it was in danger of hitting him, the pilot decided to climb higher to avoid a collision. He got above the situation. He increased his elevation. He levitated to a higher altitude. In the words of former First Lady Michelle Obama, "When they go low, we go high!" I believe this is sound advice in these circumstances. When individuals are what is causing you to curb your landing spot in success you must go high on them. Reach a place where they can longer be of any danger to you.

1) First Check Yourself

Maybe you find yourself unwittingly granting others undue influence over your actions, allowing them to wield power or control where none should rightfully exist. It's crucial to conduct a thorough examination of their influence and determine whether it stems from a legitimate position of authority or if it's a product of your own accord.

Once you've discerned that their sway is not rooted in formal authority but rather in your own consent, the next step is to transcend their influence. Next, you have to go above their behaviors, first in your mind then in your deeds. In other words, if the persons are not your supervisors, and you can avoid or go beyond them, then do so. Notice the pilot did not notify the other plane of his intention to go higher. He just did it. We too must do the same. We don't have to tell the offending person our next moves. Just do it! Just move higher. Just increase your work ethic. Just execute your plans. Just escalate your intensity. Just go up! And trust me they will eventually see it. But by the time they notice, you would have moved on to landing in your sphere of success and achievement. Go up and stay up!

2) Rain

In the story, the second thing/item/deterrent that attempted to hinder the pilot's approach was rain. Obviously, rain is a natural force that the pilot had no control over. In addition, when the pilot began his flight, I am sure rain was not in the forecast. Which begs the question, how do you overcome, prevent, or circumvent a natural element when you are attempting to approach a junction in your life? Rain represents those factors in life that are outside your sphere of influence and are truly a part of another sector. It is an outside force that comes into your realm that you must deal with. You cannot ignore it because doing so will not only dislodge your approach to success but it could possibly destroy you. It's interesting because these kinds of hindrances can be both a blessing and dangerous. On the one hand rain is necessary for the overall ecosystem in which you also abide. On the other hand, it could annihilate you. So you must confront it.

Some examples of these kinds of interruptions are illnesses, economic downturns, pandemics, or relationships. Anyone of these has the potency to force you to reconsider your approach to success. You develop a sickness which causes you to recalibrate how you're going to move forward. We live in a global economy and are impacted by markets in other countries and jurisdictions whereby what they do can have an adverse effect on how you conduct business.

Additionally, relationships can be very volatile. Like rain, relationships are necessary but so many factors can cause them to either bless or curse you. Furthermore, the timing of these elements is crucial. As stated above, when the pilot began his navigation, the rain may not have been foreseen. The same can be said about relationships. You never know what relationships you will need to develop on your approach to success. How you treated others in the past could be a blessing or a curse in your future. So just be aware the force of interpersonal interactions is a force to be reckoned with. As you continue to contemplate your approach to life, like the pilot you must be mindful of elements such as rain that could thwart the path to your destiny.

So how would you approach success if one to these "natural elements" were in your pathway? Let us consider our pilot. What did he do? He did a "go-around maneuver" to get out of the rain. That sounds good for our story, but the reality is there are certain aspects of life that you can't just "go-around". What do you do if you contract an illness that may be impossible to "go-around"? What if there is a global pandemic and you are forced to shut down your business for an extended period of time? Or maybe there is a past relationship where you were abused and although you were able to leave the relationship back there you cross paths years later in business and you can't just "go-around" them?

I bring up these scenarios to get you to think about how you are processing them. What mindset are you using to approach these situations? Are you thinking with a negative mindset or a creative one? Because these are all possibilities. And it is your approach to them that will determine how successful you will be. Sure, they are hypothetical for some, but they are a reality for others. Would you just throw in the towel and quit? Or would you dig deep within your soul for an approach that you may have never considered before? When the pilot was facing the rain, he was facing a life and death situation. And when life and death are set before, that is when you should carefully consider your options. I would hope this book will begin to churn your mind, heart, and soul to unearth the untapped alternatives to approach your life.

3) Other Things

Just when the pilot was able to get from under the grip of the torrential rain, his "go-around" maneuver put him in the path of yet another obstacle to hinder his successful landing, it's another vessel -a helicopter. Just like the first plane that was in his way, now there is another aircraft in his way. And isn't that just like life! You dodge one obstruction, only to be faced with another. Now this is where you must remain calm and not allow the frustrations of life to get the best of you. I know you passed the first test when someone was in your way, but here is another person again in your pathway.

It's one thing to have your peers or someone in authority block you, but it's entirely different when it's someone just getting in the game. They just reached the arena and they are taking shots at you. They are not a jet plane like you, but rather just a helicopter. Some may try to discount the fact that it's "just" a little helicopter. As if to suggest due to its size it can't do you any harm. When the reality is it is no less dangerous. In fact, one could argue that it's more dangerous. There's some interesting scripture that states, "It's the small fox that destroys the vines". Meaning, oftentimes in life it's the minor intrusions that can be most fatal. Therefore, we cannot take the "helicopters" for granted.

For this variety of deterrent that tries to hinder your approach, it seems there is a simple yet potent solution. In the story, when there is danger, how did the pilot get beyond this hindrance? This time he received assistance from the Air Traffic Control who told him to "descend to safety!" The idea is that you may be tempted to think you can handle it. But the reality is you must get instructions from Air Traffic Control.

What is Air Traffic Control? They are the ones who direct aircrafts through controlled airspace and on the ground. In our lives there is one who controls the various spaces in which we traverse, be it social, economic, relational, or spiritual. He knows the coming and goings of all and has put all things under his control. He is God and he is Lord of all, and we must seek him for instructions. Not doing so would be detrimental to us eternally. We would then be guilty of experiencing diseases of the soul (which I will discuss at length in the next chapter.) For now, we must realize if we don't seek God for guidance we then operate in pride or some other underlying force.

If we don't center our mind and allow God to lead us, many times we can have knee-jerk reactions and behavior in a manner that we might regret. We may react with anger, compulsion, or a distorted perception. In this case the instructions were simple, keep going and toward what is safe. In other words, don't switch destinations right when you're about to reach your goal. Many times you must just keep it simple. Some call it the K.I.S.S. theory. Keep It Simple Silly. In other words, don't over complicate it. Stay focused. You know what you came to accomplish. Now just do it. Doing anything else will throw you off course and cause you to be delayed.

Agency: Embracing Your Approach to Life

One of the things I want to be sure to convey is that you are in control of your life. You already have what it takes to be the captain of your own destiny. You may have to hone it, but you already possess it. This is important to understand. You are not waiting to get any additional physical features to be great, you are already equipped with it. Once you accept this fact it's called an Agency. Agency is the concept of coming to the understanding that you feel you are in control of where you desire to go in life. You can make decisions to impact the outcomes of life and the force to navigate your course comes from within.

This is vital. Many are stalled or frozen waiting on something on the outside to do for them what they are already endowed to do. They feel that they are helpless and have an overall sense of defeat when no one comes to save them. However, it really comes from the inside. As the pilot in our story demonstrates, as these things/items/deterrents try to hinder your approach, you are the conductor to maneuver as you need. You are the one at the helm to steer your ship in the direction you desire. It is true that outside influences will attempt to get you off course, but you don't have to acquiesce to them. In fact, some could argue that they are there to test if you really want to go in the direction that you say. However, standing up to the opposition and embracing your Agency will be pivotal to your success.

But this begs the question, why do you feel that you are not in control? We must deal with this. What have you experienced that is giving you pause? What is in your environment or in your mind that keeps you from sensing the potential that is in you?

I want to address this because if you are waiting for others to provide the plan, power, and to get you where you want to go, you will never get there and you will be sorely disappointed. Yes, we need others to assist us in the course of life, however, it is up to us to determine where we want to go in life. It is our choice to decide who we want to partner with. You can't be vulnerable to the whims of others. Embrace your own Agency, your instrumentality, your self-determination.

Even if your instruments are outdated, like the plane in our story above, you can decide to update them. The good news is that we live in the information age. A great many of us have smartphones and have access to information at the tip of our fingers. All you have to do is find the information and educate yourself. Self-study is so crucial. This is why this book is here. I hope you use the ideas, concepts, and frameworks in this book to help better equip your Agency, your approach, your feeling of empowerment to get the best life you eagerly yearn for. What does your Agency consist of? Who is in your Agency? What do you have to change to feel more in control of your life? All great questions to get a better grasp on the direction of your life.

AGENCY VS AGENCY

In the world system there are many parts to a physical Agency. Let's take for example, a small not-for-profit agency, and list the different components of the organization. Typically, there is a Board of Directors, there is an Executive Director, and then there are Directors over certain functions such as Director of Finance, or Director of Communication, or Director of Operations. Then finally, under the Directors are the staff members.

Here is a picture of a basic typical agency:

Given this example, how would this compare to the Agency that operates our lives? For individual lives, our Agency is our soul and your soul consists of three parts: intellect, will, and emotions. I will go into much greater detail in the next chapter. But for now just know these are the many parts of the soul. So the question is, who is the Board of Directors of your soul? Which part of your soul is the Executive Director? Which area is Directing your soul? And finally, which part of your soul is staffing your Agency? Knowing the answer to these questions, will indicate the direction you are going. This will help you understand how you are approaching life. If you don't like the place you are in, then your Board of Directors is who is guiding you and giving you advice. Maybe it's time to get a new Board. And may I suggest that the one who gives you the best advice is God. Just like the Air Traffic Controller, he knows what you're facing and gives you the information you need to safely land your life in success.

Agency Rating

At this point, what I would challenge you to do is, create a list of how you are feeling about where you desire to be. Write down good and bad feelings. On a scale to 0-10 (where 0 is you feel that you have absolutely no control, and 10 is you feel that you are absolutely in control) determine your level of Agency. (Use the scale provided below.)

This is a good way to measure the level of your soul strength. Once you get a number, chart down why you think you feel the number you are. For example, if you honestly rated yourself a 3, then think about why you choose 3. Maybe you had bad influences and you still hear their voices in your head. Maybe you were in a bad relationship and your self-esteem is in need of healing. Just make a list of reasons and we will address how to improve your score in the next chapter. I do this because if you don't address why you feel you are not in control, then your approach in life will not suffice. You will always come up short and not understand why you are not successful. And it's important to realize how you feel, what your Agency is, a direct reflection of your soul.

Amy's Battle

Let me give you an example of how your Agency correlates to your soul. I am a mental health counselor and over the years I have had many clients who struggled with realizing who controls the trajectory of their life's journey. One such client, let's call her Amy, is an example of this. Amy is a 20 something receptionist who has struggled with self-esteem and bouts of depression as long as she can remember.

When we first started meeting she confessed that she had never seen a counselor before and she felt a bit embarrassed and ashamed in doing so. Most times she would have issues with looking me in the eyes. She would often compare her life of depression with others and would have thoughts as to her situation not being as bad as others. But over-time she learned that it doesn't make sense to think of it that way. She didn't need to invalidate my own circumstance because others may have it worse. Some days for her were hard and because other people have it worse or better than her didn't take away from her own experiences and feelings.

As part of her background story, she was around nine years old and she didn't understand why she felt a certain way in different circumstances. She had to try to act in particular ways, depending on how she was feeling. It caused her to miss homework assignments and social interactions in school. Other times she would feel uneven and unbalanced in her life. Eventually she opened up to her parents about it because she knew she was different but didn't know why. Amy's teachers began noticing that oftentimes it took her longer to do things because she did not feel adequate enough and she reported that it would seem to occupy her whole being. Fortunately she had parents who were supportive and loving, took her to the doctors where then she was first diagnosed with depression.

She was prescribed medication which drastically helped her with day to day life. On the one hand it made her feel a little more balanced to a degree and it improved her depression. But Amy was not sure how much of it helped her self-esteem. Then around the age of 14 she was taken off medication because she felt that she could handle the depression much better. She still had some low feelings but felt that she could handle it well enough without medication at that time. And Amy has managed to stay off of medicine for many years.

At this point in her life Amy's agency was decent, especially compared to when she was younger. Before she started taking medication she stated she didn't think too highly of herself because she did not feel she had control of her life. She felt her condition dictated how she was to live for the rest of her life. She felt helpless and unable to improve. In other words, her depression impacted her self-esteem (soul) to the point where she believed that she had no choice but to fail. However, as she began her medical treatment, her self-esteem and self-worth improved. Amy felt more in control and even had her began to believe that she could make things better in her life. Thankfully for her,

Amy found a way to mediate her situation and get on a track to move forward.

Then as life would have it, things changed. And as life changed her agency was impacted, which led her to having to change her approach. As we continue with Amy's story, we now find her years later married a few years and moved many miles away from her family to Texas. At around the same time due to the new environment, she started having doubts again about herself. She felt more nervous talking to strangers and her face would become flushed if anyone came up to talk to her or her heart would start beating in overtime. Amy felt that moving away from her family was hard. Her husband worked long hours and she was unemployed for a couple months. She started experiencing depression to a degree that she had not experienced in a long time.

Although she had the support of her family and would talk to them to help her depression, her marriage was beginning to suffer. Due to her husband's long work hours she felt she was inadequate and that her husband didn't want to be with her any longer. Therefore, Amy began feeling like her depression was causing her marriage to spin out of control. Amy stated that some days, mostly when her husband was at work, she spent the whole day trying to distract herself from her depression and problems.

There were days Amy had trouble getting out of bed. She would sleep in late and not know what to do when she woke up. Although she thought about going on medication again, even calling to make an appointment was difficult for her. Amy also started to get anxious when it was time for him to come from work. She would watch the clock waiting for him to get home, hoping things would get better. But when he got home there would be minimal communication and she felt like she had no control over her life. Amy would just go sit in the shower and cry because that was her release. It was at this point Amy knew she had to do something to change her life. At the suggestion of her Mom, she sought counseling. After conducting some assessments, I felt she was not only dealing with depression but also low self-esteem. Subsequently, we started working to build up her self-belief system and get her to upgrade her agency.

As weeks passed by and Amy came to see me regularly, she slowly started to realize that she could actually improve her own situation by realizing she has the power to change her perspective. All the self-doubt and self-blame began to melt away. As time progressed, she embraced the fact that her depression and anxiety were not her fault it was not anyone's fault. It was just a part of her path. It was just the way her brain was wired. As she embodied a surer agency, she felt she was ready to be more productive. She mustered up enough courage to apply for a job and ended up getting a job at a restaurant close to her home. As she took more control over her outlook, her mental health improved, and she felt happier. And now even her marriage started to get better. It was quite a transformation. To see Amy evolve and strengthen her resolve and renew her emotions was an amazing feat. But it was not magic. It was a fight. She got so brave she wanted to go to school to get an administration certificate. Amy applied to a local adult education program and was accepted. However, all the while Amy still had some struggles. She still struggled with some anxiety about going to school due to her self-esteem. But she did it anyway.

Consequently, right after she began school her husband's job offered him a temporary position with increased pay in another state. From Amy's perspective, that was big news and on top of committing to increasing her education. She would confess in our sessions that she felt overwhelmed, and it all was very scary for her. But she agreed with me to do her best to stay positive and continued with school anyway. I helped her to understand that this was an investment in herself and it will help her to improve. Amy made a pivotal decision and decided to believe in herself and go anyway! Wow! Powerful. She decided to take a chance on her own agency.

This is so critical. I just want to pause the testimony of Amy to point out a vital lesson. When you are in the clutches of decision you will have to rely on what's within you. I know it may not feel comfortable at first but you have to believe that you will be victorious, I understand that you don't want to fail again, I know the voices of doubt may still be there, but want to encourage you to grasp the little strength that you have within and do yourself a favor and take a chance on yourself again. Be like Amy and despite what you have experienced, realize that you can change things for the better; once you do, it will be the most rewarding feeling. When you begin to see problems as opportunities, when you view negative situations as part of the options available and that you have other options, then you will begin to allow yourself to flourish in a way that you always dreamed of. Take a chance and just change your approach.

Amy took a chance and admittedly the few classes in school were the busiest that she had been in her life. And due to the stress she felt it necessary to seriously consider going back on medication. It was a really hard choice for her to make. Not only did the side effects of the medication sometimes make her feel really bad, especially if she forgot to take them and she didn't want to experience that again. But also, Amy struggled with the thought that "didn't she already conquer depression and low self-esteem?" She was doing so much better before but as I stated earlier it is a fight that you have to keep on engaging. When stressful times emerge these things tend to sneak up on you sometimes. In some instances, it can be a lifelong battle and it is okay to need help. I helped Amy to realize that there is no shame in asking for help.

There were so many times in our sessions that she tried to talk herself out of it; it took strength and courage for Amy to talk about her struggles. But as we continued our journey she found the right combination of therapy and medication that eventually led her to try again. She found a way to balance the stress and believe in herself and face life anew. In fact one of the most memorable things I heard Amy say was "I am in control of who I am." It was at this point that I knew Amy had found her true agency. I knew her soul was the healthiest it had ever been. She knew what was controlling her life, she knew where her power was coming from, and she had come to the realization that the only one who could change her life was her.

Soul Condition

Therefore, based on the condition of your soul right now, how are you going to land in success? After being honest about your Agency Rating, are you really in a good place to get you where you want to go? Is your soul providing you with the adequate approach? Based on your Soul's current status, what will be your approach? You are the pilot of your own success. What is your approach for this season of your life? Do you have the Approach of yesteryear? Is your paradigm old? Will your approach work in this new economy or environment? Come on now! What is your approach? You've got to land this sooner or later! You can't keep circling around and around and around. You're out of time! You're running out of fuel! You're running out of energy! You have to have some results soon. What is going to be your approach?

If these questions are stirring you, that's a good thing. They provide you with an opportunity to get in the correct state of mind to begin to land exactly where you claim you want to be. If you never thought about this before you are at the right place. I will now begin to delineate exactly how to have the "Approach" you need to obtain success and to be where you truly desire to be in life.

"You cannot teach a man anything, you can only help him find it within himself" - Galileo

Before I begin to delineate the tenets of an "Approach", I think it is fitting to consider this quote from the great astronomer and physicist Galileo Galilei. As I stated earlier, I believe you already have everything you need inside of you to be successful. I'm not here to "teach" anything new. In fact, you probably already heard most of what I'm about to lay out. If you discover something new, great! But I'm really here to help to take a deeper look inside of yourself to get to know what you truly want. I'm here to enrich your self-examination and self-motivation. First, I'm going to challenge you to do some deep self-examination. I want you to look inward and evaluate your own thoughts, feelings and behavior. This will help you to better understand yourself, gain insight into your personal situations in order to deal with them more successfully. Secondly, I will equip you to re-charge your self-motivation so that what may be dormant in you will be invigorated by your own beliefs and desires so that you will push yourself to be persistent until your life goals are complete. My aim is to assist you in thinking of ways to motivate yourself from within through a variety of new techniques that involve creating and following plans, identifying obstacles, finding solutions, and setting achievable goals. However, in order to find your inner motivation, it's important to know what you want. (I will touch on that in depth later in the chapters.) Once you have figured this out, it's easier to make decisions about the things that are worth your effort. Now, let's begin!

What is an Approach?

I define "Approach" as the philosophical underpinnings that inform a specific system of dealing with situations, circumstances or problems. In other words, there is a particular method of how you process, handle, and think about states of affairs. Seriously, if you think about every part of your life you have a very specific view on how you do life. You may not realize it but you have a philosophy on life. And your philosophy is how you matriculate through decisions and challenges that you face. And I am here to show you how to determine if your philosophy or view or approach is either helping or hindering you from getting what you desire. Please understand there are many approaches to life and I'm not here to judge yours. I only feel a need to provide a measuring stick to determine if this is the path you truly want to be on. Because it would be a tragedy to be working, striving, and believing in a particular destiny only to wake up one day not knowing where you are. It's terrifying to want to go West but end up in the East.

For instance, this reminds me of a recent news story of an airline that had passengers who were on the plane with a particular destiny in mind but ended up in another place. According to the BBC, a British Airways flight destined for Düsseldorf in Germany had landed in Edinburgh by mistake.

The article reports that they believe the reason for the mistake was that the flight paperwork was submitted incorrectly. And the only way customers realized the error was when the plane landed and the

"welcome to Edinburgh" announcement was made. Can you imagine? You are doing what you think is the right thing, but ended in a strange place. I'm here to help us not be in a strange place unintentionally. It's okay to want to end up in an odd or peculiar place, but if you desire to get to Dusseldorf, let's get you to Dusseldorf and not Edinburgh (which I'm sure is a very good place:
(source:www.bbc.com/news/business-47691478)

What's the Formula?

In many classic movies, there is always a secret formula. And this secret formula does some amazing things that the bad guys are always trying to steal for their own personal gain. And just as the bad guys steal the formula, in comes the Superhero that gets back the formula and gives it to the Townspeople. The Townspeople thank the Superhero and take the formula and continue to use it for the good of the people. Well, I always wanted to know, what was the secret formula? Why won't they share it with me? So, if there is a formula for success I would like to share it with everyone. Here is one of the formulas for success I learned from my spiritual mentor Bishop L A Wilkerson: "Your attitude determines your approach and your approach determines your success." It's that simple.

Many times we hear that your attitude determines your altitude, meaning how high or how successful you are. But the reason this is so is because your attitude will enable you to act or approach circumstances in a very distinct manner which will then determine if you are successful in your venture. Therefore, your attitude is vital to your results. So the question is, How is your attitude connected to your approach?

Dissecting "Approach": Two Parts Plus One

As I mentioned earlier, I define "Approach" as the "philosophical underpinnings that inform a specific system of dealing with situations, circumstances or problems". Based on my definition there are two parts of an Approach, the philosophy and the action. Meaning it's about how you think and how you behave. And although it's true that your approach or outlook on life is based on your thinking and your behavior, there is another component that sometimes is overlooked. A lot of times you may think or have knowledge of something, and you may act on it, but there are other instances where despite what you know about how you should move, it's how you **_feel_** about it that determines your actions. In other words, in addition to philosophy and action, there are emotions that guide us. If you add all three elements, we summarize the soul of an Approach: the Intellect, the Will, and the Emotions of your Approach to life. In other words, your soul reflects and mirrors your attitude. So, if I were to recalibrate my formula for success it would be: Your attitude (soul) determines your approach, and your approach, determines your success. Let's go deeper and investigate the Soul of your Success.

2. The Soul (Attitude) of Approach

What is the human soul? It's not just what you think or feel, it affects your life as well as those around you. From how we make decisions to how we treat others, our attitudes play a major role in who we are and who we become. In fact our thoughts are so powerful that every idea that enters our mind has an enormous effcct on us-for better or worse. And it's our responsibility to ensure these thoughts reflect what we truly desire. The human soul is intimately intertwined with our decisions and feelings. It provides our spiritual life with a moral compass that we rely on to make choices in life. It is a part of our inner self, housed in a material world. A person's soul can be considered as an aspect of their personality the whole sum of their thoughts, aspirations, wishes and desires. In addition to spoken word or writing, it can also bc expressed through a person's creative endeavors or projects. Furthermore, onc of the reasons the soul is important, is that it's what separates us from other living creatures on earth. Although other animals have souls, they are not conscious of their actions in the same way that humans are.

How the Human Soul is Affected by Your Attitudes

The role of attitudes in our lives is very important. Attitudes are how we think and feel about certain things. It is important that we know how to use our attitudes in a positive way. The human soul is not just what you think or feel, it affects your life as well as those around you. Every day we are exposed to the world, our experiences, and other people. We interpret all these things in some way or form. Sometimes what happens can be compared to how light travels through water or glass. If you put a piece of paper with an image on it into a jar of water half full of water, you will see that the part of the picture that is above the surface is visible but only in the area where there is no obstruction. Then if you turn over this same piece of paper and let it rest at an angle, more than half of it will be submerged underwater; consequently your view would include more submerged parts than before. But, when it lies flat at the bottom, none of the image would be visible. The same principle applies to the human soul and attitudes: in real life there is no such thing as a completely clear view because we can only see in one direction or area at a time just as you cannot read through a book without turning each page. If we analyze our feelings and thoughts we will perceive more than just what is happening in front of us. It is important that we don't drown out all the other parts of us.

We all know that in order to live a happy and fulfilling life, we need to take into account our own thoughts and feelings, aka our attitude. But what many people do not realize is that the human soul plays an integral role in this process and it deserves to be respected for its ability to influence so much. I'm sure you have seen or experienced what happens when people are negative, they often bring down the mood in their surroundings with them. A glass half empty can quickly be turned into one that is completely empty through one person's pessimistic views. We need to understand not only the effect we have on others, but they are also important for us because negativity either prevent us from achieving our goals or it will cause pain once it's achieved. Therefore, let's get a proper understanding of what makes up our attitude or soul.

Researchers suggest that there are several different components that make up soul/attitude. One can see this by looking at the three components of an attitude: cognition, affect and behavior.

We can categorize the 3 Elements of Attitude as follows:

1. Intellect (Cognitive) Element
2. Emotions (Affective) Element
3. Will (Behavioral) Element

To get a better understanding, let's breakdown each element.

Element #1 - Intellect (Cognitive)

The human intellect is a complex and fascinating subject. There are many different theories as to how it works. Understanding how the human intellect works is important because this knowledge can help us to better understand ourselves and others, in terms of actions, thoughts and feelings. This kind of insight will not only change your life for the better but also reveal hidden truths about who you are that have long since eluded you. We all want answers; we're looking for ways to make sense of things in order to be happy and feel at peace with what we know about ourselves – who we really are deep inside.

The most popular theory of 'how the intellect works' is that it is controlled by what are known as 'the five senses'. These include sight, smell, touch, taste and hearing. The senses help us to detect things or be cognitive of our surroundings so we know where they are and can avoid them if necessary. The way we process this information is through what are known as 'cognitive functions'. Neuroscientist Antonio Damasio, explains three different states of mind that people can go through to process the intellect or cognition:

1 - The first state is where we put things into memory and store them but fail to connect them or associate them with other relevant details. This means that the brain has taken in all necessary information but hasn't yet made sense of it, everything is simply stuck together like a jigsaw puzzle.

2 - Once all the pieces are in place then the second state is activated where we reflect on our experiences by making connections and associations between related information. This means that we're able to look at things from different angles which would give us more of an understanding. We can take what has been assimilated and start to use it for ourselves or put it into practice because now there's a better chance of finding out if something works/doesn't work for ourselves.

3 - The last stage involves being able to take all your experience, knowledge and understanding and process it in order to make good judgments based on rational thought processes. This is often referred to as 'intelligence' but really it should be called 'wisdom'

because only after you have experienced various things in your life can you become wise enough to make good decisions.

Each of these states are important in their own way because they impact our attitude. The first state is necessary for anything to work, but it's the third stage that develops our intellect and makes us more intelligent. When we succeed at something, this sends a signal back down to the second state which adds more meaning or significance to our actions. In turn it will send another signal up to the third stage, making even stronger judgments next time, reinforcing what we "think" we know. Meaning, what we know about a thing can determine our attitude towards it, which will inform our approach to it thereby determining our success in it. So be mindful of your thoughts or beliefs about people, circumstances, and opportunities because your opinion will influence your perspective to be victorious in those spaces.

Element #2 - Emotions (Affective)

Emotions are the feelings or sentiments portion of an attitude. It is also a state of mind in response to some type of stimulus. Meaning it refers to the way one feels toward things. The word "emotion" comes from the Latin word *emotio* meaning "to move." The emotional system is made up of many parts including the amygdala which responds to stimuli by sending signals throughout the body so that we may react accordingly. For example when an animal sees a predator it sends out a signal for adrenaline so that they can fight or run away. When humans see something frightening, their amygdala triggers a sympathetic nervous system response which prepares them either to attack or to attempt an escape. Emotions are often defined as a person's mental state that is the result of some type of stimulation; however they are also expressed physically, in for instance, facial expression.

An example of this would be frowning when experiencing negative emotions or smiling when experiencing positive emotions. Individuals vary in the degree to which they express their feelings outwardly through physical expression or their attitude. Therefore, individuals' emotional expressions may not accurately reflect what kinds of emotions they are experiencing internally. It is believed that it takes at least seven seconds before an individual can recognize another's emotion or attitude by looking at their faces. People are often unaware of how readily others can read their attitudes. For example, if someone walks into a room with a smile on their face people will assume that they are happy.

Emotions can also be categorized as either basic or complex emotions. Basic emotions are the fundamental categories of emotional response, such as anger and fear. Meanwhile, complex emotions reflect more nuanced interpretations of circumstances that arise from the basic emotions. For example, happiness is an emotion but joy would be considered a component of happiness or one possible product of it.

One thing to consider is how cultural differences influence not just what kind of expressions people make but even what kinds of feelings they have.

For instance in the United States both men and women express anger with similar frequency however in Japan women tend to express anger less than do American women whereas Japanese men express anger more than their American counterparts do.

While emotions are often seen as a mental state, they have been connected with several physiological states of being. For instance, when looking at the causes and effects of emotions one can look at how they have been linked to physical health through research on cardiovascular responses. Emotions can influence our hearts in both positive and negative ways depending on what kind of stimulus triggers them. For example, anger has been shown to cause an increase in blood pressure whereas happiness has been shown to cause a decrease in heart rate.

Emotions are often cited as predictors of behavior. For instance, empathy is correlated with helping behavior. This correlation is strong enough that certain social psychologists have focused their studies on understanding the relationship between empathy and prosocial behavior in order to design interventions that can benefit others besides just themselves. This emotional response is based on empathy; if there is no empathy an individual will not experience the emotion and so will not be inclined to help.

On the other hand, guilt is correlated with empathy. Guilt-inducing language creates feelings of horror and self-disgust in people who read it. There are also ways to induce feelings of guilt by employing techniques like audience manipulation in order to make readers feel guilty for not conforming to societal standards or expectations.

A key point about emotions is that they motivate behavior by giving us information about what kind of approach might be necessary in particular kinds of situations. This is critical because how you are feeling will determine how you will respond in a situation. The following are six different types of general emotions: sadness, anger, happiness, disgust, fear and joy that we might experience. As they are listed below, think about your approach when you encountered these feelings in life.

1. **Sadness** is a feeling that is often brought on by pain or unhappiness. You can also feel sadness when you're thinking about something that happened in the past such as the unfaithfulness of a partner.

2. **Disgust** is a type of emotion which makes us want to avoid something because we find it unappealing. For example, some people might experience feelings of disgust about an animal because it's slimy, ugly or disgusting looking.

3. **Fear** is an emotion typically caused by things we don't like and want to avoid. Such as failure and heights.

4. **Joy** is an emotion which gives us more pleasure, excitement and happiness than other emotions. This is part of what makes us feel so good when we get married or successfully complete a

difficult task.

5. **Happiness** is one of the six different types of emotion because it's an intense feeling that almost always follows joy.

6. **Anger** is often brought on by other people's thoughtlessness or actions that are out-of-line with how someone else might think they should act. Anger can also be caused by things like extreme heat, pain or frustration.

So, as you perused the above list of emotions, what crossed your mind? Was your approach helpful or more hurtful to the outcome of the situation, based on how you felt? Or based on the attitude that you displayed? Emotions can be understood as a state that has both physical and cognitive components that are linked together in some way. Emotions are often thought about in terms of knowledge because it can help us know what we need, what we want, and how to get it. Perhaps most importantly, emotions serve as a way for us to catalogue things that matter to us, not only positively, but also negatively. Hence, be mindful of your attitude and role it plays in your approach in life so that you can filter things in a way that will give you success.

The relationship between what we experience and how emotions work for us is an important one to consider when thinking about why we behave the way we do. Everyone experiences many different kinds of strong feelings during their lives, and it's useful to learn about them in order to better understand your own emotions as well as those of others. With this added knowledge, you may be able to achieve more by knowing yourself better than ever before. Emotions are often seen as the feelings or sentiments portion of a person's attitude. There are various emotions that people can experience which vary depending on their mood or situation.

No matter how you process your emotions, your brain is always changing them for you so that you can have some control over them instead of feeling overwhelmed by everything around you. Emotions are subjective feelings that result from mental stimulation which can manifest itself in different ways depending on the person experiencing it. Feelings are just as important as facts because how you feel can affect your life and how you approach it. A positive person might see the good things in life while a negative one would be more likely to focus on what's wrong or missing and respond accordingly.

How We Control Our Emotions

If you change your emotions you can change your attitudes, then you could change your world. And it would be a better place for you. Changing your attitude will not go unnoticed. How you approach things will inspire others around you to change their bad feelings and thoughts as well. Getting rid of your negative feelings and thoughts is very important in improving yourself, but sometimes you need someone else's help. One way we can change our bad feelings and thoughts is by talking them out and finding someone we trust completely and telling them. It would be advantageous to consult someone who can provide you with guidance before you address the situations. Also writing down negative feelings and thoughts is good because it makes them more final and fixed in place, so that we don't forget about them. Another procedure is visualization: imagine what kind of positive outcome would come from solving a problem or goal that has been troubling you. Imagine how it would feel if you'd accomplished that goal or solved that problem. You should see yourself going through each step of the process in a very vivid way. It is also important to think positively about your feelings and thoughts. If you're feeling discouraged, tell yourself that you can do whatever it is you're trying to do, if you believe you can, you will.

Element #3 - Will (Behavioral)

In our discourse of the three elements of the soul, so far we have discussed the Intellect and the Emotions. As we continue, the final component that encompasses the soul is the Human Will. The human will is often misunderstood, overlooked and even disregarded. We've all heard of it but what does it actually mean? The will is a set of mental capacities that encompasses our volition, desires, intentions and personal values. It's the source of human power to choose between options for action. When we are motivated by our own wills, that inner drive makes us more likely to accomplish tasks that are difficult or have no clear rewards at the end. We will explore three major concepts that govern the human will: desire, intention and power. Understanding how the human will is impacted by those components is integral in comprehending ourselves better, providing an enhanced understanding of our approach to succeed.

The *Desire* of Your Will

To understand desire, it is helpful to go back to the moment of history in which humans first began to give names to distinguish ourselves from animals. The human will is what makes us unique, it distinguishes us from other animals and gives us a greater capacity for change than they have. To show our uniqueness, Socrates chose to portray humanity's defining characteristic as a capacity for self-reflection, wonder and thought. To have the human will is to have the capacity to think for ourselves and ask questions about our existence.

Desire is what shapes those thoughts into action or inaction. Our actions can be driven by desire in three major ways: we may fulfill it (satisfy our needs), thwart it (prevent ourselves from getting what we want), or act on it in different ways. Sometimes this can be for the worse (such giving into temptation) sometimes for the better (doing something beneficial to make up for a previous wrong).

Desire marks an important distinction between the human will and the will of animals. It is what allows us to be conscious of our desires and motivations, which can in turn make it easier for us to change them if we need to. Desire can be viewed as a precursor for intention- a reason or purpose that leads us towards an action. This makes sense because without knowing what we want, it would be difficult to decide on a course of action. In order for us to make a decision, we must first have a goal or purpose in mind. Desire differs from intention in that the latter is more focused and specific. It is what leads us towards a result.

The *Intention* of Your Will

Intention can also take two forms: either we truly believe in our intention and want to fulfill it or we only half-heartedly intend to fulfill it. This is because there can be a discrepancy between what we say we will do and what we actually intend to do. When this happens, the intention of the person concerned is not likely their own. They just happen to think it's easier for them to fulfill an intention someone else expects from them rather than to explain their lack of follow through.

In addition, intention must be distinguished from motive in terms of how governed by desire they are. In other words, the difference between motive and intention is that intention is a choice while motive is not. When we do something without the conscious thought of choice, it is considered a motive. Conversely, when we do something because we choose to (and not because someone else has forced us), then the action born of that decision must be one of intention. An example of this would be if someone threw a ball at you and you caught it, your actions were governed by the motive of self-defense and not by the intention of protecting yourself.

The *Power* of Your Will

Power is what gives us the capacity to carry through our intentions and complete actions. It provides us with the agency to be dynamic beings in the world. It allows us to go from desiring or intending something to actually doing it, making power integral for action to take place. Without power, there would be no action.

The two types of power are internal and external. Internal power is derived from the individual's own faculties, while external power is derived from outside sources that govern our actions. This can come in different ways: a person may allow themselves to be governed by a force or they may use the same force to accomplish something they desire.

An example of the latter power would be using coercion to get someone else to do something. An example of the former type of power would be allowing oneself to be governed by another person's will or obeying orders because one fears the consequences if they don't obey. It should also be noted that power can stem from various sources; an individual may use his or her own power or they may use the power of an external source.

When we decide based on our will, it is because we have made a choice from what is available to us in pursuit of something that fulfills our desire. In this sense the will is very much like intention, they both rely on choice and are often used interchangeably. However, the difference between them is that intention arises from conscious choice while will originates in unconscious choice because it stems from our desire picked up by sensation. Examples of this would be if we suddenly feel like eating chips or feeling inspired to act on a certain idea, these feelings are what give rise to the actions stemming from our will.

Your Will and Making Decisions

Every day, we make a multitude of decisions. Some are big and some are small, but they all have an impact on who we become as individuals. These decisions shape our thoughts and actions in many ways that can be difficult to anticipate or predict. One way to explore this is through the lens of decision making itself from the seat of our human will. We must ask the following questions: What does it mean for us to decide? How do these decisions shape who we are? And how might our understanding of ourselves change if we see decision-making not just as something that happens from moment to moment, but rather a process with a long history? We are all born with free will, but when it comes to making decisions; our brains are wired in a way that makes us more likely to take the path of least resistance. When your brain detects an easier option, it opts for that instead. The problem is that there's no clear line between what's easy and what's important. But that's actually good news because it means you get to choose what really matters. When you become intentional about how your choices align with your values, you can reprogram yourself to automatically move in the right direction. Get crystal clear on what things are most important to you and start making decisions according to those values instead. You can keep the good things that are easy to do, but you'll be less tempted by things that go against your values. If your choices don't match up with your values, then you're going to end up feeling dissatisfied and frustrated.

However, there is the issue of temptation. We all face temptations, every day. We all know the feeling. You want something but know it's not good for you. You find yourself deliberating over whether or not to follow your desires. Eventually, you give in because of the inner conflict of good versus bad. This can lead to self-loathing, guilt, frustration, and ultimately passivity. Typically, we view temptations as an endurance challenge for our will: how much can we resist temptation before we give in. But this approach focuses on resisting external temptations like donuts when what you really need to do is strengthen your sense of purpose so you're less vulnerable.

We all have a personal will, but few of us know what our personal wills are. This is because there's such an emphasis placed on the physical and external influences in this world that we often forget to look at what our inner selves want. The biggest problem with looking outside yourself for motivation is that it can be fleeting and when we are tempted, we should rather look at core values of our inner will. This will help us make better choices and reach the level of success we truly desire. But we must rewire our minds according to our true will. Once this happens you can start making decisions according to those inner values instead and create a life worth living.

I know it may sound easier said than done. Many of us, myself included, have lost the will to go after what we really want in life because of all the pressures that come along with it. But this doesn't have to be our fate. We're living in a new age where we can easily be interrupted and disrupted by technology and entertainment. If you're one of the many who can easily find yourself overwhelmed, here are some pointers to strengthen your personal will and get things done:

1. Start with a strong vision or end goal in mind before you move forward.

2. Put your desires first. Ask yourself, what do you truly want! Keep in mind what you feel as you figure out what you yearn and aspire for.

3. Avoid distractions that can come from living your life at the effect of other people, social pressures, or desires that shift your focus away from what's truly important to you.

4. Establish several strong intentions before setting out to achieve them - this will help give you a sense of purpose and maintain your level of motivation.

5. Stay on track with deadlines and goals you've set for yourself by writing them out or creating a calendar specifically dedicated to keeping yourself motivated.

6. Find time in your daily routine to practice strengthening your personal will. This can include meditation, practicing self-care, exercising, reading an inspirational book, painting, dancing, journaling, etc.

7. Think of the positive benefits you will get once your goal is reached. This can be a source of motivation to stay on track and reach your goals.

8. Be patient with yourself during moments of self-doubt, confusion, or when you're feeling overwhelmed by all the things. Just know that your efforts stemming from your will shall be rewarded.

9. The final way to strengthen you will, practice. Stay focused on what you value most by engaging in activities that help you achieve goals, saying "no" when appropriate, and reflecting on times where your will helped you say no to something less important than the activity or thing which you were choosing not to do. One of the greatest challenges of modern life is that we are constantly bombarded with new opportunities, information, advertising, social media, etc. that can distract us from what's truly important in our lives. The only way you can protect your time and energy is by practicing personal will to remain focused on what you value most. This type of practice of saying "no" can help give us more control over our lives so we don't get swept away with busy-ness and distractions. This would be a good place to take some time and think about what activities have strengthened your personal will in the past? This reminder might help in your present moment.

Your will is the source of your power to choose between options for action. Believe it or not this all happens at the center of you will. That part of your soul that allows you to conjugate and transmit your desire, intention and power. The human will is a complex phenomenon but it is critical to interpreting how it impacts your success because your will influences how you approach day-to-day life.

Now that we've separately examined in depth all three components of the Soul: Intellect, Emotions, and Will, let's put them all together. Let's see if we can comprehensively create a system to analyze our attitude so we can ensure we are on the path of success that we are eager to fulfill.

The Attitude Approach Spectrum (AASM)

It is imperative to grasp how these three elements Intellect, Emotions, and Will, impact one's attitude. In fact, their interactions can be complex, confusing, and overlapping and yet they are so influential in your success. To help our understanding of their complexity and the potential relationship to our success, I have created The Attitude Approach Success Model (AASM), a chart that will assist in narrowing down where to focus in order to better the chances of having the right attitude and even greater opportunities of approach that will land us into success.

The Attitude Approach Success Model (AASM) is based on Vishal Jain's "3D Model of Attitude" where his model displays the different combinations that the intellect, emotions, and will could have on your attitude. However, my AASM takes it a step further by demonstrating how each combination will not only impact your attitude, but also how that attitude might help determine what success you may have. You can almost call it a predictor of success. Let's take a closer look.

	Emotions (Affect)	Will (Behavior)	Intellect (Cognitive)	Attitude	Approach	Success
GGG	Positive	Positive	Positive	Positive	Positive	Yes
GGB	Positive	Positive	Negative	Somewhat	Mixed	Possible
GBG	Positive	Negative	Positive	Somewhat	Mixed	Possible
GBB	Positive	Negative	Negative	Not likely	Tainted	Uncertain
BGG	Negative	Positive	Positive	Somewhat	Mixed	Possible
BGB	Negative	Positive	Negative	Not likely	Tainted	Uncertain
BBG	Negative	Negative	Positive	Not likely	Tainted	Uncertain
BBB	Negative	Negative	Negative	Negative	Negative	No

(*G= Element is in a Good place, B=Element is in a Bad place; i.e. GGG = means Emotions, Will, and Intellect are all in a Good place, whereas GGB= Emotions and Will are in a good but the Intellect is in a Bad place.)

AASM Explained

GGG

GGG is when all the three elements of attitude - Emotions, Will and Intellect are all in a Good place. This is where a person is in a good place emotionally, and their will is pure and their thoughts are good, healthy, and positive, toward people, places and situations. In this case, when a person has all three in a good place, they will have a positive attitude and their success is guaranteed! This is certain to be so because no matter what transpires, the person will be in a good place not only to learn from the experience but be in a good place to bounce back quickly and be ready for the next opportunity. This is the ultimate goal. Once you are in this zone the challenge is to remain there.

So how do you continuously be in GGG mode? That is a great question, which will be addressed in the next chapter. But for now, just know not only is it achievable, it is also maintainable.

GGB

GGB is when your emotions and will are well situated in a good place, but your intellect is in a bad place. In this combination a person, although they have healthy emotions and have a desire to act in a positive manner, the information about a situation is based on a negative base. This is where we enter an attitude that can be somewhat positive. This is due to two positive elements in your emotions and will to come against the one negative information. So, the two can outweigh the one and cause you to have a somewhat mixed approach. This could lead to possible success. The likelihood of succeeding is less than GGG but is still possible. It now depends on what you think you know about it which can influence how you move towards it.

GBG

GBG is where your emotions and intellect are well situated in a good place, but your will is in a bad place. Your will (desire, intentions, and power) is negative towards a challenge or problem even though you feel good about it and your information is positive. Have you ever been in a situation where you are happy and you have good news concerning it but you just don't want to be involved in the circumstance? The desire to be in that place is lacking. In this scenario, your attitude could be somewhat positive or somewhat negative, it depends. Which means your approach would be mixed because although you're happy you just don't have the motive to deal with it. So since your approach is mixed, the success is possible but not guaranteed. The likelihood of success is not secured but a possibility.

GBB

GBB is where your emotions are well situated in a good foundation, but your will and intellect are negative. This further decreases your chances of success. This is where although you may be joyous; your intentions about an event or situation are not present. Your thoughts are also contrary to a positive outcome. As a result, your attitude is not likely to be in a good place and it will show. Also, it is uncertain if you will be successful. Please note I am not saying you cannot be successful in your endeavor, however, if there is success it will mostly likely be shallow and short lived.

BGG

The BGG combination is when your emotions are in a bad place but your will and intellect are in a good place. Similar to the GGB, in that the BGG has two positives against one negative. Meaning, your emotions are all out of whack, you're not jovial about what is happening. However, you have no ill intent and the information regarding the circumstances is favorable. There is a good chance your attitude will be somewhat positive and then your approach would be a mixed bag of positivity and negativity. So, your success is possible but not assured.

BGB

BGB represents that your emotions and intellect are in a bad place, but your will is in a good place. This is a real challenge to success. For instance, imagine you are attending a party that is not really meaningful for you, so you're emotionally detached plus you've heard some unkind things about some of the attendees. But you decided to attend to support your friend because you have good will towards them. Well, your attitude while there may not be the nicest and then your approach to it will probably be sour or tainted, and it will show. So, would your presence there be considered a victory? I think it's uncertain or even debatable.

BBG

BBG is where both your emotions and will are in a bad place, but your intellect is in a good place. As in some earlier combinations there are two bad bases versus a good one. Have you ever heard some truly uplifting news that you didn't want to believe? Or really you couldn't believe it because your emotions and intentions were negative. As stated above, this is a good indication that your attitude will not likely be positive and this greatly challenges your chances of success, if you're successful at all.

BBB

Finally the dreaded BBB, which is a guaranteed defeat! This is where all three: your emotions, will, and intellect are all in a bad place. This is a synopsis that you want to avoid at all cost. The triple negative fusion of all the elements of your soul will automatically spew out a negative attitude leading to a soured approach and ultimately induce your downfall.

As I stated earlier, the above The Attitude Approach Success Model (AASM) was created to enhance our understanding of what stems from our soul (emotions, intellect, and will) and its impact on your success. It can be used to analyze and even forecast to assist you to be consciously aware of how you are presenting yourself to the world, which is vital to your success. This model I feel, would be a good framework to be implemented in various settings such as Human Resources, Businesses, High Schools, Colleges and Universities, Adult Education, and even personal development, in terms of breaking down the complexities of the soul and its correlation in achievements and advancements in life.

Truthfully, when we speak of success it does not mean to win every time. There will be instances where you will fail, but how do you bounce back and stay on the path to success. A genuine comeback requires a healthy and positive soul. And the Attitude Approach Success Model can be a gauge or thermometer to check the temperature of your soul and make the necessary adjustment to get where you desire to be at any moment in life. However, as the above model demonstrates, if every aspect of your soul is negative, your attitude and your approach will reflect that and your efforts will be for naught.

Please be aware that, unfortunately, many people are stuck right there, right in the all negative zone and don't even realize it. They think that others are the cause for their failure when in reality it stems from their innermost being, their soul. In life we must think carefully about what kind of attitude influences opportunities, events, and people. This model helps it to become easier to understand how important attitudes really are. But if you are not able to control or change your attitude you will negatively impact the level of success you can achieve. Even worse, your inability or lack of desire to change may indicate something worse. It may be indicative of a disease of the soul.

Diseases of the Soul

You might not be able to see it, but there are invisible forces at work in your life. They have an enormous impact on the way you feel and act, on your relationships with others, and even on your physical health. These forces are what I call the diseases of the soul—disturbing emotions that can lead to self-destructive behaviors or create misery for everyone around us.

We all know that we're susceptible to viruses like influenza or Ebola; just ask any doctor! But what about those other viruses that we don't hear much about? The ones lurking deep inside our souls? Just as they do for a body's immune system, these diseases of the soul are meant to protect us, but when their actions go awry, they begin to attack us instead. It's easy to think that because we live in a modern world, we're immune to diseases like these, but it only takes one small thing for us to become infected. Here are some examples of diseases of the soul and some things you ought to know about them:

1) **Pride** -As mentioned earlier, one way this disease gets into our souls is through arrogance- thinking that what matters most is ourselves and not others. This kind of pride can create an atmosphere where people feel superior or better than other people who may be different from them or have less than they do. Pride also comes up when someone claims to be more spiritual than others.

2) **Greed** - This is defined as an insatiable desire for material things—especially money, wealth, and property beyond one's needs. People who are afflicted with the disease of greed cannot be satisfied with what they have or how much they earn. They always want more, even if they already have more than enough.

3) **Lewdness** - When an individual succumbs to lewdness, it signifies a surrender to sexual thoughts that overpower rational control. This descent into lewd behavior manifests in various forms but is fundamentally antithetical to purity of intentions. When one's intentions veer away from authenticity and purity, they inadvertently pave the path towards the slippery slope of lewdness.

4) **Anger** - People who are angry have feelings of hatred or ill will towards other people. They let their anger build up until they eventually blow up in a rage, hurting themselves or others around them. When you are angered by someone who may have hurt you, it's extremely important to remember not to do the same thing back, but approach him or her instead to resolve the issue.

5) **Gluttony** - This disease of the soul I think we all battle with. This is when a person gives into his or her appetite for food beyond what he or she needs. It often leads to obesity because a person keeps eating until he or she feels overly full, resulting in weight gain.

6) **Envy** - When someone is envious of another person's traits, abilities, or circumstances it means that he or she wants to have what the other has, regardless

of whether they can afford it or not. For example, a person who is envious of another's car might steal it because he or she doesn't have the money to pay for one themselves.

7) **Slothfulness** - This soul disease manifests itself in people who do very little if any work at all. They have an "I don't care" attitude about everything. In doing so, they fail to exploit their talents and abilities and end up wasting their God-given talents and gifts. Slothfulness is not the same as laziness; it's when a person doesn't do what he or she should do, even though he or she could.

8) **Self-righteousness** - This can be caused by an irrational belief. The belief that I'm morally superior to everyone, in all circumstances. One way to change my behavior was to replace this irrational belief with a rational one: "It is possible that I might be morally superior to some people in this particular instance." If unchecked this soul disease can lead to some very erratic behavior.

9) **Worry** - Most of the time, worry is caused by a rational belief. However, in most cases, the belief lingers too long in the thoughts such as "something bad could happen at any moment." However, here is an idea that can assist in easing your soul: "In life, there's no such thing as risk-free decisions." This would help you to take more risks and therefore you would have more success.

10) **A desire for revenge against others** - Harboring a desire for revenge against others can corrode the soul,

poisoning it with bitterness and resentment. Instead of finding peace and closure, this desire festers, consuming one's inner tranquility and tarnishing their character. It perpetuates a cycle of negativity, hindering personal growth and spiritual well-being. Letting go of the desire for revenge is essential for nurturing a compassionate heart and fostering inner harmony.

The Symptoms and Causes

Given these are all real and they must be dealt with if you want to be successful in life, the question becomes, how do we know when these viruses are at work? What are some symptoms and causes of diseases of the soul? Here's what you might notice in someone with one of these diseases.

Symptoms:

1. Loss of affection for others - The person will be unable to love or show compassion.

2. Feeling drained - The person will be exhausted and barely able to function which can lead to depression and other illnesses.

3. Anger outbursts - The person may not understand why they are so mad about things that don't matter, but they still experience the anger.

4. Loneliness and isolation - The person becomes withdrawn and feels like no one can help them or understands what they're going through.

5. Lack of motivation and interest in life - This is oftentimes a sign that the interest in life has been replaced by drugs, alcohol or some other vice.

6. Depression - The person feels like there is no hope or future.

7. Anxiety - The person will feel afraid and worry all the time, often for things that don't make sense.

8. Delusions - The person may believe that they are being watched or that someone is out to get them

9. Hallucinations - The person may experience auditory (sound) or visual (sight) hallucinations which can lead to even more delusions

10. Self-harm - These types of actions are usually a sign of hidden anger and hostility toward oneself due to guilt about things one has done in life.

11. Suicide attempts - This type of behavior occurs when the disease reaches its climax within an individual, leading them do desperate acts in attempt to obtain relief.

12. Lack of ability to handle stress - The person becomes overwhelmed with problems and

begins to shut down, unable to function.

13. Over-reaction - This is usually the final stage before the disease completely consumes a person; they may lash out or take things too far.

Causes of Diseases of the Soul

1. Abuse - People who have been abused either physically, emotionally, sexually or financially are oftentimes so traumatized by their experience(s) that it infects every aspect of their life.

2. Psychological - People who have had difficult experiences in their lives, especially early on in life are more likely to be inflicted with a disease of the soul; this is due to feeling abandoned when one's needs aren't met.

3. External influences - Such as engaging in behavior that goes against one's morals or values.

4. Ignoring or denying that something is wrong with oneself.

As I close off this section, it's time for a self-audit. Having looked at all the Diseases of the Soul with some of the symptoms and causes, now consider yourself. Did any of those fit you? Did any of the Diseases of the Soul describe what you are facing right now? As you read each one did you feel as if it was speaking to your issue? If so, you are not alone. At times like these, it is important to remember that everyone has the potential to develop one or more of these diseases of the soul. It takes only one small thing, one trigger event, for anyone to become afflicted. This means that each one of us must develop the ability to recognize the condition of our soul (by using the above The Attitude Approach Success Model) then take action to change it which can then heal your soul.

Healing the Soul

"Dismiss whatever insults your own soul."
Walt Whitman

The healing of the soul has nothing to do with religion or spirituality, but it's about understanding that there is a power inside of you that will take you through your darkest days and nights. It's about understanding that there is a force inside of you that will pull you back up when you're down, no matter how low things get. It's about understanding that at the end of all things, you are capable of becoming a stronger person.

Hope - When life gets tough, it can be hard to imagine how things will ever get better. Regardless of where one lives in the world there will be harsh conditions that are difficult to deal with. Suffering isn't pleasant but it can teach us things that we would never learn in more comforting states of being. When these hardships arise, our first thought might be "Why me?" but this question should be redirected towards "What can I learn from this?". The whole point of suffering is so that one can gain insights and grow stronger, not wallow in defeat until hope is lost. It's important to remember the saying: "This Too Shall Pass". Healing the soul is about hope. No matter what your circumstances are, having hope and believing in yourself is key to making it through difficult times. Hope keeps us alive; without it we might as well give up on all our dreams and aspirations; without hope we have nothing left to live for.

Faith in Self - Healing your soul means developing faith in yourself and trusting that everything will work out for the best no matter what. You can increase your faith in yourself by reminding yourself how far you've come despite what has happened in the past or what's happening now; believe in yourself because if not, why should anyone else? Remind yourself of all the good things going on in your life, not just the bad. You can increase your faith in yourself by concentrating on what you have left even if it seems like everything is going wrong right now; focus on how far you've come and not where you are now. When things get tough, it may seem impossible to survive, but think of all the people who have been through worse and yet they found a way to make it out okay. Try looking at it from another perspective - from a bird's eye view-and be grateful for all that you do have rather than focusing on what's missing. There are times when we feel like we've lost everything and our only choice is to give up. But remember, you can't lose if you never give up. Remind yourself that you can get through this - if others have before, so can you.

It's about accepting that the only way to change your life is to first take responsibility for it, no matter how much it hurts. It's about understanding that nobody will save you except yourself. It's about knowing that this world is both beautiful and cruel, but you must learn from its cruelty if you want to survive its beauty. It doesn't matter where you start from, everyone has been through difficulties in life. The thing is, tough times aren't easy to deal with, and so most people don't know what they need to get through them successfully. If someone had never been hungry or poor or sad or lonely, then they wouldn't know what it means to be hungry or poor or sad or lonely. Only those who have experienced these things can appreciate how painful they are, and only those who feel the pain of life's difficulties fully will learn how to heal.

A prime example of this is alcohol abuse. Alcoholic individuals usually drink because they want to forget, they drink to escape their problems. But while drinking might provide momentary happiness, it inflicts damage that lasts far longer than any temporary joy. It's easy to drown one's sorrows in the bottom of a bottle, but by doing so, people are essentially stealing away time from themselves that could've been used for something much more productive - like solving their problems head-on with a clear mind.

Self-Care - The best way to heal your soul is through self-love. Self-care is understanding that it's okay to be who you are and that not everything about you is totally wrong. It's about understanding that no matter what mistakes you've made, there is always a bright future ahead of you. You need to love yourself unconditionally and learn to look at the positives in life.

There is always something beautiful in nature and even if we don't see it right away, we have an inner connection to the universe so we must keep faith and believe in ourselves even when things get tough.

It's important for us to respect our body and soul because we have a connection with the universe that needs to be honored. We should honor this connection by being mindful of what we do because every action that we take affects not only us but also other people, animals, plants, etc. It's about understanding that there is a force inside of you and learning how to listen to it so you can better understand life as a whole. There are times in life when we need an additional boost; there is so much emotional and physical pain, and we feel like we cannot go on. But after all, you can't lose if you never give up! It's about finding yourself again. You might feel like everything has fallen apart, but think about all of the things you have learned from previous experiences... And finally, self-care is very important because it's about respecting yourself by taking care of your body and mind so they don't fail you when trying to accomplish something or even survive another day!

Every word said in your mind is a brick in the wall you build around yourself when you refuse to deal with life's issues head-on. A single bad habit can ruin one's entire life, but it's not easy to break habits without strong willpower. In fact, breaking bad habits isn't even possible without some serious determination and self-discipline. It takes real courage to conquer your fears and face your problems head on, but you must realize that facing them isn't the same as conquering them forever. We're all just temporary visitors to this earth and there really is "forever." There it is imperative that you take care of your whole being: spirit, soul, and body.

Having a healthy body helps one with better mental health. It doesn't mean that it will cure all ailments, but as Hippocrates famously said " Let food be thy medicine and medicine be thy food". Proper nutrition can be achieved through eating whole foods and exercising regularly. Additionally, the foods we eat should not make us sick; if they do, there's something wrong with those ingredients and you should love yourself by disciplining yourself to no longer eat it.

Self-Reflection - Self-reflection is also important in healing the soul. This is because it's the only way to really know yourself. You can't live your life according to what others think, but you can't live it according to who you "think" you are, either. We all get fooled by our own delusions even when we're not actively trying to fool ourselves; the only way to avoid this is by stepping back and examining yourself objectively. This process of self-creation is an uphill battle with no clear road map or destination, but this journey is worth it. Our lives are cherished and the more time we spend understanding ourselves, the more time we have to make reality conform to our wishes rather than the other way around.

Help Others - In order to heal the soul, a healer must first realize that one's thoughts and feelings are what causes them pain. Healing your soul will also begin healing in other areas as well as it changes one's perspective of life. This may come from something as simple as catching someone else's laughter to participating in a spiritual celebration. The healer approach is through helping others and reflecting what they see back onto themselves. It is about coming to understand oneself and accepting their flaws and strengths so that they too can heal and go on living.

One must turn life into an adventure and embrace the beauty of the world around them. That beauty could be as simple as a warm breeze or as complex as a massive galaxy, but to ignore it is to ignore what gives our lives purpose and meaning. Imagine you're running through a forest; if you look up and see birds flying across the sky, your mood will automatically improve, and you'll probably run even faster than before (even if you can't keep this speed up for long). Nothing beats waking up in the morning with fresh "batteries" in your brain because it allows one to fully appreciate all that life has to offer. Every sunrise offers another chance at finding joy no matter how small or insignificant that moment might seem at first. Just remember nobody wants to feel alone, so do your best not to be.

Ask for Help - If you're feeling despair or hopelessness, and your soul needs healing, sometimes it's good to ask for help. This will give you a sense of purpose and remind you that there are others out there beside yourself. The more people you can help, the better your mood will be over time, if only by a little bit. When someone receives comfort from you, they may pass it on to another person someday, so don't worry about how much effort it takes because your actions have ripples that spread far beyond what the eye can see. Sometimes all that's needed is a smile, but one doesn't always know how to start this chain reaction; if this is the case then ask yourself: "What would make me smile today?" You don't have to wait for something mind-blowing or life-altering, just do whatever it is you think might make you smile even if it seems too simple. There are people who care about you and want nothing more than to see you happy. By sharing your experiences, you are helping yourself heal but also helping other people heal their souls because everyone goes through tough times.

Healing the soul is important because without your soul you have nothing left, it's what keeps us going through our worst days and nights. Healing doesn't mean forgetting or erasing memories; healing means learning how to live with those memories while finding a way forward.

There are many ways to help with the healing of the soul. Other common methods include learning how to be better at handling stress and anxiety. Meditation has been proven time and time again to be an effective outlet for anxiety and depression taking care of your mental health. You may need to heal your soul when you are in so much emotional and physical pain that it is hard to keep going, especially if this has been happening over a long period. It's important that you do not let guilt or shame stop you from seeking professional help if needed. Your life is precious and it's important to respect it by caring about yourself so you can do what is right for you.

Love - And finally, love is a powerful force that can heal almost anything. Here are a few things that love has been able to heal:

-drawing borders between friends and enemies
-turning enemies into friends
-healing a broken heart
-drawing everyone together as a community
-helping someone find the courage to live again

Love has been shown to improve health, help people live longer, and make people happier in general. It's akin to witnessing a meteor shower for the first time or being captivated by an artist's work. Love has the capacity to galvanize a person to better mental health in a number of ways: it increases feelings of optimism, decreases anxiety, reduces failure anxiety because you feel secure.

It is more likely to lead people toward destiny life goals rather than hedonistic ones. People who experience love respond better to problems and suffer less from stress and depression than those who don't. Love is the most powerful domain in the world! It's stronger than anything else that might try to hurt us or make us feel unworthy. You are loved beyond words and it is the ultimate element to heal the soul!

Soul Searching

I want to conclude this chapter with an opportunity to self-reflect and for you to do some soul searching. A lot was discussed regarding the soul. We looked at the three components – Emptions, Will and

Intellect and how they all contribute your attitude. And the main point I want to drive home in this book, is that your attitude plays a profound part in your success. But what is the benefit of getting all this information about your soul without examining where you are? Why take the time to increase in knowledge and not do anything with the information you receive? It would be a waste of time and energy. Therefore, I want to give you the chance to do some soul-searching. I want you to put in practice what you have learned. Take a moment and reflect on what you just read.

This is important because the act of soul-searching should be viewed as an opportunity for insight and understanding. Whenever we engage in the process of reflection, there is no need to fear that we are simply dwelling on past mistakes or failures. Instead, it should be looked at as a way of learning from our experiences so that they can benefit us moving forward.

Benefits of Soul-Searching

Soul-searching can help you explore what exactly it is that's holding you back and preventing you from reaching your full potential. In order to achieve success, one must first understand your strengths and weaknesses as well as your values and motivations, as these will all play a role in determining which direction you take during times when decisions need to be made. Soul-searching works by opening the space of our minds and freeing it from the constant bombardment of information that surrounds us in the modern world. The importance lies in allowing yourself to contemplate, instead of staying confined in your usual mindset.

Perhaps when you look at your life you see stress where there isn't any or fail to notice when something is stressing you out. The opposite could be true as well; inhibition may prevent you from seeing stress in places where it truly does exist. By practicing soul-searching regularly, we can learn how to properly recognize stressors within our lives and respond accordingly by formulating helpful strategies for dealing with them.

How to Soul-Search

Soul-searching requires us to focus on our values, or what is important to us now so that we may better understand the direction that our lives are taking. It is important to take some time each day, either first thing in the morning or right before going to bed, and simply be alone with your thoughts. You can write about what you think or reflect on more complex ideas by doing less literal writing activities.

As you continue this practice of soul-searching throughout reading this book, you will find yourself becoming more aware of how you are feeling as well as more conscious of your thoughts and actions. This task should not require a ton of effort on your part but instead should be something that just happens naturally whenever you have some free time during the day. If it becomes challenging, don't worry about it too much because over time it will become easier.

The best way to approach soul-searching is to not feel as though you are talking about yourself, but instead that you are having a conversation with an imaginary friend. This will help prevent you from getting caught up in your own head and allow the process to be more fluid an uninterrupted. Whenever you begin to think about something outside of yourself it interrupts the flow of your thoughts so take this issue into consideration when beginning the practice of soul-searching.

Although there are times when practicing soul-searching can be helpful, it does come with its own set of problems because it requires us to stop whatever we're doing at that moment and focus on ourselves instead of everyone else around us. As much as soul-searching can lead people to the answers they're looking for, it can also inhibit progress if a person loses sight of what they've been working towards.

As you review the soul issues listed above and begin to soul-search, don't shy away from taking this moment to assess your life. It will allow you to see things from a different perspective and help improve upon any shortcomings that you may have by allowing you to take control over your life. The only way we can truly succeed is if we learn from our past so that future decisions, future attitudes that we have, and future approaches to life are informed by what you learn from them instead of being just another blind step in the dark.

Tips on Soul-Searching

Soul-searching is a crucial component of personal growth, and it allows you to explore the thoughts that are within your mind. For this kind of reflection to have an effect on our lives, we must be aware of what's going on in them so they can make the necessary changes. If this type of introspection is new or intimidating to you, try these following steps:

1 - Start with some simple one sentence exercises before moving onto more involved ones like journaling about yourself or completing questionnaires online (answers don't need to be perfect - just go with whatever comes into your head first).

2 - Look at your expectations of yourself and other people.

3 - Ask yourself what you're doing, feeling or thinking that needs to change.

4 - Set boundaries for how you will treat others and let them know what you want from them.

5 - Pay attention to your thoughts and acknowledge if any of them are getting in the way of your personal growth.

6 - Be aware of how you're feeling and give yourself time to figure out what those feelings mean to you before making any decision.

Practice daily for thirty days and see how much progress you've made.

Happy Soul-Searching!

3. The Art and Science of Creating Your Own Approach

"Many ladies will tell you, it's all in how you approach them." – ALTPHD

I remember the girl, a beautiful sorority sister of mine. She never got out much and was shy to speak with anyone. I had seen her at parties before but never up close until this one night after a party. She looked lovely as she walked by me on the way home from the party. When she passed, I shouted to her "Hey," I said with a smirk. "I wanted to ask you on a date." The girl was shocked by my forwardness and laughed, shaking her head. "No thanks," she replied flatly before turning around quickly to walk away. She felt embarrassed but I guess she couldn't tell if I was trying to be funny or serious in my approach. "I can't believe I just did that," I muttered to myself, feeling defeated. My words bounced back at me as soon as they left my mouth and all that came out were unimpressive little ripples in watery silence.

Method to the Madness

It is interesting that many people desire to be successful, but many do not want to implement the required steps to get there. Many see the trappings of success but think the path to get there is bizarre. But you must be willing to do what others are not willing to do, in order to have what others don't have. In reality the approach to success basically boils down to operating in a fashion that may not seem feasible, but in the end, you will have the desired result. There is certainly a method to the madness of gaining success, but you will sometimes look foolish doing it.

Let me give you an example of what success looks like. I will take a page out of my own life. Not that I have reached the pinnacle of success, but I do have a degree of success. And hopefully it can be a source of inspiration to you.

My Ph.D. Odyssey

There are many things I can say about obtaining my doctorate degree, but the thing that sticks out the most is the entire process. I attended The University of Texas at Austin, and I dragged my family, consisting of my wife and two very young children, through this entire process. In fact, one month after the birth of my daughter we moved to Austin to pursue this, yet another, degree. I always desired to achieve this level of academics but looking back I was not prepared to give what was required to accomplish this goal. I thought I was, but when the time came to do it, I almost gave up.

Most programs of doctoral study require two years of course work then you must complete the last assignment called a dissertation. Traditionally, schools allot between three and seven years to complete the degree. After that, typically, the school will ask you to complete the degree at another school of your choice. And let me tell you, those years go by at a very rapid pace. Because I was married with children, of whom I had to support, I was also working while in school and it took me two and a half years to complete my course work, meaning, now I am behind schedule to finish. But that's okay because, if need be, I have another four and a half years to complete the dissertation. However, my beautiful wife, who was ever so patient, is now beginning to get a little frustrated because it is taking longer than I promised her. So the heat is on for me to get it finished. After completing my course work, I now have to prepare to take my comprehensive exams, where once I have passed them, this allows me to start the dissertation. I take and pass my exams, thank the Lord, and now you become what's called ABD, All But Dissertation. The danger at this stage is that there is a sense of accomplishment, which it is, but the reality is the real work only now begins! For the dissertation, you must assemble a committee of five persons who will judge your work and determine if you are fit to become a Ph.D. I gather my committee and start to accumulate the data for my research, but there is a problem, information overload. There is so much information that the time it takes to accumulate it is much longer than expected. In fact, it takes over a year to collect and read all the articles I wanted to include in my work. And before you know it, I spend too much effort and time all the while becoming too comfortable being ABD that I forget I have a deadline to get this thing done before it's too late.

A Beautiful Distraction (The other ABD)

Let me give you an example. One of the expectations of doctoral students is that in addition to coursework, exams, and research, you are advised to attend academic conferences and make presentations and represent the school. Based on this premise, I discovered a great conference that I felt was a good fit to display my work and gain valuable experience, however it was a very prestigious conference, and it would be a long-shot for me to get accepted as a presenter. Additionally, I am still only at the gathering information stage of the doctoral program, but I thought I would apply just for the experience of the process. Well, I applied to present and would you believe it, I got accepted! OMG!!! I was thrilled and excited and when I shared the news with my mentor and Dissertation Chair, Dr. King Davis, he thought it was great too. However, after his congratulatory praises, he graciously reminded me I had not actually completed the research in order to participate in the conference. In only the way he can, he presented two options for me to consider: First, try to hastily put together a project to complete before the conference, or secondly, focus all my efforts on completing my dissertation, so I can then legitimately join the conference on a higher level. So, I had to choose, either to present or to complete. It was at that moment that I knew this opportunity was a beautiful distraction. The conference was being held on an amazing Caribbean Island filled with scholars with whom I would love to connect. However, I knew in my spirit what I had to do. That after I presented at the conference, I still would have had to finish my actual dissertation and switching my energy from the dissertation to the conference would have delayed my time even further. Therefore, after much prayer, I graciously declined the acceptance and decided to focus on my ultimate objective of completing my doctoral degree.

Back at the Plow

After realizing that the conference was just a distraction, I had to change my approach on how to get this dissertation completed. Therefore, I began to plow away because I needed to finish. My original approach or method was not working so I had to switch up how I was going to proceed forward. There were several things I had to change. Here is a look at my new approach: First I took the advice of my mentor and Chair that the best dissertation is a completed dissertation. Meaning, just get it done. In addition, he told me at some point you just have to cut off the materials that you are reading. There is so much information out there that you could literally spend a lifetime just searching for information. In fact, there is a saying that we are living in a time where people are "ever learning but never coming into the knowledge of the truth". So, you just have to determine at what point is sufficient for your objective. Meaning, you must make a decision. Therefore, I had to decide on this new approach, in that I have adequate material and now I must thoroughly read it and write about it. This leads to the second part of my approach, I had to recognize what were my strengths. I recognize that my best time to write was early in the morning. And the best time for me to read was in the afternoon. Therefore, I created a schedule where I read materials and write my chapters at the same time, just at different time slots. I could no longer afford to spend a whole day just reading and not accomplish any writing. This decision ultimately led to another decision that was pivotal in the success of my degree.

Uncomfortable Comfort

As stated earlier, in the beginning of my doctoral studies I had to provide for my family which meant I was working as I was doing my coursework while conducting research and being a teaching assistant. In addition, I had to make time for my family and participate in the daily activities of my children. However, working did afford my wife and I the opportunity to purchase our first house. This was very exciting and fulfilling. It was a two-story home where the bedrooms were upstairs and the living room, dining space and kitchen were downstairs.

Typically, my "work office" was in our full bathroom, which was in our main bedroom. This is where I did my dissertation work. It was easy and convenient to just get out of bed and slide into the bathroom and work. However, I noticed there were times that I was so comfortable in bed that I overslept due to exhaustion and would not get up in time in order to accomplish my reading and writing dissertation task for the day. This also fed into me missing my timeline to finish this dissertation. This habit was hindering the process, again, my family was waiting for me to finish up and as time was passing the pressure was mounting. I had to get it done **NOW!**. So, I had to make a decision. I decided if I was serious about successfully completing this dissertation, I must better manage how I use my time. I decided to move my "work office" downstairs in the dining area and I would also no longer sleep in the comfort of my bed next to my wife and began sleeping downstairs on the cold couch until I finished my dissertation.

This was a challenge because I love my wife and I love our comfortable bed. Especially when it's cold and I can just cuddle up and stay warm and sleep easy. But being comfortable made our lives uncomfortable due to an unfulfilled promise to get this dissertation done. I told my wife my decision, and although hesitant she agreed in order to accomplish a goal. I had to get comfortable with being uncomfortable to obtain what I really desired. The question I had to ask myself was this, which did I desire more: sleep or accomplishment? So, I looked deep into myself and decided I must be successful. As a result, over the course of the next few months, the majority of the time, I slept and worked downstairs.

I can remember working until about midnight, then going to sleep on the couch and as the alarm clock rang out at 3 am to start working again, I would literally roll off the couch and on the floor just to fully wake up and get started reading and writing again! Wow the memories! It may seem radical to some, but this was the approach I had to have to get what I truly desired. There comes a time that you must do what others won't do, in order to have what others don't have. There are a variety of ways to get to success, but it's all in how you approach it! Obviously, I am not the only one. This is a pattern in the lives of those who are successful who have had radical approaches to achieve success. For instance, there is the story of the founder of Perdue Chicken who often slept in his office to ensure he got the work done. There is the story of those who had to sleep in their cars to fulfill the vision. There are those who make great sacrifices to get to the place called success. We all say we desire it, but how do we determine to get there? It's all in your approach.

Persistent

The last part of my methodology, I would say, was my persistence to be successful. I was persistently persistent in my pursuit. Read that again. I was persistent, not perfect, not the best, not even that great at it, but I just kept moving forward. A major component to my approach is to keep trying and keep doing it until it is complete. There were some at the school who felt my work was not worthy to be accepted. But I did not let that bother me. I just kept on working at it. I also found others who supported me and helped me find my way to victory. This is why I am a believer that dedication, persistence, and faithfulness are better than talent. Don't misunderstand what I am saying. I think talent is great, and we all have talents. But if you don't have staying power and tenacity that keeps you going forward, then your talent is useless. I've heard it said before that you just have to outlast any situation in order to be successful. Just by you showing up and as others quit, you will be the winner. Just outlast your feelings, just outlast your emotions, just outlast your mistake, outlast your discomfort, outlast your embarrassment and keep showing up. That is the definition of persistence. Employing an approach that is fueled by persistence will ensure that nothing is insurmountable to you. Can you imagine that all you have to do is keep showing up, and then in a moment the world will be yours!

Basically, I had to follow certain principles that were the foundation of my approach to success, and I was able to obtain and complete my degree. So enough about me, what is your approach to success? What are the principles that are guiding you to land in the area of success that you desire? What is the method to the madness of your life? If you don't have any answers to these questions, now is a good time to figure it out. Although you may not realize it, you are using a particular approach to the situations in your life. The question is, are you satisfied with the results? If not, now is a great opportunity to change approaches.

How to Build Your Own Approach

As a licensed psychotherapist, I have often been asked to provide clients with a readymade or cookie-cutter template on how to create change in their approach or methodology to self-improvement. On the one hand this is good because they are committed to their own growth and maturity. However, over the years I have realized that there are no short-cuts or cookie-cutter growth plans. What works for one may not work for another. At times many of these so-called "self-help" books are counterproductive and rarely contribute to one's personal growth and increase of self-worth. You have to discover what works for you. Your own tailored approach, the process of developing the approach yourself would do wonders for you. It would be an expedition in the discovery of self. The mechanics of undertaking this task is priceless! Not only will you unearth the "real" you, but the results of this bespoke plan will also be better suited to your life because you developed it yourself, using your own language and creating your own way. So, let's get started!

Your Belief System

Socrates famously said, "The unexamined life is not worth living." In other words, he believed that it was important to question the purpose of one's own belief. He felt that if a person did not understand his or her own personal philosophy, then they were a slave to whatever ideas and whims came their way without any real understanding of why those things mattered to them. The human souls are constantly changing. If a person formed a core belief early in life and stuck with it through adulthood, it would become inflexible and could hold this person back from being able to grow as an individual as time went on. Being open-minded allows for greater growth as a human being. Scrutinizing your beliefs about life is just as important as following them.

Therefore, as we begin to create your own approach to success you must first address your belief system. The reality is that the human brain is the most complex organ in the body. The average person has over 100 billion neurons, and each neuron can make about 1,000 connections to other neurons. That's more than 100 trillion connections in total! It's no wonder that people are often confused about how their thoughts and feelings affect them. But what if there was a way for you to change your belief system? What if you could train yourself to think differently?

The human belief system is the set of beliefs that people share in order to understand the world. Humans, like other animals, have evolved with certain features that help them survive in their environment.

For humans these include cognition, consciousness and language. They also include our mental machinery for understanding social relationships and abstract representations of reality.

Many aspects of our mental life are shaped by evolutionary advantage or usefulness for survival. For example, it makes sense that we are drawn to water sources where we might find food or mates because this means a greater chance of survival if you happen upon one. But many elements of thinking can also make us feel let down. For example, the assumption that if we pass an exam then we will automatically get a better paying job makes sense in many cases because there is evidence to suggest this is true. But one must also account for the relativity of what you perceive as 'better'.

Therefore, it is how your belief system processes "better" that will determine if you are successful if you do get a better paying job due to passing an exam. But if you pass the exam and you don't get the job, then your belief system will conclude you that are a failure. And it's thoughts like these that can give rise to anxiety and depression when they are built on faulty beliefs or assumptions about ourselves, others, society or the world around us. We may even act upon them without realizing it. It's no wonder scientists have analyzed common human belief systems for centuries, trying to understand how they affect our lives and minds. And now scientists can answer some important questions about how changing your belief system might improve your success in life.

It is possible to change your belief system, but it will require dedication. It takes time and effort because the brain has built up its own set of connections over years of thinking in a certain way. This is called neuroplasticity, or 'rewiring' the brain. This doesn't mean completely changing who you are or becoming someone new, but rather making slight changes that can have big effects on improving achievements in life. Learning what are known as 'cognitive behavioral therapy' skills is one of the best ways to start changing how you think about yourself and your circumstances. For example, learning that you don't need to believe every thought that passes through your mind might be helpful in managing negative self-talk which some people experience with failures.

In psychology, "belief" is defined as a mental representation that is inferred from experience or knowledge. Beliefs are very closely related to one's identity. We use them to understand ourselves and our world so if we change our belief system then our sense of self would have to change too. The good news is that despite how strongly we hold some beliefs, they aren't considered absolute truths about the universe, they are simply beliefs.

Some examples of irrational beliefs might be "I'm not good enough", "people will never like me" or "bags of money grow on trees". These types of thoughts all have in common that they are unhelpful, inaccurate and awful! The things that we tell ourselves when we believe these ways are what keep us feeling down because they're just not true.

Here's an explanation about how our minds work when we're thinking irrationally:

reality > belief > perception > behavior

For example, let's imagine there is a bear coming toward you in the forest:

reality = there is a bear coming toward you in the forest

belief = I'm going to die

You would feel fear, even though your belief doesn't match up with reality. Your emotional response of being scared isn't logical but it's still completely understandable. The first step of changing one's beliefs is to identify if they are irrational by checking if they are:

- inaccurate (does not reflect realty)
- unhelpful (does not move one towards goals)
- awful (debilitating for oneself and others)

Generally, people take their beliefs for granted and don't stop to question why they believe them or how true they are, but if you desire to reach success, I encourage this type of questioning. This could even help you change your belief if you see that there are reasons why your original belief might not be right. The way people take on philosophical beliefs shapes their lives. It is important to understand your own philosophy and approach to life. Changing your belief system can seem daunting at first, especially after years of thinking irrationally, but it doesn't have to be hard!

It all starts with self-awareness. Whether you are doing it for your own benefit or trying to help someone else with their mind, self-awareness is the key.

Steps to Build Your Own Approach

There are many ways to change your approach, but it starts with making a choice. You can either continue to live in the same way that you have been or you can make the decision to live your life with intention and direction. It's time to take control of your perspective instead of letting it control you! We often don't realize how important our approaches are until we've found ourselves living in one for so long that we forget what reality was like before it. Our approach acts as filters which dictate everything from what we think is possible, how much effort we're willing to put forth, even who among us will be friends. If left unaddressed, they can lead us into deep ruts where all hope seems lost and our best efforts yield no results. The harder we try to escape, the more stuck we find ourselves until everything around us starts to feel meaningless and hopeless. You have to put your fears aside and keep moving forward no matter what! It's time for you to take a deep breath and remind yourself of the things that are important in your life so that you can feel better about yourself. It's time to stop complaining about anything and everything and start living with intention.

Here is a Four Part system that can help you change your approach so that you can make positive changes and take control of your life. The Four Parts are Observe, Gather, Implement and Evaluate.

Part 1 - Observe

1. Don't Focus on What Others are Doing. One of the most common ways we self-sabotage our progress and happiness is by focusing on what other people are doing and comparing ourselves to them. It's time to stop focusing on what other people are doing and start paying attention to what they're doing right.

2. Look for Feedback. By getting sufficient feedback, this will improve how you see yourself. If you feel like you are in a rut with work, home life, your social life, your fitness routine, or anything else you can think of, the best thing you can do is to get some feedback. Allow someone you trust, to share what's going on in your situation at that moment and then see if they can offer some ideas on how they might improve it. At the end of the day, you might get some ideas that you never thought about before. Realizing you don't have to use all the advice given. You can pick and choose as you please, but don't be afraid to try something new or different.

3. Watch Your Tribe. Spend more time around positive people who have a good outlook on life and less time around those who always complain or judge others harshly. Another way to create a new approach in your life is to spend more time around people who have a good outlook on life and less time around those who are always negative. Excuse yourself from the negative people and thoughts when they come up. You may not realize it, but people are constantly watching how you act, including the reactions you have to difficult situations. Your attitude really does affect how other people feel about themselves because humans are very sensitive creatures. If you're always complaining, then there's a good chance you'll find yourself alone. It's up to each individual to take charge of their lives and lead it in the direction they want, even if that means being alone.

4. Set Aside Time to Think. Set aside time every day for thinking critically about something that has been happening recently. This is so vitally important that I want to spend some time on it. You need to spend 10 or 15 minutes just sitting down and thinking of all the aspects of the situation, such as what could happen if one thing goes wrong. Paying more attention will help you identify situations where there are potential risks, or things that could go wrong with a certain scenario. This is one of the many ways to develop your own approach skills.

You should try watching multiple perspectives on forums of education like podcasts or documentaries that offer different insight into particularly controversial subjects, such as politics or social issues. Not everyone will agree with what's being said in these contexts and it's important to be able to take in multiple points of view so you can compare them and decide which one makes more sense based on the logic of your project or situation. Sometimes this skill is referred to as step back reasoning. You can hone this skill at home by practicing listening to each perspective closely before coming up with your own approach of what happened/what was said between the different perspectives.

If you want to get better at expressing your approach, you can take the time to write down an explanation for each point. This will allow you to better understand where you are coming from when it comes to decision making. You should also try writing down any potential challenges or flaws with your own reasoning so that you can refine your thinking process and improve your approach later on.

I find that in order to think critically about my own approach, it's helpful to spend at least 10 minutes learning about other viewpoints occasionally. It might be hard at first if you're not used to it, but it can help open up new possibilities in terms of how we see things and how our habits affect us. Try watching videos or reading articles by authors whose opinions are different from your own. Once you have generated some fresh notions of what to do, then you start to build.

Part 2 - Gather

1. First, Identify What You're Looking For

Seek out and discern what it is you actually are trying to do. Develop an idea by defining its purpose and understanding your needs at this moment. While you may know a lot about what you want to do and why you want to do it, there may be some aspects of the plan that aren't as clear. It can be helpful to gather information about the industry from journals, books, forums and courses online. This will not only help ensure that you're on the right path, but it'll also provide useful knowledge about how others handle your approach goals.

2. Idea Factory

Generate as many potential solutions to meet those goals as possible. Sometimes just brainstorming about different options can be enough! You'll want to narrow down these ideas into three or four of the best ones before moving on to step 3. Prioritize them based on how well they work with your original goal or goals.

3. Write Them Down

It is important that you start with identifying and writing down what exactly it is that you want to achieve. You should also make sure that the goal is specific and measurable and include all of the steps needed for success. This will help ensure that the strategy is specific and measurable, and capable of being applied whenever it's needed.

4. List the Tasks Needed for Each

It is essential that you map out all the steps that are needed to succeed. These should include both short and long-term goals as well as any necessary preparations. You can't be successful if you don't know how to get there, so make sure you're not forgetting anything by including it in your plan.

5. Determine Milestones for These Tasks

Once you've got your approach mapped out, you may be wondering how you can measure your success and see if you're on the right track. It's a good idea to create milestones along the way, keeping in mind that they should be specific and measurable, so you know when you've reached them. If your goal is more long-term, then creating a final benchmark is a good way to test whether you've been successful or if there is still work to be done.

6. Set Priorities

It's important for you to be able to distinguish between relevant and irrelevant information so that we can focus on what your priorities are, and not waste time with unnecessary details. For example, when we're researching a new topic, some parts might seem more interesting than others at first glance, but if we want your new approach to be effective your focus should be on determining what's most important rather than focusing on every single detail that comes up. This will ensure that we get the needed information to develop the priorities without wasting too much time on unnecessary details.

7. Break New Approach into Manageable Chunks

Breaking your new approach down into small, more manageable chunks makes the overall project of creating a new approach less intimidating. For example, if you are planning an entire year-long research project that will culminate in a large paper or presentation, you can create weekly deadlines for assignments that allow you to focus on smaller pieces at once rather than focusing on the final product. This helps us be more productive because it's easier to stay focused when there are no looming goals right around the corner. Breaking up goals like this also allows us some time to experiment and make mistakes without worrying too much about ruining months of work. Even though these problems might not seem like they would be related, thinking about them in terms of how they apply to your new approach is the best way to really understand why it's important to break things down.

Part 3 - Implement

Idea generation and idea implementation are two distinct processes that involve different parts of the brain. Idea implementation is more mechanical and less creative than idea generation. The best way to come up with new ideas for project implementation is to brainstorm as many ideas as possible, including both original and copied ideas, and then implement those ideas one at a time until we find an idea that works.

Part 4 - Evaluate

Take some time to evaluate each option carefully so that you know which one is most appropriate for you. Remember that there are no right answers here; only decisions made through critical thinking will help guide future decision making about your approach.

A Note on Creating and Evaluation

Creating means generating new ideas, visualizing, looking ahead, considering the possibilities.

Evaluating means analyzing and judging, picking apart ideas and sorting them into piles of good and bad, useful and useless. Most people evaluate too soon and too often, and therefore create less. In order to create more or better ideas for a new approach you must separate creation from evaluation by coming up with lots of ideas first, then judging their worth later.

Creative work is all around us, but to generate the best creative quality you need to separate the act of creating from the act of evaluating. Creative work includes any artistic project, scientific discovery, or brainstorming session. Evaluating creative work is the process of considering its worth and deciding if it should be utilized or improved further. And it involves assessing value, usefulness, and understandability. For example, a movie review might consider whether the movie was engaging and well written; a critical analysis of a political campaign strategy might consider whether that campaign increased voter turnout or encouraged people to vote for one candidate over another; and a newspaper article might provide an overview of recent scientific discoveries in hopes of highlighting which ideas are most significant.

Creativity requires you to think differently in order to produce something new. This type of thinking is very different from the routine, well thought-out ideas that we see in everyday life. Before we can even begin to judge the value and usefulness of creative work, we need to generate lots of ideas first. This is because creativity involves connecting and recombining existing thoughts in new and interesting ways. Therefore, it must come before evaluation in order for you to truly understand your original idea or concept. When you're brainstorming, do not worry about whether your ideas are good or bad; instead, let them flow freely without judgment. This will make it easier for you to create lots of new connections between random ideas.

The best way to accomplish this is to separate creation and evaluation of your new approach. Separating creation and evaluation is easier said than done. It's not the easiest thing to do, but it's worth working on. I'm not sure that I can say anything that will really help you with this one, but it might be a good idea to try out some different ways of finding balance. For example, you might want to spend more time on activities that are result-driven and less time on ones where you are continuously evaluating what's happening or worrying about what could go wrong.

It would also be helpful to notice when you're shifting back and forth between these two modes of thinking, at times, it might make sense to just think about what you're doing without worrying if it achieves something. Evaluate your creative work after you've created it. But make sure to separate the act of creation from the act of evaluation. Create first! You can't drive a car in first gear and reverse at the same time, likewise, don't try to use different types of thinking simultaneously. A lot of the time, when we're actively trying to generate ideas or think differently, all we need is a break. It can be helpful to take a few minutes for yourself and have a snack or go for a walk. If you come back even more energized, you may find that you've thought of tons of new ideas!

Conclusion

Changing your approach to your world is one of the most effective yet overlooked ways to change your life. Everyone's approach is different, which means that if you have a bad perspective of something, then you can find a new one and it will make everything better. Challenge yourself to approach situations with an open mind and be willing to work for the things you want instead of taking them for granted. This cannot be done in isolation. But you have to gather information from various angles. This can be difficult when you are facing challenges in your life, but with time it will become easier. It will only get better when you are armed with the understanding that when something is not working in your life, you must make a change.

Manifesto!

Another option on how to develop a new approach to success is by creating a personal manifesto. A manifesto is an expression of one's beliefs, usually in writing or speech. It can also be thought of as a public declaration of the intentions and motives of the issuer. A manifesto often presents a person's philosophy or goals and describes what they want to happen in the future. Examples include Manifesto for American Progress and Margaret Thatcher's The Path to Power (1979). Maybe this is what you need in your life. This may give you the needed assistance in helping you keep on task to your destiny of success.

When we talk about creating your own manifestos, it means coming up with your personal statement of beliefs or objectives. Something like "I believe X because Y" statements. When you create a manifesto for yourself, it's like creating your own personal mission statement. The idea of creating a manifesto often points to an occasion where someone makes known and announces who they really are or what they believe in. Think about political candidates, their campaign managers work with them to create an official platform that they will follow and proudly announce to the world. Their manifesto is a great tool for their constituents to keep them accountable to their actions. This is similar to proclaiming and sharing something very personal and meaningful with those around you.

Additionally, by creating a manifesto you establish boundaries and guidelines for what you do and who you are in the world. Creating a manifesto is setting out all the traits that make you unique. It is for those who are brave enough to declare their beliefs and ambitions in life.

How to Get Started

Think about the reasons you want to create a manifesto. What are your thoughts on these topics? What are your thoughts on the world/society around you? What type of change do you want to create in the world? Create an outline for what you think should be included in your manifesto. What things are important to you and what issues you want to address. Make sure that it's clear, easy-to-read, and concise. Once it's complete, print out copies for yourself to read in your hearing.

A Sample Personal Manifesto

Here is a portion of my, Albert Thompkins', Personal Manifesto:

-I am a Great husband
-I am a Great father I am a Great man
-I believe in happiness, health, and wealth
-I believe in Good success
-I am an overcomer
-I am faithful
-I believe in traveling the world
-I am Loved

All these statements are the bases of my entire approach to life. When things are not going as expected I pull out this manifesto to remind me who I am. These are things that I wrote down over 10 years ago. It really helps keep me grounded and focused on my path of success. If your current approach is not yielding the results you want, try it again and this time start by writing down your own personal manifesto. It's okay if it changes over time. Just don't stay in the same rut and regret what you could have changed. Give it a shot and change your approach to life and see if you have a better outcome in life.

There is an old adage that states, "What you see is what you get". Meaning, what is in front of you is some total of what to expect, no extras, no frills, and no fluff. Even though when people quote this phrase, they desire people to take them at face value, however, there is a dilemma: How are people interpreting what they see? It truly all depends on the angle they view the situation. The assumption is the receiver will have the exact same angle as the sender. That is a fallacy. There is a popular meme that shows a number, however, depending on the angle you are viewing it from the number could be either a "9" or a "6". It all depends on your angle; it's all contingent upon your approach. So, what is your angle on success? Do you see obstacles or do you see opportunities? Are you looking at situations or are you looking for solutions? One solution could be to just change your approach.

I will end as I began with the earlier story of the *A Pilot, His Instruments, and His Approach*. Like the pilot navigating a turbulent landing, despite making errors and nearly colliding with obstacles, he persevered. It's a reminder that setbacks are inevitable, but the key is to remain resilient and adapt your approach. Learn from the pilot's example: if you fall short of your goal, recalibrate your approach and press forward with determination.

Now, go for it!

BOOK THREE

THE WORK

by **W**alter Barrett

"By the sweat of your brow
   you will eat your food
until you return to the ground,
   since from it you were taken;"
            Genesis 3:19.

The Curse of Work: 7 Steps to Getting It Done

Throughout history, the philosophy and institution of work has remained a constant staple in every society, from the very primitive to the most developed. It is the 'holy grail' of the family, the community and the nation, passed on in some instances from one generation to another through a meticulous succession plan that involves training, resourcing and even the transfer of wealth. In other instances, there is nothing but the unspoken expectation that those who come after will ensure that what has been put in place for their comfort and sustenance will continue to be nurtured long after their predecessors are dead and gone. The reality is that one of these approaches yields far more productive results than the other, determining whether a man leaves behind a legacy or a loss.

The failure to relay the ultimate importance and inviolability of work is the successful start to a pending tragedy. The absence of work, or by extension, the absence of a healthy, positive work ethic, leaves in its place an unrealistic feeling of entitlement that is always fueled by greed and pride. The proverb says, "Give a man a fish, and you feed him for a day. Teach a man to fish, and you feed him for a lifetime." The problem is, many people in the world today just want to be handed fish. They don't want to go through the hassle of learning how to set bait, cast a line and wait patiently for prey to bite. No, just give me the fish and I will be fine. What that creates, however, is a dependency mentality. That person becomes no different than a bird that learns you throw seeds out the window at six o'clock every morning, so it starts landing on your window sill every day at five fifty-nine. At first, it's cute. No problem. You look forward to helping out mamma bird so she can start her day off right. But then come the days when you were planning to sleep in late. Or the days when you have no seeds. Or the days when you leave earlier than the usual time and so you skip breakfast. Mama bird is suddenly banging her beak all over your window, reminding you that she is there and you owe her her daily ration of seeds. Worse yet, when you open the window to chase her away, she starts attacking you with wings, claws, beak and whatever else she can throw at you.

The scenario may sound funny to some, but in reality, this is what happens when people are conditioned to believe they don't necessarily have to work for what they want. Now, there is absolutely nothing wrong with helping someone who is in genuine need and you are in a position to either help them, or point them in a direction where they can be helped. But again, as the proverb says, it is always better to teach people how they can provide for their own needs in a more meaningful, lasting and productive way, than to simply become their Salvation Army, because this type of dependency can easily turn into resentment, or even anger, when you are unable to supply their need.

We are seeing more and more societies where young people, especially young, black males, are trading in their work gloves for latex ones, opting to commit burglary or armed robbery rather than to perform an honest day's work. Prisons are infested and overrun with this demographic of our populations and the numbers keep rising exponentially, with no possible solutions in sight to curb the pandemic. So while the world fights to find vaccines for COVID-19 and other diseases that are indiscriminately taking lives, there is no investment in finding a cure for the disease that is taking our nineteen-year-olds and placing them in systems that are designed to lock them up and lose them for life.

To some, it may sound overly emphatic to say that the absence of personal work ethics can lead to an entire nation's demise, but the growing disappearance of a desire to aspire toward and achieve is a societal illness that can not only infect, but eventually kill both the individual who lacks such motivation, as well as those surrounding him. If we were to even remotely examine this theory as a possibility, the question one would then have to ask is, "How do I reinstall the drive that produces a strong, positive work ethic in the minds of the people around me?" This is the challenge, because when we speak about work ethic, we are not merely speaking about the ability to seek meaningful employment, to toil, to labor, to use some skill in a way that in return generates some genre of remittance. That may in reality be the easier goal to accomplish. Rather, when we talk about work and work ethic, we are referring to one's very will. Their will to try, their will to succeed, their will to rebound from a failed experience, their will to not simply dream a thing, but to fully commit and conform to it; whether it's getting a job, starting a family, making a difficult marriage work, attaining a degree, whatever it is, the will that keeps you in the race despite all the obstacles that come your way is the determinant of either success or failure.

Why doesn't everyone have the capacity to conquer?

Why is it that some people can come from such humble beginnings, claw through the most harrowing of experiences, yet come out as success stories, while others would fail during the same journey, even if they had the ideal start to their story? Why does one seed grow into a strong, lush, rooted tree, while another struggles to grow in the same soil, in the same climate and in the same environment? How does one child grow through the echoes of violence and abuse in the home, finish school and go on to become their own entrepreneur, while another who experiences the love and support of a nurturing home drops out of school, joins a gang and fails to exit their teenage years? In many instances, it is as simple as the will to succeed. The will to work hard. The will to change one's circumstance and to fulfill what one believes to be their destiny.

The will to work toward a goal – and to work hard and to work well – has been the impetus to the successes of men and women who were counted out because of their familial background, their geographic location, the social class they were born into, or the color of their skin. While others talked, they worked. They devised a master plan to transport them from people's perception of them, to their own reality of themselves. And the journey is seldom ever easy, because success is a living entity that does not succumb to well wishes and high hopes. Rather, success is wooed by inspiration, aspiration and perspiration and is drawn to such virtues as commitment, resilience and resourcefulness. The idle cannot court, much more dare to marry success. She is a sophisticated woman who can tell when someone is truly ready to settle down, or simply driving by for a brief moment of satisfaction and self-gratification. Success is enticed by hard work and success will only couple with the one who is willing to work to have success.

Taking into account the various interpretations of success already posited in the previous chapters of this book, we will use the following abridged definition for success as we try to now understand the critical role that work plays in attaining it. Simply put, success is, the achievement or fulfillment of an aim or goal. Therefore, no matter how big or small the goal, success is measured by the ability to shift from planning to execution. I have not succeeded because I have started the race. I have succeeded when I have crossed the finish line. Whether it's getting a degree, starting a business, building a house, or traveling to an unfamiliar destination, it is quite possible to pick up some trophies along the journey. And there are some who would sacrifice the bigger picture and simply relish in those acquired landmarks, because it seems like too much to keep going all the way to the end.

There have been and will continue to be arguments surrounding who is truly the greatest basketball player of all time. Many players have amassed various titles throughout their careers. Most Valuable Player for the longest consecutive period. Most assists in a season. Most back-to-back triple-doubles. Leader in three-point shots attempted and made. Yet, not all of them make it to the table when arguing who is the greatest of all time. Because, as amazing as many of their accomplishments are, there is one ultimate mountain that must be climbed in order to be crowned the G.O.A.T. You have to have earned the elusive championship ring. Sorry, Tracy McGrady, with all your high-flying antics and magnificent dunks that thrilled us for years. Sorry, Charles Barkley, who now, at the end of his professional career, sits in the chair as a sports analyst and converses about today's superstars. Sorry, Allen Iverson, Dikembe Mutombo, Reggie Miller, Patrick Ewing, Steve Nash, John Stockton, Karl Malone and the plethora of other Hall of Famers who despite their undeniable skills, passion, drive and tenacity, ended their careers without a single championship title, which is the most defining feat in the sport. Now, no one will ever deny the fact that all of these athletes lived for and worked toward winning a championship. Yet, as the twilight of each of their careers approached, I would imagine the dreams of one day boasting a collection of five or six rings dwindled more and more with each passing season, until they would have just been satisfied to have won just a single one. But the curtains dropped on each of these basketball greats, leaving all ten of their fingers bare, with no championship title to show for their devotion to and love of the sport.

And then, there's Michael Jordan. A man who ended his career with six NBA Championships and numerous other titles to go along with them. A man who even after announcing his retirement – twice – would return to the court and bring the same motivation, drive and will to win at forty that he did at twenty-one. A man who no matter where you go in the world, someone knows the name and the symbol for 'His Royal Airness'. What separated Michael Jordan from the rest? It was more than his agility, his natural strength, his ability to fly. It was his work ethic, which, to this day, remains unmatched in the basketball arena. According to his biography on IDMb (Internet Movie Database), "At Laney High School, as a sophomore, he decided to try out for the varsity team but was cut because he was raw and undersized. The following summer, he grew four inches and practiced tirelessly. The hard work paid off as he averaged twenty-five points per game in his last two years and was selected to the McDonald's All-American Team as a senior."

What if the young, raw, undersized Michael Jordan had simply allowed what others saw in him to overshadow what he saw in himself? What if he had decided to throw away his dreams of playing professional basketball because it would have taken too much out of him to make it? The world would have never known the man who today, is arguably the best athlete to have ever played in the NBA. Understand, though, that Jordan's success did not just happen. It was a long, meticulous journey, one that had no shortcuts or fast-forward buttons. In his own words, Michael Jordan said this of his will to win: "Nobody will ever work as hard as I work." Fellow teammates and former coaches throughout his career said that whenever practice was over, Jordan still wanted to run drills, take shots or shoot free throws. Again, in his own words, Michael Jordan notes, "I've missed more than 9000 shots in my career. I've lost almost three hundred games. Twenty-six times, I've been trusted to take the game winning shot and missed. I've failed over and over and over again in my life. And that is why I succeed." Michael Jordan's success was due to more than just mere skill. It was the direct result of continuous hard work. Even when his body was broken, Jordan's work ethic remained intact and that is why he boasts 6 championships today.

There is something that happens when a dream is tied to desire. Desire, or will, is the engine that moves and motivates us to go past the challenges and to remain focused on the goal. There will always be stuff thrown at us. There will always be man-made and natural obstacles threatening our progress and making the path seem impossible to navigate. But even then, desire says, I am going to work toward it, come what may. It is at these moments we must look past what is directly in front of us and fix our gaze on the object of our affection. It cannot come easy, because then everyone would be able to sit in the seat that was carved out just for you. It is therefore up to you to ensure you don't abort your purpose. Although this may seem easier said than done, it is possible when we apply certain principles to our lives that can help us grow healthy work habits. Work does not have to feel like a curse. Rather, it can be a blessing in the hands of the individual who has learned to cultivate healthy work ethics that drive their daily routine. So, in this chapter, we will discuss seven steps that we all can take in our quest to foster healthy work habits that guarantee success.

Do you want to be successful? If you really do, then, let's get to work.

ONE
Don't Just See It – Speak It!

I love to hear children talk about what they want to be when they grow up. Every child has their own perception of life and particularly, the world of work. Somehow, in the mind of a child, getting a job and staying employed is, "easy, peasy, lemon squeezy." They don't grasp the challenges that many of them will face when that time comes. They don't grasp the reality of such responsibilities as bills, deadlines, discrimination and overtime at their early ages and as a result, their excited recitations of professional aspirations are unadulterated and genuine. The list usually sounds the same, ranging from doctor to firefighter. Fast-forward some ten years later, however, and less than a quarter of those same children – now young adults – are pursuing the same passions they had when they were toddlers. For some, their passion simply morphed over time into something else. But for others, they were daunted by the sudden, overwhelming awareness of what it would actually take for them to accomplish their dream. I have had to counsel countless teenagers who were determined that after high school, they were never setting foot inside the classroom again. Yet, in order to become the doctor, lawyer, technician, engineer, or whatever it is they were planning on becoming, I had to remind them that some level of education would be needed, as well as training in the particular field. I had to encourage them not to give up on their dreams, just because they won't materialize overnight. The challenge? Not everyone is dedicated enough to work toward what they want in life. They get intimidated by the sight of the journey and choose to settle for something else.

If we are honest with ourselves, there have been a lot of places in our lives that remained stagnant because of fear. Fear of failure, fear of rejection, fear of loss, fear of not being capable enough. As a result, there are some pursuits that we either abandoned, or never even started. Perhaps it was someone else who planted that seed of fear in us when we allowed their doubt to overcome us. They questioned our ability to do what we said we were going to do and they met us with skepticism and ridicule instead of faith and support. Couple that with issues of insecurity where in many instances, there is the feeling that the doubters were somehow in a better position than we were to determine what was best for us and so, we succumbed to the words spoken over our lives and we changed course. Today, we all have regrets for some road we never took. Those, "What if" moments knock at the back of our minds from time to time, resurrecting every now and then, causing us to imagine what life would be like if we had dared to pursue our passion, rather than fold to our fears. Is there some way to guarantee our commitment to success?

It is easy to have a goal in sight. There is no difficulty in saying that at age fifty, I will have my own home, my children would have all graduated from school and I would be enjoying retirement with trips to places never seen before. However, chances are that a lot will happen between now and then. Unexpected expenses, a pandemic that disrupts the education system, a change in an academic major, there is just a host of stuff that can happen to throw the best plan into a tailspin. It is human to become discouraged when things don't go according to plan, but is there some way to press through the whirlwind, stay on course and complete the mission? There may not be any formula that guarantees success, but there are some actual steps that one can take to increase the likelihood of being successful at the end of the day. With all these steps, that healthy work ethic mentioned earlier is the fuel that fires the entire system. There must be that commitment to seeing whatever it is through to the end.

So, think about something that you are excited about. A relationship, a job, a project, an innovative idea that you think can change the way we live. Whatever it is, it has a name. Think of it by name for a moment and in your mind, silently call it out. Now, repeat that name. Not just once, or twice, but several times, over the course of a minute. See how many times you can call that vision out by name in your mind within that time. Now, open your mouth and speak it. Again, not just one time, or two times, but repeat it over and over. Repeat it when you wake up in the morning. Repeat it as you go through the day. Repeat it before you go to bed at night. Make it the first thing in your thoughts as you start your day and the last thing on your mind when you end it. Why? Because repetition breathes life to a thing. I read an online blog entitled, The Power of Repetition: the Secret of Successful Leaders by Lighthouse, a company that prides itself in creating better managers within large and small companies. A portion of the article reads thus:

"The power of repetition is in its simplicity. A
message heard repeatedly is more
likely to stay in your mind."

Are you serious about succeeding? Repeat your
plan over and over by name. Yes, successful people
who have achieved what they set out to do in life will
tell you that part of their regime was to write down
their plans in detail. They would remind themselves of
those plans every day, making adjustments as they went
along, but ensuring that they followed the blueprint as
closely as possible. I want to add to that principle. I
want to encourage you to not only see your goal, but
speak your goal. There is power in your words. Words
can tear down, but words can also build up. There is
creative power not only in your mind, but in your
mouth. So when you think about what you want to
achieve and then you speak it, you bring it into
existence by birthing it into the atmosphere. You are
releasing a time capsule of purpose and destiny into
your environment and like a seed, once you add other
principles to it and begin to water that spoken word, it
will germinate, it will find root and it will grow.

Your success is not only dependent upon your
thoughts. It is equally dependent upon your words.
Your words are a declaration over your life that you
will complete that which you have begun. Words are
vibrations that attract like-frequencies. Positive words
will yield positive results. Equally true is that negative
words will also obey your command. There are people
living beneath their potential today because of the very
declarations they made over their lives yesterday, not
understanding the power that is attached to what we

say. Constantly declaring curses such as, "I'll never have money", "I'll never get a job", or, "It will never get better" only create an air of frustration and depression, two soils that cannot produce, but rather, stifle. It is incumbent upon anyone who desires to be successful that they change their language and cultivate a garden that bears only the fruit they are willing to eat. So, speak life. Tell yourself, you will get the degree. You will have a happy marriage. Your children will be healthy. You will receive the promotion. You will own your own home. You will be financially fruitful. Declare your words even louder when there seems to be no reason for you to be speaking them. At your weakest points, when you feel like throwing in the towel, that is the time to remind yourself even more about where you are going, rather than where you are. You aren't doing the things you do simply to get by. You aren't persevering through pressure just because you're trying to prove a point. There are people whose own destinies are tied to yours. The success of your children is dependent on whether you are able to provide for them or not. The success of your marriage relies heavily upon your ability to work past the differences and learn to forgive. The success of your business is hinged on whether or not you can find a way to become even more relevant and necessary when competitors turn up.

So, the first set of work you need to put in to achieve your goals is to plant them into the fertile soil of the atmosphere through your words. Just as you would nurture a child, or a spouse, or any relationship by speaking kind, positive words of affirmation into them, speak those same words of affirmation over your own life and destiny. Even when everything is saying, You can't, sing a different song. Tell your environment, I can. You are working toward creating the life you want for yourself and your words are each brick that will form the wall that keeps positivity in, while locking negativity out. If you were not already housing the capacity to do what you were created to do, that passion would not continually keep you up at night. You believed in your purpose before someone or something dropped a thorn of doubt into your being. Instead of speaking against it, you believed it and that thorn grew and wrapped itself around your vision and choked it. But I want to assure you that it's not dead. And you have the power to speak life over that thing and rekindle the passion for your purpose. Every word you speak that aligns with your potential is like a weedicide sprayed over those toxic vines. Strip them off of you and root up any and everything that is not what you desire to be planted in the garden of your soul.

I know how discouraging it can be when the ones speaking against your vision are the very ones you love. I know how it feels when you share your plans, hoping to receive additional motivation to drive you to your expected end, but instead, you are confronted with detours and roadblocks on every side, so you give up. Maybe you are reading this and recalling your own experience of being shut down instead of shot up. As ridiculous as it may sound, I dare you to speak over that dream again. Speak it until you are able to see it clearly and believe that you can achieve it. The only obstacle in the way of you accomplishing your purpose is your lack of faith in what you have already been endowed with for the journey. The only impossibility you face is expecting to get to your destination without ever moving. What is wonderful about moving is that it does not matter if you walk, or crawl, run, or drag yourself forward inch by inch, because it is not a race, but a journey. And your journey doesn't need speed. What it needs is commitment.

Speaking your success into action isn't just for you. Is there someone in your life that you want to see succeed? Speak over them. Speak over your children as they sleep. Call out their success while they lay dreaming about it. Speak over your spouse, who may not be as motivated as you are about their own giftedness. Let your words manifest in the air and become the very breath they breathe. Speak over your employees who don't seem to have caught hold of your vision. Speak over your mind that oftentimes allows fear to manipulate your thoughts. Speak over your health that prevents you from performing the tasks that you desire to do. Speak over everything in your life that you want to bloom and likewise, speak over the things that hinder you and block your progress and command them to get out of your way. Your mouth is a gateway to your success and everything connected to you – from your mind to your very spirit – must fall in alignment with your spoken assignment.

I'm not saying that simply speaking words will bring the finish line closer to you, but I guarantee you that it will bring you closer to the finish line, because your mind was created to respond to commands. What commands are you feeding your mind? Give up? Abandon the mission? Take an easier journey? Forfeit what is waiting for you at the end of the road? Whatever you feed your mind is what will feed you. It's time to start feeding your mind the kind of food that will motivate your spirit in the midst of any problem, pandemic, pressure or perplexity. It's time to start commanding your mind to get back up, even when the rest of the world is telling you to stay down and quit. Only you can keep yourself from succeeding. You've been through so much already, if you were built to break, you would have. But you can't be broken, because that purpose inside of you is far greater than the situation around you. So, if you've never done it before, begin now to speak your desired future into existence. Your feet will move in the direction that your mind commands them to go in. Will you always feel like you actually believe all that you are saying over yourself? No. Will you always feel like declaring something over your life that contradicts what the majority might be saying? No. But speak anyhow. And everything else must come into agreement with your declaration, starting with your will.

TWO
Think 'Colossal'

A lot of people have been told that their dreams are too big. I've had people I confided in tell me all the reasons my plans would not get off the ground. Had I listened to people each time they failed to affirm my vision, I would have tried nothing in life. The truth is, it isn't that your dreams are too big. It's just that not everyone has the capacity to handle your greatness.

One of the biggest mistakes we make is constantly trying to adjust our purpose to fit someone else. It is good to seek counsel, to accept advice, to listen to what others have to say. In fact, those are all signs of great leaders. The problem arises when we let people talk us out of the construction zone and they suddenly become the developers of our destiny. Don't let anyone tell you what the size of your achievement should look like. There is no limit to what you can accomplish, or what you deserve. In fact, question the motives of anyone who continuously douses your passion for success.

Not everyone is going to buy in to your dreams. I'm certain that many of the inventions that make our lives so convenient today were scuffed at in their embryotic stages because unlike their inventors, people couldn't conceptualize them. It just seemed too impossible at the time. Catching and projecting light from a glass sphere? A device that facilitates communication while being miles apart? Transportation with four spinning circles in the place of four stomping hooves? What madness. But, just think about this for a moment. If everyone were able to see your vision as clearly as you did, then anyone would be able to do what you do. When it feels like no one understands what your purpose is, don't become so discouraged that you throw in the towel. It simply means that what you have to do is so unique and so different, that not everyone is going to be able to join you for the journey. That can be disappointing, because some people aren't comfortable going the journey alone. Sometimes, the company you roll with can be your greatest distraction, prolonging the completion of your mission, or sabotaging it altogether.

I always encourage people to rethink whatever they've heard about purpose and destiny. We hear a lot about making 'realistic goals'. I challenge that school of thought, which suggests there are some things that you just can't accomplish. I would like a list of those un-accomplishable tasks, because I would gently immerse it in kerosene, then ever-so-lightly lower it on to a struck match and watch it burn. Forever. There is no greater lie than telling someone, "You can't." Says who? Why can't you bring that idea into fruition and watch it prosper? What hinders you now, that you can't remove in time and clear the path later?

One of my favorite advertisements of all time features a young boy that runs up to a man named Ralph who is standing outside a barn, eating from a pack of Doritos. The boy asks, "Hey Ralph. Can I have a Dorito?" Ralph stops eating, looks down at the boy, laughs and answers, "Sure. When pigs fly." The young boy places his hand under his chin as if in deep thought, and the scene cuts to our young hero as he starts on his master plan. He goes into a nearby barn, rolls out some blueprints across a wooden table, starts hauling in some materials from around the barn in his little wagon, begins measuring the back of one of the pigs on the farm, and gets to work off camera. All the viewers see are sparks flying everywhere. Finally, the young boy emerges from the barn with a giant remote control in his hands. He looks at Uncle Ralph, who is still standing where he left him, eating his Doritos, and calls out to him. "Hey, Ralph," the boy says. The man pauses and looks down at the young boy and his contraption, as the boy presses a red button on the control with the word, 'Launch' under it. Suddenly, there is a loud rumbling coming from the barn, and something bursts through the roof in a huge puff of smoke and flames. There, flying through the air, is a pig with wings and a rocket strapped to its back. It swoops down, zooms right past Ralph who is standing in disbelief, blows Ralph's cap off his head and shoots back into the air. In the closing shot, as Ralph stands staring speechless and open mouthed at the flying pig, he hands the little boy the rest of Doritos. And the boy takes it with a look of accomplishment on his face.

Perhaps you've seen the ad before yourself. Not only is it hilarious, but it also holds some deep-rooted lessons that I want us to extrapulate and apply to our lives as we look at not merely thinking big, but working big. While this advertisement only lasts thirty-one seconds, there are three lessons we can extract from it that can last a lifetime.

1. Don't Let Fear and Doubt Rule Your Faith and Destiny

It would have been easy for the little hero in that Doritos ad to have become discouraged by Ralph's response. Clearly, Ralph was someone that the boy knew and trusted, so he was not expecting the response that he got when he simply asked for a Dorito. One measly, little Dorito. After receiving the snide response, he could have just walked away and licked his emotional wounds. He could have stood there begging, but it seems like he was too proud to grovel. Instead, he devised a plan. In Ralph's mind, his Doritos were secure, because, after all, pigs never flew before. I want to believe that Ralph himself was so accustomed to hearing about the proverbial flying pig that it was easy for him to regurgitate the saying to others. But on that day, he would learn a lesson that would change his perspective of the word, 'impossible'. That little boy was determined to find a way to get what he wanted and as far as he was concerned, nothing was impossible or out of the way.

That is the mentality you need to have when approaching the things that pertain to your personal success. There may be a plethora of reasons you should listen to all the naysayers and just abandon your dreams, but what would happen if you resolved in your mind to honestly give it a try? Sure, your present situation may not resemble your future aspirations, but that's where the journey and the approach come in. There is a path you are going to have to take if you are serious about being successful. Want to pass a test? Study. Want to get a job? Apply. Want to learn a trade?

Understudy. It's good to have the dream, but that dream requires effort to move from fantasy to reality. You may not see the means to the end right now, but that can't stop you from getting up and starting the journey. One thing that I've learned along my own walk thus far is that even when the resources are low or even non-existent, once you are diligently moving toward fulfilling a task, resources find you. For those who define success simply as financial fluidity, another lesson that I've learned is that money is not just a currency, but an actual current. It thrives between conducive conductors. I'm not talking about metals, or staves, but plans and ideas. I tell people over and over again that money should be the last thing that keeps them from fulfilling their purpose, because once you cast your vision far and clear enough, others will catch it. Investors will come. Donations will come. Money will find you. Because money thrives on great ideas. On the other hand, when you are chasing after money with nothing to attract it with, this living currency will always run away from you. And trust me when I say that money can outrun the fastest of us. Again, it isn't about how swift you are, but how committed you are.

So, that big dream you have been trying to get others to believe in for the longest while, but keep getting shut down? It's time to stop telling it to the dream killers and to start finding ways to make it happen. Just because something has never been done before doesn't mean that it cannot be done. And just because people are determined to count you out doesn't mean you have to count yourself out also. Make your pig fly. The people who have initiated the most positive, meaningful change in the world are people who dared to go against the status quo. They were willing to question the norm and most times, it was in pursuit of betterment. They were not satisfied with just following the crowd. They had a deep rooted, gut feeling that there was something more. So they asked and they planned and they swam against the waves of negativity until they arrived on shore. You have a purpose in the earth. That purpose involves you discovering your passion and understanding how it fits into the overall plan for your destiny. It does not matter how you got here, or what conditions you were born into. Yes, I know and accept that your environment plays a major part in shaping and molding you into who you are, but ultimately, you decide if you are going to be a statistic, or a success story.

Too many spend their years playing it safe, living out their time camouflaged in the background out of fear, rather than standing out in faith. You don't have to limit your imaginations to the size of your surroundings, or people's evaluations of you. You don't have to be an eternal slave to your limitations. For every weakness that you have, there is a strength that far surpasses your failures. It's easy to become a victim of words spoken over us that were meant either directly or indirectly to cripple our conscience. "You're just like your father." "You'll never amount to anything." "You'll always be in the same position." "No one is ever going to love you." "You'll never be successful." Hurtful words can hurt even more when they come from people who we expected to encourage and love and nurture us. They can cut like knives and force us into reclusive lifestyles and in an instant, our dreams that once ignited and excited us are thrown aside and abandoned, because we shared them with dream crushers instead of dream builders. I'm encouraging you to take a breath of fresh air and resuscitate that passion you allowed to suffocate. It can still live. Fear and doubt can only live where they have been invited in. You don't have to be afraid of failing. You don't have to question your ability to succeed. The only thing that you have to be afraid of is never becoming who you were created to be. The only way to ensure that does not happen is to get up and get moving. If a little boy can find a way to make pigs fly, there is no reason you can't attach wings to your vision and cause it to soar. You are bigger than your doubts and your fears and as long as you conquer those demons by simply getting started along your road to achievement, then you've already begun your journey to success.

2. It's Time to Get in the Barn

Sometimes, you have to take the same posture as the little boy in that Doritos add and just get in the barn and shut the door. Shut the door from the naysayers, the haters, the doubters, the scorners, the jeerers. Just shut out all the negativity and get to work. If our little hero had spent all his time and energy begging for what he wanted instead of devising a plan to get it, before he knew it, he would have been staring at an empty pack in Ralph's hands. Instead, he locked himself in the barn, put his ideas down on paper, brought his ideas to life and presented his creation to the world, earning him his prize. Well, just like that young boy, you have something to present to the world that is going to blow their minds, just as assuredly as a flying pig would. But commitment calls for cancellation. You have to learn to cancel every sound that is not in tune with yours.

The world is filled with distractions, vying for our attention, bidding to rob us of our most precious commodity - time. Social media is constantly competing for the attention of every man, woman and child that owns a device capable of receiving content from the worldwide web. In that sea of information, many plans have drowned and died. Persons have exchanged their own stories for someone else's, following the lifestyles of others rather than writing their own script. While there is so much good that can be garnered from the digital realm, there is so much damage done when we allow the distractions of cyberspace to take our focus off the finish line. Academic and entrepreneurial pursuits are placed on hold while Netflix, Facebook, Snapchat, YouTube, Instagram, Twitter, LinkedIn and more take center stage, numbing the conscious mind to the urgency and the nearness of the time. We are lulled into believing that time is the one thing we will always have, when in fact, it is the only thing in life that we can never get back. We sit back and watch as others graduate from college, or are promoted on the job, others who started out the same time we did, but somehow, we watched them pass us by and advance along the way. We even have the nerve to entertain feelings of jealousy, when in fact the only emotion we should feel is shame, because the only difference between them and us lies in our use of time.

Success is a direct by-product of hard, dedicated work. You must endeavor to devote your time to the process of making success happen, or it will simply remain a desire. To be successful, you have to block yourself in with your vision and guard it from thieves. Go into the barn and shut the doors. Close the windows. Block out the sounds of laughter that mock your efforts and the sounds of criticism that want you to walk away from the desire of your heart. The barn is your safe place. The barn is your work space. The barn is wherever you can turn to and find encouragement in the midst of the noise and the clatter. Nothing good comes easily and that is a fact. But when you have toiled for the prize, you value it more. Your vision always exceeds what you have in your possession. That's why it's a dream. The tangibles aren't always present the moment you receive your download, but the blueprint always shows you what resources you need to gather along the way. The young boy in the advertisement had only two things on him at the time Ralph issued him the challenge. A plan and determination. It was upon these two pillars that he went to work. His plan told him what he needed to pick up along the way in order to fulfill his mission and he gathered all those essentials together in his wagon and began to build. His determination chased away any opposition that popped up and threatened the execution of his plan. With these two ingredients, he made what everyone thought was impossible, possible. And you can do the same.

Find literal people and places that you can go to and find refuge for the purpose you are carrying. They are safe havens where you can plant your words and they will water them with support and aid you along your journey. Not every friend is family and not every family is a friend. Learn the difference. The barn keeps you safe from jealousy and envy. They will always be present, but they do not have to get to you and suffocate your drive. Find people who speak the same language you do. People who want you to succeed as much as they do. People who aren't just speaking about building, but you see them constantly putting aside the steel, the cement, the blocks and all the materials necessary for it to materialize. Find places that nurture your best thoughts. Places that bring out your greatest ideas and fertilize the seeds of your prosperity. Distractions will come and not all of them will be external. Some will come from within, taking the forms of insecurity and anxiety. You have to want the end result so badly that the process becomes worth it. Get selfish with your success. Don't let just anyone and anything in that can contaminate your progress. You've worked too hard already and come too far, just by deciding to start this journey. Don't let people and stuff sidetrack you and cause you to regress rather than progress when it comes to working toward your goals. Whatever you want in this life is accessible to you. That's a fact. It's up to you to prepare and safeguard your mind for the journey toward that goal and to stay committed to giving it whatever it requires of you.

3. Make Your Plan and Stick to It

Sure, you want to be successful, but what does it actually look like? How do you arrive at this coveted place called, Success? What do you need in your possession right now to get from where you are to where you envision yourself being? The truth is that many people drift through life's treacherous sea without any form of direction. They look at others who seem to have it all together, sailing comfortably into the sunset and decide that this is the life they want to live. They never took into account what type of boat they would need, or how much it would cost. They never considered if they would hire a captain, or learn to sail themselves. They never compensated for bad weather, pirates, breakdowns, or any other inhibitors to their arrival time. That, my friend, is how many people are living their life today. Looking at others, wanting to live the kind of life they live and never stopping for a moment and thinking about what such a life really costs.

Looking back once more at the young, determined inventor who was the first to make a pig fly, we see someone who was not only determined, but someone who was so committed that he put a plan in place to get what he wanted. It is one thing to want something. It is another thing to get to it. The bridge between the two is not as complicated as it sometimes feels. In fact, it is as simple as having a plan of action that takes you from one point to the other. A plan that takes all of the intangibles and puts them together in a way that your idea can become both visible and operational.

Many people lack the discipline required to plan. The thought of putting something together frustrates them and turns them off. It is always easier to jump to something else that is simple and requires no effort. Yet, those things are usually temporal and we end up sitting in the places we were before, still wanting more for ourselves. You are not going to accomplish anything of value and substance without a plan. Think of your journey as a literal trip to another country. You don't just close your eyes and arrive somewhere else. First, you have to choose a destination. Where do you want to go and why? Florida, for the summer sun? Alaska, to experience the extreme cold? A cruise, for the endless buffets and onboard entertainment? After you've settled on where you want to go and why, you have to figure out how you're going to get there. Are you going to enlist the help of a travel agent, or go online and book everything yourself? How long you plan to stay away is another question that you would need to consider. Then, you need to look at the cost for the entire trip. How much is it to get there? Will you be staying with a family member or friend, or staying at a hotel? If the answer is the latter, then obviously, cost goes up. Food is another factor that must be taken into account when considering cost. What is the best route to take to get there? Are there any restrictions that you need to be aware of? Do you have the required documents needed for this trip and are they up-to-date? These are some of the pertinent questions that must be asked when planning your trip, because they will make the difference between a memorable experience and a disaster you'd want to forget.

Sometimes, it is good to turn the planning over to someone who can make the process easier, such as the travel agent in the example given above. Planning can seem overwhelming to some, especially at first, or based on the magnitude of the project. There is no reason to leave a goal behind because it requires too much work to get done. You can reach out for help. You can seek the assistance of people who have gone down that road before, or who are good at figuring things out. The important thing is making sure you have some sort of map that guides you along your journey, so you don't get lost or distracted along the way.

Having crafted your plan of action, it is important that you stick to your plan. Yes, it may be adjusted and altered along the way and that is normal and natural, because variables change. Costs fluctuate, routes may be altered due to unforeseen circumstances, but you must always keep the final destination in sight. Even when the plan does not seem to be working, don't just throw it away. Find another way to get it done. See what areas of your plan need amending and keep on the journey until you arrive at the end. Your vision matters. It was given to you for a purpose. You are the one entrusted with the responsibility of fulfilling it, because all the tools to accomplish it are already in you. Yes, there are other tools that you may not possess that might be needed for the excavation of that master plan, but those additional resources will only come into play when others see your plan and latch on to it.

Whether it is writing a book, opening a restaurant, getting a degree, starting a family, building a house, or whatever it is, you need to plan. You need to take the time to carefully and strategically outline the steps it will take to fulfill that vision and you have to stick to your plan. As was mentioned before, there will always be distractions that seek to pull you away from you purpose, even in the form of family and friends. Are you willing, though, to give up your permanent position for a temporary temptation? It is up to you to ensure that you keep at the forefront of your mind why you started out on this journey in the first place and to see it through to completion. Understand, too, that success does not look the same for everyone. Success for me may be motivating a room filled with people to pursue their dreams. Success for someone else may be finishing the shed to the back of the house, or planting that garden they purchased seeds for years ago. Success is never one size fits all. It isn't what we see on music videos or movies. It isn't simply the possession of material wealth. Success goes deeper than all of these. It is the satisfaction of knowing that a simple task was seen through to the end and completed, even in the midst of opposition.

Your plan is unique to your purpose. Not everyone is going to agree with it, see the need for it, or support it. But stick to your plan anyway. Be open to advice. There may be genuine persons who care enough to help build on your idea and that's great. Be mature enough to accept their advice and to adjust as you go along. But know when there are also people whose plan is to derail you from your purpose, simply because they don't believe in you. So, be careful who you share your plans with, because there are those who simply want to compete with you, so they can complete before you. Guard your plan, but get going on your plan and don't give up. Challenges will come. Distractions will appear. You have the responsibility of finishing what you started, because that, my friend, is success, no matter how big or small the achievement may be.

Nothing of significance just happens. The largest companies, the greatest songs, the biggest blockbusters, every accomplishment that has been of major significance and marked history in some way all started as a simple idea, but developed over time through a systematic approach that resulted in what we have come to see and know. Whether it's 'Amazon', 'I Will Always Love You', or the 'Star Wars' franchise, someone took an idea, put pen to paper and created a plan to move from thought to reality. Someone planned while others dreamed and those plans manifested into something so great, that to this day, others are benefiting from it. Being successful requires having a plan for your success. It does not just come to you. You have to tell it how to get to you. It means remaining true to your plan, even when it requires you putting out more time, more finances, more energy than you may want to. The end result, however, is that you get to celebrate your achievement, all because at some point, you planned for your success and you did not give up on that plan.

You have to have a plan for your life. You aren't going to stumble into your place of success. You have to work toward it. Like an archaeologist seeking a precious find, you have to dig your way through all that stands between you and your treasure. But like the archaeologist, it all starts with a plan. Where am I now? Where do I want to be? How am I going to get there? What do I need to take along with me? Have your plan. Stick to your plan. Success will find you as sure as you will find success.

THREE
Divide! Then Conquer

There is anxiety in uncertainty. When we don't know exactly how or when a particular season or circumstance will end, it can leave us in a state of worry and despair. We love to feel in control and when situations take our hands off the wheel, it can be a struggle for us to adjust to that reality. That same level of frustration can creep in when we can't seem to accomplish a given task, or reach a goal, be it personal or professional. It can be a drainer watching everyone figure stuff out while we are still there, struggling with our own battle. It's these struggles that prevent many people from even venturing out into deeper waters, because they already feel overwhelmed just fighting with the waves near the shore. All the while, our thoughts are in direct contradiction to our desires. Why should I risk the little I have left when I've already lost so much? It didn't work the last time. Who says it will work now? I don't have the strength for any more disappointments. Maybe this was never meant for me in the first place.

We have all had moments of doubt in our lives. We've questioned whether that picture we're pursuing is worth it, or even possible. Sometimes, the mountain that stands between you and your destination can seem insurmountable and you just don't think you have what it takes to get over it. I want you to know that there is always a price for your progress, but whatever that is, you have what it takes to own it.

Most times, the bigger the goal, the tougher the road. And that road can be so intimidating that we tell ourselves it just isn't worth it. There is another approach that we can take when it comes to putting in the work required for our journey. We don't have to throw in the towel, just because it requires too much work. There is a way to succeed, despite how impossible things may appear, or how many times we have already tried to annihilate all that stands between us and our progress. Divide the task into parts and get it completed one part at a time. It's the same approach we take when it comes to devouring a huge meal, for example. It's always more believable that it's achievable when we cut that huge hamburger into quarters and tackle it one fourth at a time. Smaller tasks are easier to manage and to get done. Even at work, we break up our to-do list into various categories, either based on due dates, timelines, projects, available resources and so on. If you want to be successful and avoid becoming overwhelmed by the magnitude of the work standing between you and that success, divide your workload into portions and then get it done one part at a time.

As was said before and as you've already figured out by now, success takes time. Whatever it is, it takes effort and it takes time. One way to avoid becoming overwhelmed is to break your journey down into short trips. Divide the work into sub-tasks and complete them one by one. This avoids the burnout that many people experience on their road to success. That burnout, sometimes, is so debilitating that some never rebound from it. So, learn to pace yourself. Don't be your own worst enemy and beat yourself over the head for not sticking to the schedule you gave yourself. Yes, it is important to make sure that you are progressing along the way, but you don't need to feel that you've failed just because you didn't meet the date highlighted on your calendar. There is still time and you are going to get it done.

Here are some practical steps you can take to help you manage your workload. As you contemplate these steps, remind yourself that while work is necessary, it does not have to be a nuisance. There are ways to manage your workload, without having your workload manage you.

i.   Be Realistic About Self-Imposed Timelines

I remember when I was writing my first book. I had it all planned out in my head. It would be a two-hundred paged bestseller, over twenty chapters long. I began writing in January of 2000 and I was going to finish it before my birthday in March of the same year. I always had a passion for writing and this was going to be my first book. I was excited, I was driven, I was motivated. And most of all, I was wrong. About a lot of things.

I had a misguided perception that the journey would be easy. Therefore, my approach was all wrong. When I was confronted with the reality of how much work it entailed to become the bestselling author I dreamt of becoming, everything started to change. My passion turned into pain. My excitement turned into excruciating effort. My drive was replaced with days of discouragement. My motivation was marred by mood swings. It was taking far too long to get through a single chapter, much more twenty. I remember times when I abandoned the project for days, which stretched into weeks. My twenty-second birthday came and went without any book launch, book signing, or even a completed manuscript. It took me four more years to finish and publish my first book and furthermore, it was not even the one that I had started writing in 2000. It was less than two hundred pages, less than twenty chapters and to date, it still is not a bestseller.

That year, as I looked back on my journey and my approach, along with all the work I finally committed to getting done, I was reminded of two important lessons. One, words cannot express the joy and satisfaction that come from seeing your work through to completion and standing at the end of the journey with the reward in hand. Two, it takes a made up mind to succeed at anything in this life. I also recognized a simple but profound truth that year, which to this day, I still share with others who are aspiring toward writing their first book. If you can wake up every morning and commit to writing just one page a day, you can have a three hundred and sixty-five-paged project to share with the world at the end of the year. Just by committing to writing one page a day. The problem is that we think we have to write the entire book in one sitting, so we often slave in front of the computer, forcing the words to come out of our fingertips, instead of allowing our natural thought processes to flow. Many miss the opportunity to present their best work because instead of focusing on a theme, they focus on the time and all they do is try to beat the clock instead of taking the time to produce their greatest creation. The question is, who placed a timeline on you? Most times, it's actually you. There is no need to place undue pressure on yourself, because all this does is takes away the joy that comes from working toward your goal and replaces it with stress. This isn't just for those who are trying to finish their book, but whatever your aspiration is, you need not cripple the process by implementing self-imposed deadlines that must be met, or else.

Timelines are important. They help measure progress and indicate areas that need adjusting in order to stay on course. At the same time, though, there is no rule that says timelines can't change. It's okay to give yourself some extra space to operate in. It's okay to take time along the journey to pause from working and just enjoy the process. It's okay to change one's approach if it is determined that such a change can actually result in greater success. Always remember that it is better to arrive late than not to arrive at all. Many people burn out during the work and never get to celebrate the accomplishment of a completed task, all because they feel pressured to produce through panic, rather than persuaded to produce through patience. So, I am here to tell you that it's okay to breathe. It's okay to laugh, to pause, to reevaluate, once you remain committed to seeing that thing through to the end. There are no deadlines to your success. As long as you are alive, you are perfecting the journey, the approach and the work that it takes to get to your mountaintop.

There is a difference between benchmarks and timelines. Benchmarks are guides. Timelines are restrictions. When your boss tells you to get the report in to them before the close of work day, a series of events begin to unfold. That overdrive button in your head is pressed hard and fast and the pressure is suddenly on, because now, there is a deadline that you have to avoid. You're more likely to make uncalculated mistakes in times like these. While there are those who will tell you they actually operate better under strenuous circumstances, the majority don't share that luxury. It is always better to pace yourself to the finish line, rather than try to do it all at once, when it comes to success. Whereas the media will try to get you to believe that you can arrive at your destination overnight, reality follows a much more logical process. Put in the work and bit by bit, you will see the fruit of your labor.

So, the key is to give yourself space to fail, before you succeed. It is said that Thomas Edison made one thousand failed attempts at inventing the light bulb before finding success. He could have given up right there and then, but he persisted, determined to make his vision a reality. He didn't beat himself over the head each time the switch failed to elicit the desired glow from the glass sphere. In fact, instead of seeing it as a thousand failed attempts, he said, "The light bulb was an invention with 1,000 steps."

Perhaps your journey will also incur a thousand steps before you reach your destination. It can be a long, frustrating process, but despite what it may look like, every day that you keep moving is a step closer to the finish. Don't be a slave to the clock. Don't think that because the date you set for completion comes and goes, it means that you can no longer get it done. You can. And you will, if you continue to stay true to what motivated you to start in the first place. Your enemy is not time. Your enemy is fear. Fear that you cannot do what you have set out to do. But you can. And you will, if you continue to press forward and refuse to give up.

ii. Beat the Urge to Procrastinate

The biggest and most silent threat to one's success is procrastination. It is most times subtle, unassuming and can take the guise of simply taking a break. For many, that break never ends and the vision is left to flicker and die. The line between giving oneself enough room to breathe so they can enjoy the journey and spending too much time putting off the task at hand is an almost invisible one. It takes serious dedication and commitment to cross over safely and ensure the race is won.

There are a lot of reasons behind why people fall prey to procrastination. Some embarked upon tasks that were never theirs to begin with. When they realized they had no resources, skills or passion for it along the way, they simply jumped ship and moved on to something else, leaving the original task incomplete. Some people have all the skills and resources necessary to get the job done, but they allow the wrong people to speak into their ear, convincing them that they are not accomplishing what they should really be doing. Others are bombarded with idea upon idea and the mistake that they make is to try to start them all, instead of concentrating on completing one goal at a time. The result is that they fluctuate between so many varying projects that none get the attention they need and again, they all become dormant and some even die.

How, then, does one avoid the urge to sleep on their success? One way to ensure that stagnancy doesn't overtake you is to find an accountability partner. This is simply, as the name suggests, someone who will keep you accountable when it comes to what you should be doing. So, you're writing a book. There are days that you may wake up and just not feel like writing. Or, you may get up all ready to make a dent in your masterpiece, but as you sit before the computer, the thoughts refuse to flow and you find yourself stuck in the corner of the room with writer's block. Here comes your accountability partner to the rescue. They are someone who have caught hold of your vision and are as passionate about your success as you are. They aren't going to try to sabotage or side-track your success. They genuinely want to see you succeed and will do whatever they can to get you to that place.

Your accountability partner will call or visit or WhatsApp or tweet and offer support and motivation at the moments when you feel like throwing in the towel. They will continuously remind you of the reason you're doing what you do in the first place. They will push you past your sticking point and encourage you through your dark days. They will offer constructive criticism and let you know when you're straying off course and you can trust that whatever they say or do is with your best interest at heart and in mind. Get yourself a good accountability partner and your productivity will definitely increase.

Another way to ward off the urge to keep putting things off for far too long is to work your project from the end up. Sounds crazy? In actuality, it is one of the most productive ways to get things done and to finish them in a timely manner. And this approach can actually be taken with almost any venture you can think of. The trick is that while you may not be able to do this physically, you can when it comes to preparing your plan outlining all the steps necessary to get it done from start to finish. Imagine your goal is to lose weight. You have tried several things in the past, but they all proved unsuccessful for whatever reason. The fact is, the weight is still there and you want to get it off. Your plan would include, of course, how much weight you want to lose and the time by which you want to actually see your progress. So, perhaps you want to lose twelve pounds. You could put a six-month plan in place, which would see you shedding two pounds each month. Next, you would put your diet plan together. What foods would you have to cut out? What foods would you have to replace them with? How often will you eat throughout the day? What time will be your first meal, last meal and those in between? Finally, you want to document your exercise plan. What days will you be working out? How many days a week and which days will they be? How long will you spend per session and what exercises will you be doing?

So, this is the actual plan that you are going to follow in order to achieve your weight loss goal. Through this plan, you are actually able to see the end result because of the progressive steps all outlined between where you are now and where you intend to be by the next six months. You can make the workload appear much more manageable by seeing yourself at the end of the entire journey and work your way back from that image. That means seeing yourself in the mirror not just at your present position, but also your purposed place. You can begin to look for the clothes you want to wear when you've dropped those twelve pounds. You can even explore various activities you'd like to pursue that you were unable to before losing the weight.

Keep in mind, up to this point, you have not shed a single pound.

When you know what the end is going to look like and you know exactly how you are going to arrive there, it becomes easier to work toward it. Waiting at the start line without a plan, without any direction as to how you are going to arrive at your final destination, can be overwhelming enough to deter you from the venture all together. But just as was said earlier about not biting off more than you can chew at any given time, it is possible to complete the entire task and do it within a reasonable timeframe as well. Most of all, starting with the end result in mind and working backward allows you to mentally complete the task before you actually do physically. This approach towards your work allows you the luxury of operating from a place of expectancy rather than complacency and decreases the likelihood of suffering burnout or becoming so overwhelmed that the journey no longer seems worth it.

Procrastinating is a real enemy of progress, but it does not have to be your portion. Pacing yourself is important, but know the difference between that and becoming complacent. Learn how to mentally stand at the finish line and celebrate even the smallest achievements along the way. Surround yourself with cheerleaders, not dream stealers. Research on the area of your interest and learn how others have successfully navigated the waters before you, because you are not alone. You don't have to fall prey to procrastination. You have success encoded in your DNA. You were born to succeed. You were resourced to succeed. You were empowered to succeed. So, leave the excuses behind and do what you were created to do. Achieve success.

iii. Know Your Limits

I always had a passion for motorcycles. There has always been something about the look, the sound and the feel of bikes that would cause me to run to the window from the time I heard one of them revving its way toward our house. I just loved watching the machines as they zoomed past, admiring their sleek lines and aerodynamic features. To this day, wherever I am, once I hear an engine approaching, I am making a beeline for the door so I can watch it race past me.

One day, when I was about twelve years old, a friend of my father came by our house riding a trail bike. I was not a fan of trail bikes, but it was the closest thing to a street bike I had seen ride into our yard in my life. My father knew that I loved bikes and he called me outside to see it close up. I was really excited and wanted to prove that I was a true bike fan and a worthy candidate to eventually have my own someday. I walked up to the bike and excitedly started getting on to the seat when my father touched my shoulder. "You can't handle that, son. It's bigger than you." I was somewhat embarrassed by his words, as the owner was standing right beside us, waiting to see what I did with the bike. I never took my eyes off the prize, I never hesitated, but instead, I sat securely on the seat and stretched out and grabbed the handle bars. "I can ride it", I told my father confidently, although I had never ridden a bike in my entire life. I didn't even know at the time that switching it on was more than just turning the key. But, I would learn an important lesson that day before ever even hearing the 650cc beast rumble.

As I positioned myself as best I could with only the tips of my toes touching the ground, I rocked the bike forward a couple times until I managed to get it off its stand. As the weight of the bike was no longer supported by the stand, I was suddenly left trying to balance the three hundred plus pound Yamaha to the best of my ability, with my feet barely touching the ground. My father saw my struggle and did not intervene. He was going to allow me to learn the hard way that morning. Fear gripped me as in a matter of seconds, the bike threw me down with it as it tilted to the side and crashed to the ground, pinning my leg under it. I could not move and could not even budge the bike. I just waited until Uncle Errol finally reached down, grabbed the bike by the handle and the seat and lifted it back on to its two wheels, freeing me. That day, I learned that as much as I loved motorcycles, I was not ready to ride one.

Sometimes, we have the goal before us, but we never measured the distance to determine what it would actually take to get to it. We see other people with what they have, admire their lifestyle and decide we want the same thing, too. The reality is, someone else' success may not be your own. Uncle Errol rode that dirt bike like it was a tricycle. He whipped it around with ease and made everything he did look so simple. I never knew that riding entailed compensating for weight, learning how to handle the throttle and how to change gears, breaking with one hand while accelerating with the other. All I knew was that I loved how bikes looked and sounded and I wanted my own. Unfortunately, that is how many people live. They like what they see and hear and they want it for themself, but they never consider what it takes to handle it. The expression, "biting off more than you can chew" comes to mind. And while I am a firm believer that anything is possible, I also believe that success does not just happen. The very people and things that we admire did not just arrive where they are. It took work. Hard work. Some had to work harder than others, but they all had to extend some level of effort in order to accomplish what they did. It is no different with you and me. If we want to be successful, we have to work toward that success. Not just work, but work smart.

Just as I learned that there were some things I could not do at certain points in my life, we must accept the fact that we all have limitations. Those limitations, however, don't mean we cannot achieve successes. There are some things that we may not be able to get done immediately, or on our own. There are some things that although they aren't impossible to achieve, they will take extra effort and may require us tapping into resources outside of ourselves. It is important for us to know what our limitations are and the faster we acknowledge these limitations, the faster we can find ways to work around them and push beyond them.

Many people see their limits as deterrents to their success. I can't read. I am not good with money. I have a physical or mental disability that puts me at a disadvantage in many areas when compared to others. Whatever it is, we allow it to defeat us and cancel our assignment. We leave the pursuit of success to everyone else, while we dress back into the concealment of the shadows so that no one has to see us fail. Who said that limitation equals failure? If anything, discovering our limits should propel us to work even harder at discovering ways to maneuver them, because we should be determined that nothing is going to come between us and our success.

Knowing your limitations is not the same as surrendering to them. It isn't enough to just find out what your limits are. In many instances, those limits can be overcome. The person who cannot read can learn to read. The person who is weak with money can take a financial management class. There are limitations that we can overcome, if we apply ourselves to what it takes to get over them. Truth be told, in my opinion there is no limitation that can prevent you from fulfilling whatever it is that you truly desire to. It may mean employing more time, energy and resources, but if you are willing to do whatever it takes, then eventually, you can accomplish your mission.

Know your limitations, so you can begin making the necessary adjustments that would prevent the unnecessary discouragements, sticking points and setbacks. Will I be able to handle this venture on my own, or will I have to seek out some dependable help? Can I do this out of pocket, or am I going to have to secure a loan to get it done? Don't allow the pitfalls and obstacles that you can avoid to spring up and cripple your assignment. Be honest with yourself. Listen to those who you trust that may caution you to consider the areas in your life that you may be struggling in. Those areas don't have to spell the end of your journey. Rather, if properly approached, they can be catalysts for improvements, and motivators that propel you past your potholes. Don't just ignore your limitations. Deal with them, and get them out of the way. You can, you must and you will.

iv. Share the Load

If you're anything like me, you probably had a hard time learning to say, "No", or letting others know when you need help. I was afraid for a long time that it would be misconstrued and perceived as a sign of weakness. I thought that people's confidence in me would begin to dwindle if I said, "I don't think I can take on any extra responsibilities at this moment." It took me a long time to realize that this was far from the truth and that people respect you even more when you are able to admit that you need help.

A lot of people have failed to finish what they started because along the way, they literally burned out. Their inability to properly manage their journey led to depression, burnout and in some instances, even mental break down. Taking on too much at once is not only a sign of poor managerial skills, but can also lead to the onset of conditions that can severely debilitate one's physical and mental health. Many people remain in jobs where they know they are being taken advantage of, carrying the bulk of the workload and never even being compensated for their labor. Overworking oneself is not going to speed up the rate of success. In fact, quite adversely, it can retard or terminate success instead.

Successful people do not operate alone. They create systems that help to increase the likelihood of maximizing output. These systems are assessed and reassessed periodically in efforts to identify what works and what doesn't. No successful person sits at the top alone and simply folds their arms and hopes they remain there. They understand that success is not a place one arrives at, but rather, success is a lifelong process strewn with achievements along the way, but requiring constant commitment and dire determination. Success requires work and the greater the size of the success, the greater the measure of the workload. And many times, we are going to need to reach out to other sources outside of ourselves to get the job done and to get it done well.

There are many reasons so many people choose to try to do it all on their own. Some are fearful that if they ask for help, others will get the credit.

Others are skeptical about bringing persons along because they may discover their weaknesses. There are those who prefer to work alone because they simply do not have the capacity to embrace and get along with others. Whatever the reason, it is best to work on those challenges rather than jeopardize the opportunity to create something great that can benefit not just them, but the ones they employ also. Sharing the amount of work needed to accomplish any given task gets the work done in a faster time, allows more than one pair of eyes to evaluate the process and lessens the anxiety level that is especially associated with projects that have deadlines attached to them. All in all, sharing the work wherever and whenever applicable can significantly raise the possibility of succeeding at a given task.

I may not be the best artist in the room. Perhaps I know who is. Am I going to allow either pride or shame to keep me from approaching that person and sharing with them my idea for an illustrated children's book and asking them to be my artist? The difference between me approaching them and staying in my own corner may be signing a book deal with an established publisher. You have to know what you want and what you need to get it. You also need to be willing to accept your limitations and reach out to the people that can bridge those gaps for you, if you cannot do them for yourself. Your success depends on your ability to do that.

Your willingness and ability to share the workload is tied to what your idea of success is. Maybe, your idea of success is selling a few bottles of your product each week. Someone else's idea of success with the same venture may be selling the same number of bottles you sell in a week in one day. In order for them to meet that goal, they may have to get some extra hands to help with the mixing, the bottling, the labeling, or the distributing of whatever the product is. Again, the bigger the project, the more work it will require and the more resources you will need to employ to get the job done. Always remember that success is not the absence of failure. Failure in and of itself is a sign of success, because it means that you made an attempt in the first place and it also eliminates one way of doing things that you now know does not work. So, the question you need to ask yourself is, what is the size of my success? How big is the goal that I'm aspiring toward? Is this journey one that I can realistically take on my own, or do I need to ask others to join me along the way? Be honest with yourself and be prepared to make the necessary lifestyle changes you need to make in order to facilitate your growth. Success is never stagnant. It is always changing. It always requires more of us than we are sometimes willing to give. If we really want to be successful, though, we will make whatever changes we have to in order to succeed.

Successful businesses regularly conduct what is commonly known as a S.W.O.T. Analysis. It is a breakdown of various measurables that can be individually examined in an attempt to help grow the business in a healthy, realistic and competitive way. S.W.O.T. stands for Strengths, Weaknesses, Opportunities and Threats. The S.W.O.T. Analysis is a tool used to gather as much information within these key areas as possible. Let's use Billy's Barbershop as our example. They will reach their first six-month milestone on Christmas Eve. They are a small business with just two barber stations and a few machines and equipment. They bring in about ten customers a day and operate from Mondays to Saturdays, from 9:00 a.m. to 7:00 p.m. Haircuts cost eight dollars for adults, five dollars for children, as opposed to the ten dollars for adults and eight dollars for children charged by the barbershop a few buildings away. What would their S.W.O.T. Analysis look like? Well, it may go a little like this:

Strengths

Although they are only operating with two barbers, Billy and his accomplice, Bob, are the best barbers in the area. Customers are always satisfied that they get what they ask for and in addition, Billy and Bob are really good with their customers, referring to each of them by name and taking time to treat each of them as if they are their favorite customer. This gives Billy's Barber Shop a constant flow of regular clients every week. So, what are Billy's Barbershop's strengths? Great cutting skills, excellent customer service and competitive prices.

Weaknesses

Billy's Barbershop is only operating with two barber stations, whereas the competition down the street has four. That means that the competition is able to facilitate more customers, especially during rush hour periods. Despite their regular client status, many persons opt out of even giving Billy and Bob a chance due to the long line that always exists at their shop.

What is Billy's Barbershop's weakness? A lack of manpower for the workload required to sustain a healthy turnover of customers.

Opportunities

One of the opportunities that Billy's Barbershop can easily capitalize on is the fact that they are celebrating a significant milestone during a major holiday period. Their six-month anniversary occurs on Christmas Eve and one of the things they can do is put up flyers throughout the area announcing their big achievement. They can choose, for Christmas Eve, to go even lower on that day and take a dollar off every cut. Or, they can give two lucky customers a free haircut for that day. The opportunity is the season in which they will be celebrating their landmark and the various ways they can capitalize on customers who would be ensuring they look sharp for the holidays.

Threats

If you hope to have a successful, long lasting business, you better pay attention to whatever threatens your existence. For Billy's Barbershop, their biggest threat is the barbershop that stands just a few blocks away from them. More customers frequent that establishment not because the barbers are any better, but because it is more time efficient for them to head to the barbershop that can tend to them in a quicker time due to more manpower and other resources. When someone runs away from work to simply line their beard or mark out their hairline, they don't want to spend their entire lunch hour waiting for a seat to become available. So, as good as Billy and Bob are at what they do, their greatest threat is that their competition has more hands on deck and has a faster turnover time when it comes to serving the customers.

Most S.W.O.T. Analysis go into much more detail and include a lot more information under each subject area, but this gives you a basic idea as to what to look for when covering the evaluation. I placed the S.W.O.T. Analysis here because Billy has a real decision to make. Is he going to share the workload, or remain satisfied with the ten customers a day, as opposed to the competition who sees in excess of forty customers a day? If Billy really wants to start thinking about success, he is going to have to swallow his fears about dishing out more money for a larger space, more stations and additional salaries and he is going to have to share the workload in order to expand his business and increase his revenue. He has to capitalize on his strengths, overcome his weaknesses, take advantage of every opportunity and eliminate the threats. That is what success calls for and one major way to accomplish this is to ensure that rather than closing up shop and accepting defeat, we spread our wings and take on persons with like minds and passions who are as passionate about our dream as we are. They will join the journey, accept the approach and be willing to work. You don't have to stifle your dream because of fear. Thinking big means thinking greater than any one man show. Start sharing the workload and increase your potential for success.

v. Break it Down, Before it Breaks You Down

Some things look relatively easy at face value and we never take the time to compute the effort needed to actually carry the load. At times, we take on some gargantuan tasks without stepping back and considering what we would need to do to not only complete it but to maintain it also.

I love food and I love watching any show that deals with food. One show I was particularly fond of was 'Man v. Food', where the host would visit various restaurants and food outlets throughout America. The highlight of each episode was when the host would be presented with some challenge, where he would be given a certain time by which to consume either a mammoth of a meal or something not particularly considered a delicacy by the average person.

On one such episode, Adam Richman was presented with what to this day is considered one of the worst food challenges in the history of the show. While filming at a restaurant in Hawaii known for its 'Killer Pancakes', Richman took up the challenge to be in the one percentile that was successful at completing a meal consisting of three pounds of pancake and a pound of topping in one sitting. Richman took his seat before the huge plate of carbs, cut the stack into four quarters and began the challenge.

At first, the host seemed poised, confident and in control. He breezed through the first quarter of the challenge almost effortlessly and started his attack on the next. But slowly, he began to show signs of discomfort. He began to sweat, his bites became smaller and he started taking longer rests between each forkful. Sadly, Richman was unable to complete the challenge. With the final quarter of the stack untouched and almost half the topping still standing, Richman conceded and had to settle for the Hawaiian lei draped around the necks of losers, rather than the first prize which included his name being added to the Wall of Fame.

Later on, Adam Richman would make an interesting comment about that challenge. He said that he overestimated himself and underestimated the number of carbs on the plate that was placed in front of him. He also said that he should have paced himself more and taken smaller bites than he did. Believe it or not, that is actually sound advice for everyone as we endeavor to bite into our success.

It's easy to think that we can start the business, build the house, take the trip, get the degree, or whatever the goal is, all in one go. We don't think about the challenges that we will face as we try to consume it all at once. We don't consider the financial constraints, the emotional tolls, or the physical demands attached to the work it takes to accomplish whatever it is we are striving toward. When the bloating begins and the pain kicks in, we curse what's on the table and we walk away dejected because we thought it would be easier than it really was.

One way to raise the chances of coming out on top of the challenge is to break up the work into parts, rather than approaching it as a whole. Allow yourself to achieve mini successes along the way that would motivate and encourage you to take on the next part of the whole while allowing you to go into that next phase of the work feeling confident and sure, rather than deflated and uncertain. If you are writing a book, for example, don't just jump in front of the computer and begin writing whatever comes to mind on the selected topic. Cut your task down into parts, like a tangerine. You don't just bite into it, because you would only make a mess. You peel apart the various segments, which makes it so much easier to consume.

So, before you even begin writing, you have to break your work down into its various parts. What are you passionate and knowledgeable about? What do you have to share with a particular niche that would benefit from your work? Who are you writing to? Is your book going to be a biographical or expository piece? Fiction or non-fiction? What additional research are you going to have to do? How many chapters, words, and pages, will your book be? Is it going to include any illustrations, graphs or photos? All these questions should be asked and settled as they could spell the difference between a bust and a bestseller.

It may be a book or a business, a degree or a diet. Whatever lies ahead of you, it is up to you to get it done. The idea is easy. Making that idea come to life is what matters. That's where the real effort comes in and that is when the obstacles will begin to present themselves. You aren't going to get it done all at once. As the saying goes, "Rome was not built in a day." But if you can commit to laying one brick at a time, eventually you will see the walls begin to form and your kingdom will begin to take shape.

Start with your plan. Break your task down into sections. Decide what area you will start with and don't deviate from it until that part is complete. Chew it up one bite at a time and give it time to digest. Allow yourself enough room to rest and take deep, fresh breaths. Stand back now and then and examine where you are. Is everything the way it should be? Docs anything need changing? Remember, you can't start putting on the roof if the wall is uneven. Take it all step by step. There is no rush, and success has no expiration date. Learn to enjoy the work it takes to succeed. If you can do this, then you will always be able to conquer the challenges and make it to your destination.

FOUR
Become an Expert at What You Do

There may be nothing more frustrating than listening to someone who has the most to say on a subject matter that they know the least about. Some are able to fake it because they possess the gift of gab. They are eloquent speakers who have mastered the art of saying nothing in a way that sounds like something. The danger with those types of people is that they are usually so persuasive and manipulative that they are able to amass large groups of followers along the way. "I have no idea if what they're saying is true, but boy, does it sound good." When the truth comes out, though, what was once a devout group of followers can quickly turn into an angry mob and a lifetime of success can quickly turn around into a moment of failure. Success takes work. And a huge part of that work is becoming as informed as possible about the area you intend to pursue. If you plan to become successful at something, learn as much as you can about that thing.

In today's world, there is absolutely no excuse for failing because of lack of knowledge. From the moment you decide to pursue something, be it academia, employment, entrepreneurship or whatever else it may be, your next course of action should be to begin your research. You can either jump into something haphazardly and hope you make it, or you can have the mindset that you are going to become the best at what you do. That is the mindset of successful people. It is not necessarily because they had the best resources, or the greatest advantages, but because they took the time to find out what it takes to be successful.

They learned as much as they could about the area they hoped to excel in and they continued learning, because life is never stagnant, but rather, it is fluid, ever changing and evolving. To become successful is one thing. To remain successful means being able to change with the times and knowing when the time has changed.

The Jheri curl (jerry curl) was popular among men and women in the 1980's and even the early 90's, but a man would most likely receive several confused and amazed stares if he were to rock that hairstyle today. Knowing what is relevant and what is no longer timely is an important element in the pursuit of success. Don't waste your time running after something that no longer matters. Is what you are envisioning relevant to today's lifestyle? Have you examined the demographic of your proposed area of influence and determined whether or not what you are proposing is something they will be willing to buy into? Maybe your vision is not for your current environment, but it will call for you moving to a whole new place and space. Or, perhaps you will be a catalyst for migration. If you are going to succeed, you need to ask the right questions and do the research necessary to make sure you are the expert at what you do.

I always believe that one's passion is directly tied to one's purpose. In other words, what you are most motivated about may very well be an indicator of your calling. Some children go through the traditional school system and suffer because they are unable to grasp the concepts necessary for mastering such subjects as Mathematics, Chemistry and Physics. Yet, these same children are able to easily use their hands and minds, take something apart without having ever seen it done before and put it all back together again, nothing left behind. The same child that is labeled slow, retarded, dyslexic, or having some cognitive disability is able to fix the broken radio, bypass the cellular phone's password and download any app on the tablet. We are all wired differently and not being proficient in one area does not exclude us from being totally efficient in another.

My son, now twelve years of age, was a Beyblade fanatic at age nine. One day, I observed him as he sat watching the Beyblade animated series on Netflix. I was shocked as he was able to give the names of each of the tops, and announce their 'stamina' as well, Stamina refers to the level of charge/energy each Beyblade uses to out-spin their rival in battle. I asked my son, "How do you know all these Beyblades and their energy levels?" His response was simple. "I watch them on YouTube."

Here is my point. If my then nine-year-old son could research what he was passionate about to the point of knowing them all by name, why can't we all put in the work required to find out all we can regarding whatever we are passionate about? At one point in my life, I was sure I wanted to start a screen printing and graphic arts company. I was always a good artist, so I didn't really consider all the other aspects that starting such a major venture would entail. I knew nothing about burning screens, nothing about the chemicals involved in preparing them, nothing about exposing the chemicals to a light box, nothing about how important it is to remove the paints from the silk at the end of each use as fast as possible. I just knew that I was a good artist and I was going to make a lot of money designing and printing banners, signs, clothing and any and everything else that could be printed.

I remember when I went to the art store in the mall and purchased silk, paint, blades, paper, everything I thought I would need for the job. I raced home, knocked up some wooden frames, stretched the silk over them and stapled away. I had my screen, I had my paint, I had my paper for my stencils, and I was ready to go. I ran upstairs, grabbed a brand new white tee shirt from my dresser and raced downstairs. I recall the stencil I drew and cut out from the Bristol board. It was the Nike logo, with the words, Just Do It neatly written underneath. I decided I would mix multiple colors and use my old, uneven rubber squeegee that was used to clean windows to pull the paint across the surface of the stencil which I had placed against the shirt. I didn't think of a bed to place the shirt on, so there was nothing separating the front of the shirt from the back. I had no machine holding the screen in place either. It was all freestyle. Confidently, I dragged the multiple colors of paint splashed on to the screen with the old, uneven squeegee. Excitedly, I lifted the screen off the shirt and identified my first problem. The stencil was still on the shirt, stuck on to the paint. I had to remove it without paint dropping, dripping, or dragging across the shirt, or messing up areas of the shirt that won't supposed to be painted. I used what little fingernails I had to pry the stencil up, but to my frustration, paint had seeped under the stencil and my

Nike swoosh looked more like a swish at this point.

Paint blotted along the edges of the stenciled artwork, breaking the clean, crisp edge work I had done with my stencil. This was not a shirt I was going to wear. Furthermore, because I hadn't placed anything between the shirt, the paint soaked straight through from front to back. I was so disappointed, as I looked at what turned out to be a horrible representation of the vision I had for my business. No one would want me to do any work for them if this was the type of work I would be producing. I bundled the shirt into a ball and flung it into the garbage. I focused my attention on the screen, which needed to be cleaned. I took it over to the hose and turned on the water. I grabbed some soap and a scrub brush and began scrubbing away, but the paint was not going anywhere. It had already hardened and all the holes on the brand new silk screen were clogged up. I grabbed some nearby turpentine and threw it on the screen. That made matters worse, added to the fact that the scrub brush began to tear away at the screen. What was going on? Why was this turning out to be so difficult? I was angry and frustrated, and could not let my family know that after spending all that money, I had nothing to show for it. Not even my mother's squeegee, which I had to throw away as the paint had coagulated on the hard strip of rubber. I was angry and frustrated. And disappointed.

A few weeks later, I decided to visit a professional screen printing company. At the time of my visit, they were placing Rossi logos on warm-up suits for the Trinidad and Tobago national soccer team, who were preparing for World Cup qualifiers.

That day, I learned a lot of things. For example, I learned that there are certain paints used on certain materials of clothing. I leaned that a machine is important for holding the screen in place which not only prevents things from moving around unnecessarily, but also frees up both hands to maneuver the squeegee evenly. I learned that there is a special squeegee for screen printing that distributes weight in such a way that there is a smooth application of the paint. I learned that a light box is important for burning the artwork on to the silk, so nothing passes between the stencil and the material on which the artwork is being applied. I learned that there are chemicals needed to help burn the screen, and these chemicals decide which areas of the screen light gets to pass through. What I learned most of all that day was that I knew absolutely nothing about screen printing, and if I was going to embark upon this journey and succeed, I would have to spend time with people who knew the trade. I would have to understudy. I would have to sap up as much as I could, and learn not just how to do it, but how to do it well.

So, I stayed with that company for a few weeks and was allowed to make mistakes, to mess up some uniforms, to spoil some screens, to waste some paint, until I learned. By the time I left, I was more confident and knowledgeable than I was before. I returned to the art store and purchased some new silk, chemicals, various paints and a host of other materials, including fluorescent bulbs and material to build my first light box. Within a week, persons in my neighborhood were bringing pictures or sketches of various things they wanted done on tee shirts or jackets or hoodies and I was printing one off originals for extremely satisfied customers. Although I never started the graphic arts company and my time spent on my screen printing dream was short lived, it was a learning experience for me that shaped the rest of my personal and professional life. I learned an important lesson through that experience. You have to prepare for success. You have to make space for it. You have to be willing to learn, to fail, to try again, and to adjust your sails to pick up more wind each time. You can be successful, no matter how shaky your start might be.

One of the most influential motivational speakers I have ever listened to is a young man named Nick Vujicic. Born in Australia but living in America, Nick was born without arms or legs, due to a condition called tetra-amelia syndrome, a rare condition characterized by the absence of the limbs. Despite the many obvious challenges he faces every day, Nick continues to face life with an amazing level of positivity which he shares with millions around the world each time he speaks, whether at seminars, or via his online media outlets. He could have allowed his physical disabilities to relegate him to a less productive life, but he was determined to make a difference. To be a difference. Most of us are blessed to have hands and feet that work, yet, we refuse to put them to their best use. Because while the arms and legs may work well, we don't work our minds the way we can and should. And so, we settle for far less than we are capable of and we become comfortable in complacency. Then we scorn the Nicks of the world who push past their personal plights and go on to become legacy makers.

Permit me to encourage you, whoever you are, to exercise the greatest, strongest muscle you have – your mind. Begin to think outside of the norm, and start focusing on what you are passionate about. How can you develop that passion and use it to grow yourself and others? How can you begin to earn off of doing what you love? If you have not begun to ask these questions, then you are not ready for success. The possibility largely exists that before reading this book, you were good enough in your comfort zone, living paycheck to paycheck, ruffling no feathers and just blending away into the background where no one had any expectations of you and you had none of yourself. Well, I am glad that you picked up this book, because it is time to become your biggest supporter.

For the next seven days, you are going to brainstorm and become intentional about pursuing your success. Start by writing down the things you are most passionate about. Things that you consider a pleasure, rather than work. You may recognize that some of the things you identify are connected to each other. For example, you may write down music, singing, playing an instrument, as some of your passions. Or, eating out, cooking, watching Food Network. Pay attention and look out for unifying themes in some of your answers. If you find any, group them together and place them in a circle named, 'Music', or, 'Food', or, 'Art', for example.

After you've made your list and placed similar passions into groups, rank them according to two separate markers. On one side, make a list ranking your answers from what you are least passionate about to what you are most passionate about. On the other side, rank your answers starting with the passions you already possess skills for, to those you love but have no experience in. An example of possessing skills related to your passion may be that you love music and the arts and you can sing or play an instrument. The adverse and lower down on your list may be that you have a passion for banking, but you are horrible at Math and Accounting.

Next, identify your top three strongest and weakest passions based on your skillsets. Place the three strongest to one side and the three weakest to the other. Under the strongest areas of interest, write down all the skills you possess that you believe can help you excel in these three particular areas. Then, under the weakest areas of interest, write down the skillsets you believe you need to develop in order to turn those areas into three additional strengths in your life.

Finally, develop a plan of action around the areas you are passionate about and hold some level of skill in. Your plan should incorporate all your skills in this particular subject, as these are strengths you both naturally possess, as well as acquired along the way, that are geared toward feeding your destiny. I believe that even in the subconscious mind, we are continuously collecting tools along life's journey that will eventually become fuel for our purpose. When your plan is complete, just as you did in the areas of your weakest passions, write down the areas that need developing under your strongest ones if you are going to become the best at whatever it is you desire to do. Let me just help you cross that highway called,

Narcissism very quickly, because some people can get stuck right there. We all have weaknesses. Don't fool yourself into thinking that there are no areas in your life that need improving. You can be the best singer in your group, choir, band, or community. There is still more you can do to become even better. The moment you believe that you have achieved all you can, is the moment you get overtaken by the person behind you who wants the same thing a little more than you do, because while you sleep, they work. You should always be learning and bettering your craft, no matter what it may be.

It is essential that you acquire a wealth of information on whatever it is you want to excel in. I had the privilege of sitting in an audience where Author and CEO Dr. Cindy Trimm was presenting on the topic of wealth and success. There was one thing in particular that she stated from the podium that resonated with me and shifted my whole thought process. She said, "People must pay you for what's on your mind." For as long as I could remember, everything I did in life, I did out of the goodness of my heart. I felt embarrassed whenever someone offered to pay me for any service I performed. Even if I wanted to accept the money, I never knew what I should charge them, so I always said, "That's okay." I never realized that I was pimping my talents, permitting everyone to use me for my time and resources. Had I sat in Dr. Trimm's seminar years earlier, I would have been much richer today. Not only richer financially, but mentally and emotionally also, because I would have been treasuring my own worth and appreciating that the work I do and the services I provide for others has value to it. Value that can be compared to what anyone else does and that should never be compromised or taken for granted. While it is okay to give of your time and talents freely, it is equally important to recognize that whatever gifts and talents you possess are tied to your purpose and your purpose has a cost to it. Don't feel bad about charging for what you do. Feel bad about selling yourself short because you refuse to accept that you are good enough to be paid for your work. The more you know, the more valuable your work becomes.

So, keep learning. Keep finding out more about your craft and discover additional ways of bringing it to the people around you. Starting the business is not enough. You have to find out how you can service new audiences, meet new needs and fill new gaps. When Covid-19 suddenly appeared, hundreds of thousands of people lost their jobs globally. Yet, in that trying environment, hundreds of thousands more saw opportunities and pushed through the darkness and found light at the end of the tunnel. The pandemic saw the birth of entrepreneurs who had to be laid off from their regular nine-to-five in order to unearth the champion that was buried beneath the rubble of doubt, fear and skepticism. The greatest way to motivate, encourage and empower yourself is to learn.

I work at a prison where I run various behavioral modification programmes within the Rehabilitation Department. Apart from helping inmates address their index crime, the Rehabilitation Department also offers academic programmes for persons desirous of acquiring their secondary or tertiary level education. One of the most rewarding things is seeing an inmate who came in illiterate learn to read and write. It is like the world suddenly opened up for them. The persons who left the prison were not the same persons who came in. They now had plans for their future, as opposed to having each day planned for them. I had one such inmate come to me to help them create a short-term and long-term plan for their life, which included starting a landscaping company. They left the prison with a business plan, logo, and twelve thousand dollars from the Small Business Development Bureau, who partnered with the prison to offer financial assistance to inmates who showed initiative and drive and who presented a proper business plan that was not necessarily perfect, but showed that they were serious about getting started. What set that inmate apart from all the others who simply wanted the cash was that he did the research. He spent hours in the prison library each day, learning all he could about landscaping. He utilized the internet to check on the various tools and equipment he would need and he sourced all the equipment, putting a real budget together that was attached to his final proposal. This was an inmate who wanted to succeed. And he came out and did exactly what he planned so hard for.

Do you truly want to be successful? Then get to work. Even if you are already living your dream and pursuing your passion, there is always room for improvement. Keep learning. Keep refreshing yourself on what you already know and find out all you can about what you don't know. There will always be obstacles in your path and sometimes, those obstacles can seem insurmountable. But there is always a way to overcome. You may have to embark upon an entirely new journey. You may have to change your approach. You may have to increase the workload, all in an effort to stay relevant and meaningful in fluctuating times. But if you are willing to keep learning, then there is literally no limit to what you can achieve and how high you can go.

FIVE
Chart Your Own Course for Success

Social media has become the expert at defining what success looks like. Instagram, Facebook, YouTube, Snapchat, Twitter and the like have all crafted their perfect image for success that so many gravitate and aspire toward. Today, success is defined by material things. Big houses, expensive cars, platinum jewelry, brand-named clothes, yachts, private jets and, of course, an entourage. Nothing could be further from the truth.

I could remember the first time I saw Sir Richard Branson in the flesh, business mogul, investor, author and former philanthropist and founder of the Virgin Group, which currently parents over four hundred companies worldwide. Like many people, I had heard of Sir Branson, but I had never met him, nor did I ever expect to. One day, however, while at the airport on Beef Island, Tortola, someone whispered, "It's Richard Branson." Of course, I started looking around to see if I could catch a glimpse of the millionaire in the flesh. My eyes gravitated from one corner of the lounge to the other, but I saw no one that fit the description of the Virgin Atlantic, Virgin Mobile Executive. Not wanting to miss out on this opportunity, I turned to the one who identified him and asked, "Where is he?" The man turned to me and then shifted his direction, standing right beside me and pointing to the tarmac just beyond the glass window that separated the waiting area from the outside. What I saw was not what I had envisioned. A gentleman with golden hair was walking intentionally away from a jet that I had watched land just moments before. He wore a plain white tee shirt, plain blue jeans and a pair of brown flip flops. That was it. Unassuming, not drawing any attention to himself, but on a mission. He had a broad smile across his face and shook hands with the ground crew as he passed them by. As he passed the glass window where almost everyone had gathered to watch him walk into the V.I.P. lounge, they waved as he got closer to them and he waved back, never relinquishing his smile.

It was strange for me, seeing a man of Sir Richard Branson's caliber carrying himself so...normally. Had it not been for the whispers and the alerts and the groups gravitating toward the window, I would have never seen the man who walked off the jet and even if I had, I would have never assumed that it was Sir Branson. Why? Because I had been wired up until that time to believe that successful people all had a particular aura and appearance to them. I believed that success must be recognized from the moment you see it. Success must be loud, expensive and most of all, success must fit the mold that media has shaped for it. Many people think the same way I did up to the point when I saw Sir Branson take his walk down the tarmac. That is why the majority of the world is brainwashed into believing they can never achieve success, because they equate success with financial and material gain. While these may be byproducts of living a successful life, they are not in and of themselves the definition of success. Here's an interesting, thought provoking question. What is your definition of success?

Always remember that success stories differ from person to person. What may be a major accomplishment for me may be an everyday norm for you. What takes you a great amount of effort to fulfill may require nothing of me but to do it. We are all different, endowed with varying strengths and weaknesses. In addition, we are all wired to accomplish different things. Our journeys differ. Our approaches differ. Our work ethics differ. At the end of the day, though, we all want to know we have gotten the job done. Everyone wants to eat, sleep and dream well. No one enjoys the feeling of lack or inadequacy, whether that feeling exists in the context of our individuality, or in the sphere of the home and family. We were all built to be successful. Unfortunately, some struggle through life never grabbing hold of that fact and so success eludes them, although they house unlimited potential to create and to conquer.

One of the biggest hindrances to success is envy. Without even counting the cost of the sacrifices someone made to get to where they are, we decide within ourselves that we want to be just like them. I see countless young, black men who are gifted and strong and full of potential enter the judicial system because of this mentality. Instead of building their own success, they decided to try to rob someone else's instead. There are no shortcuts to success. You can't cut your journey short and still expect to arrive at the chartered destination. You can't manipulate your approach to suit you and expect that the outcome will still be what you were hoping for. You can't refuse to put in the work, yet expect that you reap a reward at the end of the day. Success is possible, but there is a process and that process has to be honored.

If you are going to ever truly celebrate a life of success after success, it is paramount that you discard every false ideology of success you have adopted along the way. How do you know which ones to keep and which ones to throw away? Well, one of the simplest ways to differentiate between the two is to figure out which of your philosophies of success call for self-actualization as opposed to self-impersonation. Success does not call on you to be like someone else. Rather, true success forces you to plot your own path and to become the best version of yourself. You were never created to be a clone of someone else. You are a trailblazer. A trend setter. You are here to find solutions to problems that you alone possess the answers for. But you need to stop focusing so intently on the things that exist outside of yourself and begin to identify the giant that dwells dormant within you.

What is it that you desire to be successful at? Remember, success is not punctiliar. It is linear. It is constant, and always happening. It is infinite, because it has no end. Even after we are dead and gone, many of our achievements will continue to bear fruit and create opportunities for success for others. Success is an energy that has the potential to generate wealth, opportunities, and multiple streams of income. It can positively impact a community, a nation and the world. Your success is bigger than you, because it serves as a motivator for those who follow in your footsteps, because they now see that ordinary people, just like them, can aspire toward something and attain it. In other words, you aren't just succeeding for yourself, but for those who are waiting to see if that idea you chose to pursue can actually work.

Instead of looking at others and trying to emulate them, focus on creating your own path to success. It may not look like the neighbor's, or that family member who always comes up every time there is a get-together, or the celebrities that you read about on TMZ, but it will be your path, that no one can take away from you. It starts with having a goal, one that should be centered on your areas of passion and strength. Don't be afraid to ask for advice, or even help financially or otherwise, as you attempt to get your vision off and running. Anticipate obstacles and even criticism along the way, but determine that none of them will stop you. Rather, learn how you can capitalize on them and use them for your growth. You may not be able to make it to the finish line in a quick, record-breaking sprint like Usain Bolt, but you may be able to get there over a longer distance, like Lelisa Desisa, if you are committed to enduring through whatever comes with the journey.

It's okay to pause, or stop along the way. If your eyes are fixed on your own lane, if your mind is focused on running your own race rather than being consumed with what is happening in the lanes around you, then it won't matter when the house on the corner goes up another level before you even get to lay a single brick. Be content with the fact that you were able to secure the land. When it is your time to start building, it will happen. It won't matter when the neighbor buys a second vehicle when you are still trying to save toward purchasing a second-hand jalopy to get you around. Be satisfied that you are on the verge of getting your own, because of sacrifice and discipline. It won't matter when your fellow classmate graduates from college a year before you do, because they had the finances to attend full time, while you had to work your way through. Rest in the fact that come next year, you will be turning your tassel and watching your options rise thanks to your hard earned certificate. Don't let it bother you when they get married first, start a family first, travel first, get promoted first, or make it to whatever first they happened to aspire toward. Cheer them on and know that your time will come, because the only one who can deny you success is you.

Just think about it for a moment. Many of the luxuries you enjoy today were made possible through the often discomforting, unnerving sacrifices of somebody else who at times had to endure ridicule, jesting and even isolation before they finally succeeded. They could have given up, but they pressed through the pressure and today, we herald them as pioneers in their own right. Colonel Sanders started selling his experimental chicken recipe at age forty in a service station where he worked, after years of turmoil that included the loss of his father at an early age, dropping out of school, enlisting and serving in the army, divorce and eventually, battling thoughts of suicide. It was at age sixty that he sold his first restaurant for around two million dollars and began to reap the rewards of his hard labor. Steve Jobs was a college dropout who loved working with electronics. After a disillusioning trip to India where his hope to seek enlightenment ended in even more cloudiness and confusion, he joined with a friend of like passion and they developed and began selling personal computers. Despite its success, there were several ups and downs in Jobs' road to success, including separating himself form the Apple Company which he cofounded, in an attempt to remain true to his vision for the personal computer. After some disappointing sales with some of his solo creations, Jobs eventually rejoined Apple and after receiving renewed interest in his computer ideas from investors. Today, we know Steve Jobs as the name behind the iPhone, iPod, iPad, Mac computers and so much more. There are countless other stories of men and women who believed in their dreams so much that despite being knocked down on more than one occasion, they stayed in the ring and fought their way to remarkable victories. They saw their dream through to its fulfillment and that, my friend, is what success truly looks like. It is refusing to give up, because what you are going after matters to you that much, even if it doesn't matter at the moment to anyone else. Because you know deep within that in the end, the very naysayers in your circle will turn around and become your biggest cheerleaders.

Perhaps you have children of your own and you want to ensure you leave something behind that they can hold on to when you are no longer there. Or, maybe you have siblings or other relatives who, for a long time, have been struggling with their own breakthrough. Your desire to succeed should encompass more than just you and your desires. Whatever you accomplish will break ground and create new trails that others will be able to pass through, making it possible for someone else's success too. Barack Obama showed the world that people of color can succeed when he became the first African-American President of the United States. Tom Wittaker showed the world that disabled persons can succeed when he became the first paraplegic to climb Mount Everest. Amelia Earhart showed the world that women are as capable as men when she became the first ever female pilot. What are you going to show the world?

Deep inside you, there is a journey that you want to embark upon. There may be things that you don't possess at the moment that may make the journey, the approach and the work much easier. What you do have, however, is the will to begin and honestly, that is the greatest resource that one can possess. There are persons who have all the emotional, financial, academic and material support that we often think are necessary to ensure success, yet, they still fail to make their mark. Why? Because none of these things can guarantee success. What was missing for each of them was the will to succeed. No one can will you to success. You have to want it for yourself and at some point in time, you have to begin to work toward it. Not work toward someone else's success, but toward your own.

I speak to parents many times when dealing with juveniles through the Restorative Justice program, and I often encourage them to allow their children to choose for themselves. A lot of parents try to fulfill their dreams through their children and while it is okay to want your child to have the privileges you may not have experienced as a child, it is another thing to try to live the life you never got to live through them. Don't force your child into a guilt-ridden corner and tell them what they should be in life. Yes, you ought to guide and encourage your child to develop his or her full potential, but it is wrong to decide the career or lifestyle path for your child, simply because that is what you want for them, or what you wanted for yourself. They may not want to continue the family business. They may not want to attend college. They may not want to become what you want them to become and that is okay. Find out what they are passionate about and try to nurture their dream rather than feed yours and understand that their success does not necessarily have to look the way you envision it. If they don't continue the family tradition, it does not mean that you failed, or they failed. It may just mean that it is time for a new tradition to be birthed. Accept that the change is happening before your eyes and be grateful that your child has the vision to venture out into a new place.

The British Virgin Islands, where I have lived and labored for the past two decades and more, is a tourist destination. So much so, that tourism is one of the territory's two strongest economic pillars (financial services being the first). As tourists enter these shores, like many other countries, one of the things they look for is a souvenir that they can take back with them to show the world that they were here. I can recall an elderly couple searching through one of the stores I happened to be in, just in the heart of Road Town, Tortola. They kept picking up items and turning them up, down, around, side to side and eventually, placing them all back on their shelves. After a few minutes of this routine, the store clerk approached the couple and asked if she could help with anything. The gentleman looked at her and said, "We're just checking the labels.

We're looking for something that was made in the B.V.I." Immediately, I started to follow suit, picking up items from the shelves and checking the labels. Although many of the glasses, mugs, dolls, paintings and even books had the name 'British Virgin Islands' painted or printed somewhere on them, the labels all indicated that they were in fact made somewhere else. Tourists didn't just want something that read, B.V.I. They were searching for something different. Something original. Something that was completely indigenous to the place they took the time to visit, so they felt they were taking a piece of that place back with them whenever they returned home.

You are an original. When people see you and hear you, they should not see a copy of everyone else that is around them. They ought to be introduced to something completely different that meets a specific need in their life. That is why you are here, and that is why you possess the skills and talents you possess. Not so you can live a life purely of self-aggrandizement, but so you can meaningfully pour into the lives of the people around you, wherever you may be called to serve. Your success is not just for you, but in order to be the blessing that you can be, you must step out of your comfort zone and venture on to your own path. Don't allow present fears or past failures to keep you from future fulfillments. Chart your own path to success. Even when it gets difficult, keep your feet faced forward. What lies ahead of you far surpasses what is behind. You are not working tirelessly, sacrificing earnestly, and enduring faithfully, just for the sake of achieving some temporary satisfaction in your lifetime. Your success envelops far more than a few fleeting, materialistic accumulations. Your success is a thread in the fabric of your legacy, which you are sewing together with every single stride you make. None of your achievements have come by chance. They have all been strategic, purchased with hard work and determination. Speak to yourself every time you are tempted to jump ship. Encourage yourself whenever you begin to question the worth of your work. Learn to be your biggest motivator, because no one knows your goals, your dreams, and your aspirations better than you do.

Has anyone ever approached you and said you would do well in a certain position, or encouraged you to pursue a particular path? There are times when what people say resonates with us, and rather than being a revelation, it comes more as a confirmation or an affirmation of what we already felt or knew about ourselves. In such instances, you basically have two options. You can bury those affirmations along with your own personal convictions of what you should be doing with your life, or you can take it as fuel for the fire that already burns within you regarding the work you have always felt inclined to do. As you prepare to launch out into the deep (or even get your feet wet at the shoreline), learn to surround yourself with people who believe in your potential. The unfortunate reality is that most times, the greater part of your support system isn't very supportive at all, especially when you start speaking about self-development and growth. The saying, "misery loves company" is true. Human beings have a natural tendency to gravitate toward others who are at the same place in their life as they are. When anyone within that circle starts to excel, or experiences certain levels of success, there is an automatic fear that their success will result in their departure from that circle. Some people will actually discourage friends or family members from pursuing a degree, or applying for a job, because it might result in that person leaving their physical space. You owe it to yourself and the future of your success to embrace the dream builders, success pushers and destiny motivators and to let go of anyone whose plan is to paralyze your progress. You have no reason not to succeed, once you water the seeds planted within you and guard against the weeds and thorns that threaten what is inside you, waiting to be exposed.

Today marks a new chapter in your life. Whatever failures you may have encountered before are simply learning curves for your next move. It's time to be intentional and strategic about planning your success. No matter what you have seen, heard, or been told, you aren't going to magically walk through a door labeled, 'Success' and arrive there. You have to work toward it. Take the time from now onward to plot your own individualized course that will take you to wherever it is you want to go. You have already seen where you want to go. Begin the process of moving toward getting there. Yes, there will be challenges, but as the one holding the map, find a way over, under, around or through whatever form those challenges take and keep going. You are the author of your success, so write it.

SIX
Celebrate the Small Successes,
as Much as the Big Ones

The majority of society has become programmed to recognize mammoth moments in life, while the small movements are filed in the 'insignificant' bin and hardly ever remembered. We cheer for the philanthropic efforts of the celebrities who build schools for underprivileged children, buy homes for the homeless and invest millions into development projects, but we quickly scroll past the daily stories of personal accomplishments achieved by ordinary men and women, because they aren't big enough. The young man who became the first black entrepreneur to emerge from his entire family, the sixty-two year old lady who received her high school diploma despite, the lone firefighter that broke into the locked vehicle and rescued the baby in the rear seat, they all go unnoticed, uncelebrated, even unmentioned, because we are wired to look past what are considered to be the little things. Only when we secure a victory in our own lives that others fail to celebrate with us do we feel the pangs that accompany the blow of ingratitude and we understand that no matter how small, every successful step matters.

Like any journey that we embark upon in this life, it does not matter the distance between us and the destination, the mode of transportation used to get there, or even who is traveling with us. What matters is that to get there, we must take an initial step. Then another step. And another. And we must keep taking steps until finally, we arrive at the target. But, as we say, the journey of a thousand miles starts with a single step. A lot of times, that first step is the hardest. Starting a business with little or no capital seems crazy. Traveling for a necessary opportunity during Covid seems senseless. Planning to pursue a degree when your grandchildren are already in college feels weird. The question you need to ask yourself is, "How much does the end result matter to you?" If it is something that truly moves and motivates you, something that will transform your life positively as well as the lives of those around you, then that first step matters and you need to shrug off whatever inhibitions may be tying you to a state of stagnancy and move.

Getting started is a victory. Right now, you ought to pause for a moment and acknowledge every move you have already made in your life that took you from one place into another. Understand that it took courage to make that move, to get past comfort zones and negative words and most of all, to overcome fear and step out into the unknown. You may have completed that chapter of your journey, or you may still be on the road heading toward it. But recognize all that you have done thus far and celebrate your successes. Not just the major ones, but the ones that aren't that big, but they were your successes. Celebrate them. If no one ever said it to you before, I want to say, "Congratulations. I am proud of you." And let that sit with you for a moment and resonate with your soul. You are a success. And your best is yet to come.

Here is a short, simple but meaningful exercise I'd like you to participate in. Take a piece of paper and write down everything you have ever started to do in your life, for as far back as you can remember. It doesn't have to follow any particular order, but try to capture every venture you at least started to pursue at some point. Next, from your list, write down on a separate sheet of paper all the projects you embarked upon that you have either accomplished, or are still pursuing. Finally, on one more sheet of paper, write down a list of all the starts you had that eventually dwindled and died.

Take that last list you created and carefully examine it for a moment. What prompted you at one point or another to take on those tasks? Were those things you were passionate about, or did someone else push you into areas you weren't really interested in? If they were your desires, what stopped you from fulfilling them? What made you lose that drive and cause you to totally abandon what you started? Was it a lack of finances or other resources? Was it a lack or absence of support systems? Was some discouraging word spoken over your life that caused you to put down those dreams and quit? Or, did you simply lose interest? Whatever the reason, you can start to work on those dreams again. A lot of times, we believe that becoming successful requires accessing some proven formula or blueprint that for some reason is out of our reach, but nothing can be further from the truth. Anyone can be successful, but we must understand that success is not one-size-fits-all, nor is success measured in terms of big or small. Someone's 'small' success may actually be far more significant than someone else's 'big' one, simply because of the levels of adversity the one may have had to overcome when compared to the other.

If you have left a passion to wither and die, there is hope. You can breathe fresh life into any project you once started and you can still see it through to completion. You can still be successful at fulfilling that task and meeting your goal. Here are three simple, realistic steps you can take to rekindle your drive and get back on track on your road to success.

1. Invest in Yourself

A lot of times, we find ourselves doing so much for others, going the extra mile to help them bring their own dreams to fruition, while failing to place the same amount of effort into fulfilling our own. Somehow, we become comfortable in the role of 'supporting cast', while our own plans suffer and even die. There is absolutely nothing wrong with helping others, but the hard, cold truth is that if you find yourself helping others at the expense of your own self-development, it's time to step back and start investing in you.

If you aren't developing your own personal growth, you are going to eventually find yourself in a position where not only are you unable to help yourself anymore, but the same people that depend on you are now going to have to look elsewhere, because your streams have dried up. You cannot give to others what you do not have to give yourself. What we all need to realize is that self-care is the best care and that is okay. Many relationships die long before they reach separation or divorce because one partner ends up carrying so much emotional baggage after giving their all to someone who gave nothing back. Yet, they continued to give, simply because they wanted the relationship to work. One day, though, they reached the place where they had given all that was possible to give and now, they were completely empty, unable to even help themselves. Perhaps that sounds familiar to someone reading this right now. Maybe you've either been there, or are currently going through it.

I want to let you know that there is absolutely nothing wrong with wanting the best for yourself. You deserve to be successful at everything you do. You deserve to accomplish your goals and to fulfill every one of your dreams and you can. Learn to make this a priority in your life and let your success be independent of anyone else. Yes, you will most likely need to reach out to others to help you in some areas of your journey, approach and work, but your success should not be dependent on their ability or inability to help you. Don't allow anyone to hold your success hostage. Determine that come what may, you are going to find a way to achieve everything that pertains to you and keep moving toward those things no matter what. As I have reiterated several times throughout this Chapter, the only person that can stop your success is you. It may be delayed, but as long as you remain fixed and focused, it cannot be denied.

When last did you take a self-help course, or attend a workshop that spoke to an area of interest in your life? When last did you read a book addressing something you are passionate about, or watched a YouTube video to help sharpen one of your skills? Too many people sit around, doing nothing to improve themselves, yet expecting more, when the fact is that you get more when you put in more. We are jealous of others who move up before we do and don't realize that their elevation was a direct result of their dedication. They kept searching for new ways to be relevant and effective and they did not remain at the same level they were when they took on the job. They exercised their intellectual capacity, learned more about their role and responsibility and grew. Don't envy people who move up in life. Keep focused on your race and learn to run smarter. Not faster, or longer, but wiser. Constantly ask yourself questions like, "How can I become more productive in my area of influence?" "What can I do to make my work more meaningful?" "How can I be more productive today than I was yesterday and how can I ensure from today that I can be even more productive tomorrow?"

Investing in oneself takes time and effort. It takes work. Work that many people are not willing to put in, even though it spells a better future for them in the end. It just seems like too much of a hassle, especially for those who have already settled into their comfort zone and are satisfied living every day the same as yesterday. But for some, there is the inert conviction that living this way is not enough. There is something internal that continues to desire more. For those, failure is not an option. If you are one of those who are dissatisfied with the stagnant places in your life, begin to reinvest in you. It does not have to be anything that costs you a dime, at least to start off with. It may be as simple as surrounding yourself with people who are already accomplished in your areas of interest and allowing them to share with you what steps they took to get to where they are now. You can pattern your own plan of approach from them and begin your journey with small, simple steps, working your way forward to bigger strides until you are mastering your own mode of achievement. But you have to find a way to start pouring the right materials into your mind and increasing your capacity for growth.

Yes, investing in your self takes work, but again, there is no need to take on too much at a time and become overwhelmed by what ought to liberate instead. Focus on one task at a time. Develop one skillset and when you see growth in the form of productivity in that area, begin to develop another. Whatever you do, however, never stop working on any of these areas, because there is always room for growth and improvement. Every Prison Officer has to undergo Control and Restraint training, where they learn safe, non-lethal techniques that can be used to manage inmates when in vulnerable and hostile situations. Although the Officers go through the training in their rookie year, it would be remiss of any Officer to complete the training and believe that it would suffice for the rest of their time serving in the area of corrections. Techniques are constantly changing and new methods are being introduced almost annually that cater to changing times, which bring with it changing circumstances. Prisons are dealing with more ingenious inmates, as well as more violent ones and it has become increasingly important that Officers stay up-to-date with the most recent training available. That means continuous training in the area of Control and Restraint.

It doesn't matter what field of interest you may be in. You need to remain abreast of what the latest techniques are, so you don't get left behind. You can't think that because you have attained a certain level of knowledge in a particular area that it is enough. You have to keep putting in the work and make sure that you are actually still operating with a relevant manual in hand. What may have been useful yesterday may very well be useless today. You aren't going to go to war with a musket in your hand, when your adversary is armed with an MDRx. The latter fires off more rounds, targets a further distance and does more damage upon impact. You want to be well-equipped to give yourself the best opportunity to win. Go into every situation armed with the most recent knowledge there is about it. Be as informed as you can as you prepare to launch once more. Your probability of success raises significantly the more resourced you become. So take the necessary time to invest in your area of interest and to invest in you. Read, inquire, research, practice, observe. Do whatever it takes to ensure that the next time you pursue that passion, you see it through to completion.

2.   Find the Time

Time truly waits on no man. The older I get, the more I am convinced that time is the most precious gift that we have. You can get back everything in this life except time. Once time is gone, there is nothing you can do to retrieve it, no matter how hard you try. We've all seen the science fiction movies that play with the concept of time travel, watching heroes and villains alike going through some time portal, black hole or time machine, in an attempt to revisit some period in time where they could make good on a missed opportunity. Unfortunately, that only happens in the movies. There is no way to go back into the past and magically or scientifically undo or redo something that we wished we had done differently when we had the chance.

If you are hoping to become successful at anything in life, you are going to have to find the time to work at it. We find the time for so many trivial things that have nothing to do with our growth or development. It is easy to carve out slots in our schedules for things that excite us and make us feel good. When it comes to the things that involve us exerting time and energy into places that we aren't too fond of, we suddenly find it difficult to spare a second. Always remember that the places we invest in today are the places that will sustain us tomorrow. Ask yourself, "Am I investing in a sustainable place?" Too often, we hang around streams that cannot restore us in the long run. We blow our savings and other resources on temporary fixes that do not have the ability to permanently provide for our most relevant needs. Who and what you spend your time on matters. Successful people are as careful with their time as they are with their money. Most times, we only equate success with financial investments and returns, but effective time management is a necessity if we are going to be successful at what we set out to do.

Two people can set out on the same mission. They enter an orchard and both have been given the same hour to harvest as many oranges as they can.

Both are tooled with a picker and a set of boxes in which to place the oranges after taking them from their source. They both settle themselves in a nice, shaded area of the orchard and the clock starts ticking. One of the men quickly gets into a systematic routine which he believes will help secure as many oranges as possible within the allotted time. Clip, pick, turn, box. Clip, pick, turn, box. Like a song, he keeps the four commands in his head and repeats them as he moves to the tune in his head. Clip, pick, turn, box. Within the first half hour, he has already filled two of the four boxes and is on track to fill all four by the time the clock stops.

The second man had no strategy. As far as he was concerned, an hour was a lot of time and four boxes were not a lot. He was sure he would get the job done in no time. In fact, he was so confident that rather than getting himself into a steady rhythm like the first man, he clipped, picked and ate the first ten oranges before finally boxing the first one. He boxed a few more and then decided to take a seat in the shade, as he was now a bit tired after consuming so many of the sweet oranges. Thirty minutes in to the given time and the second man only had half a box full of oranges to show for his work.

Finally, the hour expired on both men. The owner of the orchard came to inspect the boxes and to pay the workers for the time they spent picking the oranges. When he got to the first man, he was impressed to see that he had actually filled all four boxes, but had also managed to pick a few more oranges and pile them neatly beside the last box. Not only was the man paid for the four boxes, but he received a dollar for each of the extra oranges he managed to harvest.

When the owner of the orchard walked over to the second man, he was shocked to find that only one and a half boxes had been filled. In addition, he found dozens of orange peels strewn across the grass that was always cared for and kept clean. The second man was only paid for the one box he had managed to fill. Irate, he turned to the owner and asked, "What about this other box that I managed to fill halfway?" The old man turned to the second worker and said, "I would have paid you, but I had to deduct the cost of all the oranges you stole along the way."

We all have the same twenty-four hours to work with each day, but we all utilize that time in different ways. Some capitalize on every second that they have, while others squander it and take it for granted. Wasted time robs you of the rewards you could reap at the end of that day. You have to discipline yourself to find time to invest in the things that matter. Dreaming of starting a business is one thing. Finding the right location for the business, outfitting it for the purpose intended, stocking it with the relevant goods, hiring the appropriate staff that have your vision at heart, that's where dream becomes reality and that takes time to materialize. You have to find the time to work on the plan that bears you fruits of success. Success thrives on a routine. Have a time set aside for working toward your craft. Whatever it is, create the space to allow that thing to be developed and to work for you in return. You can look back at the end of the day with regrets that you didn't accomplish what you set out to do, or you can look back with the satisfaction that you were successful at fulfilling your plans. Yes, there are times when things do not go the way you intended, but put another plan in place. Don't just roll over and accept defeat. Keep managing your time and experimenting with what works.

Perhaps your creative juices flow best first thing in the morning. Then set the alarm and maximize that moment. If it's late in the evening or at nights when everyone is asleep and you have the entire day to reflect upon, then try to get the children to bed earlier and carve out that time necessary for you to work on your plans. Learn how not to overbook your day. This means turning down some additional responsibilities that you may be asked to take on. You have to be selfish about guarding your time. No one is going to give it back to you and you don't want to look back on your life with regrets because you never took the time to enroll in the course, or buy the extra equipment, or take the trip to meet with the investors. Nothing is worse than those "What if" moments that flood our minds ever so often. Tell yourself that you will never again lament on a missed opportunity because of mismanaged time.

Today, we all have smartphones, tablets, email accounts, electronic calendars and other gadgets and applications that we can utilize to help manage our time better. Get into the habit of setting reminders and notifications that assist you along the road to becoming more productive and time conscious. Developing the discipline for time management can be a task at first, particularly for the regular procrastinator like I was, but with consistency, it can become one of the greatest liberators as you see your plans coming together and the load become lighter and lighter. When there is no longer the usual hassle to get things done at the last minute, or the realization that you overlooked an important piece of the puzzle because there was no structure to your approach, what was once a burden can suddenly become a joy as you learn to pursue your purpose with a passion. So, don't just want success. Make time for it.

3. Failure is Not an Option

Failure is a subject that no one likes talking about. For some, it is an emotional topic that evokes feelings of sadness, disappointment and even embarrassment. It is difficult knowing that you went into something feeling totally prepared, gave it your best, yet you didn't manage to produce the desired result. Such experiences have kept many from ever trying again. Here, though, is the question. Who determined that you failed?

A lot of what we have been taught, needs to be untaught and we need to be retaught. The world has its grading schemes and measuring sticks that it uses to decipher who has been successful and who has not. Hardly do we examine the complete set of factors surrounding each person being evaluated, because we presuppose that everyone entering the race is coming in at the same level, when this is not the case. Truth be told, we are all coming from different backgrounds, facing varying challenges that affect us cognitively, financially, emotionally and even physically. Yet, we are expected to perform, to excel and to win. For many, this is not as easy as it sounds and in some instances, it is even unfair to expect such. But the pressure is on the individual to overcome the challenges and to succeed, according to society's definition of success.

I personally have my own definition of failure, which I stated earlier. Failure, to me, is not so much the inability to succeed, or to meet a particular mark, as it is the unwillingness to try. You fail when you decide, "I can't do it", or, "I won't do it" and you allow that proclamation to cut you off from taking your step into the unknown. That, in my estimation, is the true definition of failure. And in that regard, failure is not an option.

You have to be willing to take the test, knowing that you may not pass. But not passing does not mean that you failed. Not taking the test in the first place is the greatest failure of all, because you have no way of knowing what grade you'll get if you don't. You have to be willing to get married, amidst the countless stories of divorce swirling around you. You have to be willing to start the business despite the news of several businesses being forced to shut down to economic instability. Whatever the challenge, face it head on, even in the presence of fear. You cannot and will not know what you can achieve if you do not step out.

Yes, you put a lot of stuff down over the years and you never looked back. But what if one of those things has the potential to positively change your life, as well as the life of others? What if that manuscript you were writing turns out to be a bestseller? What if pursuing the degree opens new doors for you to share your ideas on an even greater platform? What if learning that trade allows you to open your own business? You have wealth just waiting for you to release it, but you need to be willing to step out and bring that dormant dream to life. It doesn't matter why you buried it the first time. All that matters is that you find the courage to try again.

There is no reason why you should watch the rest of the world succeed at what they do while you struggle. You have as much potential and hold as many possibilities as they do, and the only difference between those who succeed and those who don't is that one actually gets up, and tries. So, you attempted something and it did not go as planned. Instead of calling it quits, why not try another approach? In other words, never stop working toward it. That is the true definition of success. It is the ability to continue to keep going, despite the odds. So, not making it the first time, or the second time, or the third, or fourth times is not failure. Failure is for those who allowed the challenges they encountered while working toward their goals to sidetrack them and deter them from what they set out to accomplish. Don't be jealous of those who stand on the podium to receive their medals for completing the race. Don't even scorn those who are ahead of you, although you all may have started out at the same time. Celebrate them. Cheer them on. Be happy for the ones who even got on to the starting line and took off. Many never started. You may not have even started. But today, I encourage you to. The only way you fail is if you refuse to try.

Don't disregard or discredit what may be huge to you, simply because it doesn't seem so huge to someone else. The people judging you and measuring your success seldom take into account what it took out of you to get to where you are. You need to learn to appreciate and celebrate the small steps with as much enthusiasm and pride as you do the big ones. There is nothing insignificant about getting up and pressing back against the pressures of life because you want to achieve something great for yourself. You deserve to succeed, but it means you have to get up and get moving.

I challenge you to reconfigure your thought process as it relates to success. It's not about the fancy cars and the big houses, or the seven digit bank accounts. There are successful people who do volunteer work and don't make a dime. Their success is measured by the sacrifices they make every day to improve the quality of life for others. Success is not confined to my own individual growth and achievements. The greatest successes are those where others have been positively affected by what we do. Society has taught us to seek things that make us happy and satisfy our desires and we equate this pursuit of happiness with success. If I am not happy, if I am not financially rich, if I have not amassed a particular amount of material wealth, then I have not lived a successful life. It is time to throw society's definition of success away and to begin focusing on the things that really matter in life. Those are the things that utilize our gifts and talents in ways that build up society, rather than just individual people. Success is measured by how many seeds we plant, rather than how many trees we grow.

I have used my position as a pastor, a counselor, an author, a Restorative Justice Officer to try to help as many people as I can along life's journey. There are many that I have proudly watched start a job, or mend a broken relationship with family, or come out of prison and become a strong pillar in their community. But there are also those who I have tried to help along the way who either never took the counsel that I gave, or who regressed after a period of seemingly doing well on their own. I cannot look at the latter and beat myself over the head, telling myself that I failed, because the path they took was not the one I hoped they would have. I have to find solace in the fact that I was there in their time of need to offer support, to encourage and to assist in a time they may otherwise have gone through alone. I planted seeds. I invested time, money and more into trying to get them to climb higher. Sometimes, that may be the end of our responsibility. The rest is up to them to take what we have offered and use it for their self-development. They have to want to succeed as much as you want them to, or even more. If you have helped someone along the way, whether emotionally, financially, academically, physically, or in whatever form it may have taken, then you have successfully poured yourself into the life of another. That is success. That is something worth celebrating, because although it may be insignificant to others, it matters to the person whose life you have affected.

The philanthropist may be able to raise and donate millions of dollars to the private school that is on the verge of closing its doors because of inadequate resources and funding. You may not be in a position to make such an impact on the entire school, but perhaps you can feed one child for a day, or a week, or help purchase the books they need for a term. Maybe you can tutor a child or two and help that family save on hiring someone else to do it. That is success. Celebrate whatever it is you can do, not only for yourself, but for others also. Don't take it for granted. Recognizing what success really looks like matters, because when you do, you will see that you are actually being successful in so many ways every day and you will be motivated to continue stepping out and pursuing a purpose, despite the challenges you may face while doing so.

SEVEN
Be Your Greatest Motivator

One of the most demotivating experiences we can have in life is doing our best and being told it was not good enough. We stayed up all night and studied for that test, went into the exam room and did our best, yet when the grade came, it wasn't enough to pass. We lived at the track all summer, training as hard as we could and even improving on our Personal Best time, but on the day of the big race, it seemed no one would be able to see and appreciate any of that, as by the end of the race, we came in dead last. We worked exceptionally hard all year, putting in extra hours and creating new systems at work that helped the rest of the staff with working smarter and better. We went in to the meeting to discuss that promotion with confidence that our employer would see the merit in our request, but instead, we were told that the position was already promised to someone else, someone who we know doesn't even work half as hard as we do. It is difficult when our success seems to lie in the hands of someone else. Many times, it can cause us to wonder, "Will I ever be successful?"

Motivation plays a huge role when it comes to working toward success. Studies have shown that employees are more dedicated and committed to their jobs when their employers or supervisors show appreciation and utilize motivational tools within the work place. Even through my years working at the prison, I have seen that inmates who feel motivated by those in authority are more likely to participate in behavioral modification and work programs.

Motivation is a tool that can build morale, boost esteem and foster unity in any circle. The adverse, however, is equally true. Persons who feel demotivated and discouraged most times simply do the bare minimum, or decrease their output, as there is no longer any drive that pushes them to go the extra mile. We all need motivating every now and again and when it comes, we feel a renewed will not only to work, but to even motivate those with whom we work, because motivation is contagious.

We are all motivated by different things. A large, universal motivator, for example, is money. People will be motivated and encouraged to work harder if they know that there is a financial reward for them at the end of the day. Some, however, are not motivated by money, but if they are promised a higher position, they will go the extra mile, because their motivation is power. There are those whose motivation is knowing that they are helping others, while there are still others who may be motivated by simply hearing words of appreciation from those above them. Whatever the incentive may be, motivation matters, as it can significantly increase the probability of success. All good employers motivate their staff and ensure they let their employees know that the work they do is valued and valuable. In fact, when you see a constant turnover of staff in any workplace, start by checking the motivation level of those walking out on the job. Even in the midst of difficulty, persons are more likely to stick it out if there is someone there motivating them to stay.

Motivational speakers around the world understand the importance of being motivated. They are called upon annually to speak to students, employees, couples, individuals, inmates, professionals and just about anyone in any sphere of life in an attempt to get those persons to operate at their optimal best. The right word spoken at the right time is so critical, that sometimes, it is the difference between life and death. I've spoken to groups where at the end of the discussion, I was approached by one or two who confided in me that before hearing what I had to say, they were about to walk out on their job, their academic program or even their marriage. Some people may be entertaining suicidal thoughts and the next words they hear will be words that literally either make or break them.

Many of us stopped dreaming about success because we were demotivated along the way. The closer that someone is to us, the greater the injury they can cause and the deeper the wounds we sustain. One of the most difficult forms of demotivation is when it comes from the people who are closest to us and who we expect to be in our corner, prodding us on. It is painful when those are the ones who discourage us and who speak over our vision and stifle the passion we had when we shared our dream with them. It can be difficult rebounding form the disappointment of lack of enthusiasm, encouragement and support from those we confided in, but it does not have to culminate in cutting our course. We can still finish the journey. What we need, though, is to learn how to motivate ourselves.

Not everyone is going to catch your vision. That is why the vision was given to you. *It is yours.* Truth be told, no one is entitled to see that thing the way you do. No one has to pick it up and run with it but you. Sure, that does not erase the fact that we would love to know there are persons affirming our decisions, letting us know that we are on the right path or assuring us that we will make it. That is not always going to be the case. There are times when we will be laughed at, ridiculed, scorned and even despised because of what we choose to do in life, but even in times like those, it is important to engage that next gear and overtake the feelings of hurt and disappointment we feel, rather than allow them to consume us. Motivation matters and you need to learn to motivate yourself, because sometimes, no one else will.

In his book, 'The Power of the Law of Repetition' by Dr. J. B. Jones, Dr. Jones speaks about the power of repetition and the effect it has on the conscious as well as the subconscious mind. Dr. Jones writes:

"Well, each time we control our attention and express our word along a certain line, repeating over and over and over again and again and again a certain concept or a certain idea, we are making a track in the subconscious. We are building, what we call in practical psychology, a conditioned consciousness. We are building a habitual feeling, or a condition, from which we express a habitual feeling in the subconscious.

And it has been proved that when we go through this process, through repeating and repeating and repeating over and over again, a concept, that it will become established in the subconscious, as a condition from which we will react with feeling habitually, and then that is known as a part of us and as Solomon said, 'As a man thinketh so is he.'"

According to Dr. Jones, repeating certain words over our lives helps to fashion not only how we think, but eventually, how we act. Words have power. They can build up, or they can tear down. They can encourage, or they can discourage. Motivate, or deflate. What words people speak over our lives is one thing. More importantly are the words we speak over ourselves. What words are you speaking over yourself? What words are you saying over your goals and dreams? What words are you speaking over your success? Your words matter. They hold weight. They can either limit you and your ability to fulfill your potential, or they can maximize your thinking and cause you to explore your fullest capacity. Tell yourself, "I have to watch my words."

Self-motivation may be a totally new concept for many. We are all wired differently and our personality types play a major role in determining our attitudes, our outlook on life and how we handle situations. Personality traits also play a huge role in relation to our work ethic and our approaches toward success. Some persons reading this book – and particularly this Chapter – may be opposed to the idea of having to work hard in order to achieve, because they may believe that life owes them happiness, achievements and success after success and they should not have to work hard or sacrifice to get it. Others may appreciate the fact that nothing good comes easily and they may be adjusting their sails as they read, preparing to catch more wind so they can go further and get to their desired destination. Whichever category you may fall into, I encourage you to learn to pair self-motivation with your success.

Life is not always going to go according to plan. No one plans for the natural disaster, the illness, the sudden death in the family, the divorce, the termination from work, none of these experiences are ones that we readily welcome and look forward to. Some of us have already experienced one or more of these crises and know the emotional turmoil they have the potential to bring. For some of us, there were no support systems present for us to lean upon and we had to circumnavigate those unchartered waters on our own. It was difficult. It was painful. There may have been times we literally just wished we could die. But somehow, we go through it. Somehow, we got back up and we started to step back into periods of normalcy, until we were able to rebound and get to where we are today. Does that mean the experience has left us completely? That we still don't carry the scars that they left behind? No! We remember them all and they have the ability to even draw us back into places of depression, anger, fear, sadness and doubt. What kept those of us who went through those times alone from giving up? It was the faith we had that the storm would pass. It was the motivation that this faith gave and the words we held on to that assured us, things would get better if we kept on pressing.

We will not always be surrounded by people who see, understand or believe in the direction in which we want to go, but self-conviction precedes success. You must own your journey, your approach and your work ethic and make it the vehicle that drives you. Self-motivation is the power source for that vehicle. You may have the fastest car, the toughest truck, the sleekest boat to take you where you want to go. If your battery is dead, all you have is a good looking ride that can't even get you started. Having a conviction is important and necessary for your success, but conviction in and of itself won't move you. You may be persuaded that you should get your degree so you can increase your chances for a promotion. That certainty, however, is going to be accompanied by a bunch of negative thoughts that try to counter your conviction. There has to be something that pushes you to push past the obstacles and clear the path so you can see your target clearly. You have to be motivated enough to the point where you at least believe you can make the first step, although there may be no clarity on what the next steps may look like.

Motivation is like the lungs you use to breathe every day. Everybody knows that the moment you stop breathing is the day you die. Could you imagine that someone else other than you had control of your lungs? What if they could determine how much air you consumed with each breath, if any at all? That person could decide, for whatever reason, to shut your lungs down and just leave you there to suffocate to death. No none would want someone else in charge of something as important as the breath they breathe, because that person would have authority over their life.

Just like your lungs, you are endowed with potential. You house the capacity to inhale creative opportunities and exhale greatness. Your lungs are yours. Your potential is yours. It is essential that you guard your potential and don't allow others to determine the measure of success you achieve. The greatest weapon you have to ward against attack is self-motivation and you can increase the amount of air in your lungs by taking deep breaths of positive words every day that expel negativity and doubt.

Let's do an exercise right now. Take a deep breath and hold it for ten seconds. With your eyes closed, think about an area in your life that you are perhaps stagnant or struggling in, but you are still believing for a breakthrough in that area. Now, slowly, begin to exhale that breath. As you exhale, begin to saturate that breath with motivational words that will enter your atmosphere. "I am going to finish the journey." "I am going to be successful." Take another deep breath and hold it. This time, whatever you are thinking about, personalize it. Call it by name as you exhale and motivate your conviction. "My business is going to thrive." "My marriage is going to work." "My children are going to graduate." Repeat this exercise for ten minutes. Keep your eyes closed throughout, because opening your eyes may cause you to see things and become distracted. You have to zero in on your target and intentionally breathe life into your success. For some of you, things may literally be on life support right now. Your dreams are barely clinging to life, hooked up to other people that you are depending on and allowing to do the breathing for you. A family member. A friend. A spouse. You feel that you are unable to do it on your own and things are being held back because they aren't as motivated about your passion and purpose as you are. It's time to take a leap of faith and pull the plug. Take away the responsibility of your happiness, your encouragement and your success from others and be your biggest motivator.

Think about this. No one knows more about your victories, your defeats, your trials, your tests, or your sacrifices than you do. Likewise, no one has the right to judge you on your success by virtue of the fact that they were not part of your journey. They don't know what you had to give up, what you had to take on, what you lost, who you lost, they have no idea what approach you had to take, or the amount of work you had to put in to get to where you are today. All they know is what they see and what they hear while observing from the sidelines. Don't allow other people to stifle you and dictate whether or not you deserve to have what you desire. Tell yourself every day that you do. Know that you are deserving of the best. Despite where you may have started from, or how many times you faltered or fell along the way, regardless to how many may have gotten there before you, motivate yourself and keep on pressing until you have accomplished everything you set out to achieve. Your only competition is yourself. Your biggest obstacle is yourself. Your greatest challenge is yourself. Likewise, your most dedicated motivator ought to be you. Learn to live under a new atmosphere of positive words of affirmation and be the creator of that atmosphere. Determine that only positivity will thrive over and around you and that nothing will exist in your space that is counterproductive to your survival. You will succeed. You deserve to succeed after all that you have been through and you will succeed, because you are the creator of your destiny.

EIGHT
Work Smart

In this section, we focused on the work that is necessary for success to become a reality. We looked at the fact that real success does not just happen. It is the result of a systematic approach toward achieving a desired outcome. Although sometimes that outcome may seem unreachable, it isn't. At times, we may have to look outside of ourselves and get help and that is fine. It does not take away from the fact that this is all a part of your process and your journey toward success. Whatever approach you take, the fact is that you have to work toward your success. You cannot simply sit still and wait for things to come your way. You must work for it. But even as you work toward your goals, it is important that you work in a way that limits the possibility of exerting all your energy in a way that in the end, still does not achieve the result you are hoping for. In other words, you have to work smart.

Working smart requires having a plan in place. You may have a desire, for example, to start your own business. Perhaps it is your dream to be the first entrepreneur in your family. What it that going to look like in reality? No matter how many times you say that you are going to work for yourself, nothing is going to change until you put a plan in place and begin to work that plan. You have to know what type of business you are going to embark upon. You have to know where you are going to operate from and what resources you would need to get it done. In other words, there must be a plan in place that takes you from perception to reality. This plan, at some point, has to be developed to the place where you are able to answer all possible questions surrounding your idea. Company name, cost, competitors, location, work force, expected monthly and annual income and expenditure and more. You can't go to the bank for a loan to start up your business without a plan. They are going to want to see that you have put some work into planning out the steps required to get that plan off the ground and they definitely want to see measurable evidence to satisfy that you will be able to repay this loan in the required time period. A plan is important because it shows the probability of success for whatever it is you are setting out to do. A lot of good ideas never materialized not because they were unrealistic or unachievable, but because no one put in the necessary planning that would have equipped them for the next step. Of course, there are many things that your plan would not cover that will pop up along the way, but having a plan makes it more likely that you will be prepared to handle whatever comes along the way.

Having a plan is not going to ensure that your venture works. It's important to establish that fact. Having an architectural blueprint for your house in hand does not build the house. You still have to get materials, employ laborers, and there is an enormous amount of work that has to go into taking that vision and developing it. However, having those blueprints ensures that everyone knows where everything is supposed to go and gives you an idea as to what goes first, last and in between.

Too many people are living their lives without a plan and that is why it is so difficult for them to see their breakthrough coming. Marriages are melted because two people come into a relationship with no plan whatsoever, yet there is the expectancy that both husband and wife are automatically going to know what to do and how to do it. Then when one party fails to live up to those unexpressed expectations of the other, there is disappointment and frustration, which creates undue pressure and stress on the relationship. It is important in a relationship to declare what your expectations are. Simply put, there has to be a plan. You plan for your finances as a couple by putting a budget together. A lot of marriages suffer painful deaths because of mismanaged money. You need money to run a household. If the husband is taking his salary each month and gambling it away on some passion or addiction he has, then when the bills come along, there will be no money left to take care of the responsibilities of the home. This has serious implications in and of itself, because a woman is created with a need to feel safe and secure in a relationship, and a big part of that security is knowing that the household is financially capable of handling its responsibilities.

A budget tells your finances where to go. You can track your spending and see what is consuming the majority of your money, as well as what you are hardly spending on. As with everything in life, there will be the occasional things that pop up that you may not have catered for, but generally, budgeting keeps your wallet in check and offers you a particular peace of mind as you can control your spending, rather than your spending controlling you. But again, planning takes work. It takes both the husband and the wife agreeing to put in the time to put all their responsibilities on the table and devise a plan for not only dealing with those responsibilities, but finding a way for savings to happen as well. Planning takes time, but it generates so many positive rewards in the end that it becomes worth the work.

Apart from the financial part of marriage, there is the question of expansion. Are we planning to have any children in the marriage? If so, are we simply going to deal with children as they may come, or are we going to agree upon how many children we are going to have and at what point in our marriage we will have them? This is what you call, family planning. Many marriages are bursting at the seams because there was never a plan in place to deal with when the family expanded. Some couples got together without thinking about children and when pregnancy happened, there was fear and frustration and even anger in some instances. The fact is that most pregnancies, whether in or out of wedlock, were unplanned. One of the worst things that you can do is to bring a child into the world that you are not prepared for. Not just financially, but emotionally, physically and otherwise. Children are born daily into disadvantageous situations due to unpreparedness. The wife was just launching out into her new career. The husband was just about to travel on a business venture. There was no room set aside for a baby and the news of an addition to the family means hunting for a new apartment, which also spells higher rent. Pregnancy that is not planned can place pressure on the partnership. What you want to do is remove every possible challenge that you can from your marriage by starting out with a plan for as many areas of the marriage as possible.

Marriages can even meet a crossroad when one partner decides to pursue a passion that the other partner was not aware of. Or, perhaps they were aware, but there was never a discussion or a plan put in place that spoke to when that passion would receive attention. Whereas marriage is about supporting each other, it is still not fair or right for one partner to suddenly get up and announce that they are going to buy a car, or start a business. Certain questions have to be asked and answered that remove any ambiguity or concern, such as, Do we have the money to get the car right now and still fulfill the responsibilities of the home? Or, If you start the business right now, is the other party going to be left with the task of running the home on their own? Again, planning removes the element of surprise, which can be a major stressor in a relationship of any kind.

Planning is not only important for marriages, or businesses, but for your own personal life as well. If there is no plan for how you will live, then whatever happens around you can easily become the driving force for your decision making and ultimately, your actions. Your environment should never be what drives you. You should command and drive your environment. This can only happen when you have established who you are, what your purpose is and how you are going to fulfill that purpose. You have to have some sort of plan for your life, or life will create its own plan for you, which may be counterproductive to your success. How many times have you heard someone say that they wished they had started on a particular journey sooner? This does not have to be your testimony. Even if it already is, though, you can prevent yourself from staying even longer on a road that is never going to take you to your destination. You can plan your way out of your prison.

Are you in a marriage that isn't working? Plan your way to a more successful marriage. Plan for counseling with a professional that is agreed upon by both you and your spouse. Don't just choose someone that you are familiar with and that you believe will hear your side of the story and sway things in your favor. Get to someone who will be unbiased and honest, so your marriage doesn't just get what you want, but rather, it receives what it needs. Plan for date nights that can encourage time spent with each other, rather than time apart. Dates even within marriages are healthy tools that can help you discover new sides to your spouse that you never knew existed, as well as rediscover those sides that were buried over time, but that caused you to fall in love with them in the first place.

Is your business struggling? Plan your way to a better business. Put together strategies that make you relevant again in an ever-changing market. Accept the fact that what may have been working ten years ago might no longer be working today, because everything in life changes. Including what people's demands and interests are. Changes in lifestyle, location, taste, health, even religion, can all play a part in what drives and motivates the people who we depend upon to patronize whatever business we may provide. Planning for the success of your business includes committing to constantly familiarize yourself with the fluctuating temperature of your clientele.

Are you still struggling to meet the academic mark you set for yourself decades ago? You can still be successful and achieve that diploma or degree if you formulate a plan to get there. Plan your way to the podium. Yes, you now have a job to manage. Yes, you are now a single mother with added responsibilities. Yes, you are financially unable to see how that course is going to be pursued. Plan it anyway. Go on and enroll. There are many online, highly accredited universities that will allow you to take courses and pay in installments, or at the end of your academic pursuit. Plan your time. Decide what times of the day you will set aside for your school work and stick to the plan. Every good thing requires some level of self-sacrifice and I can tell you, academics demand much from you. But you have the capacity to fulfill whatever you put your mind to, especially if you plan for it.

Whether it is family, work, health, or whatever it is, success is driven by a plan. That plan is subject to change, to tweaking, to developing, but it demands our attention and it is critical to true success. Your plan may not look like anyone else's, but the truth is, it isn't supposed to, because you aren't like anyone else. As unique as you are, so will be the plan that directs your steps. Understand that as assuredly as you are destined to succeed, you are required to take the time to create the blueprint for your life. No one has the authority to design that blueprint but you. Don't live your entire life bending and bowing to the demands and expectations of others. Know your worth, know your potential, know that you house greatness in you and own your destiny. You have been endowed with the tools and resources to create your own success. Failure is nothing but the inability to accept this as fact and to live as such. Success is yours for the taking. Not success as it is defined by the world, but success in its truest sense, which is fulfilling the tasks that you have been placed on this earth to accomplish.

You make plans for so many things and people in your life every day. Why not plan for your success? Define what success looks like for you. Develop the steps that you need to take in order to make that success materialize. Put all the buffers in place that you can to mitigate against the challenges and obstacles that you anticipate would come against your progress. And constantly examine and reexamine where you are on your plan to success. I have repeated time and time again that success is not going to simply run into you. You have to run behind success. You have to not just want it, but you have to be willing to work toward it and if you do, you will have it. There is no way to have it without working toward it and you cannot work wisely toward your success without having a plan in place that instructs your work.

Begin working on the plan for your success today. If you already have your plan, work it. Don't ignore it, or put it down and try to manage without it. Your plan is your marching orders and it will determine not just how you start, but how you finish the work that must precede your success. So, don't spend another day wishing to be successful. Plan the meeting between you and your destiny and let it unfold while you are able to see it come to fruition. Nobody said that success would be easy. The journey, the approach, the work that success calls for, can all be tiresome, frustrating and downright demanding. Success is like a child that you have to care for and nurture until it grows and matures. At the end, the sacrifices are all worth it. You deserve to be successful and that is why you have read through this book. You want more out of your life. You want to produce more. You want to receive more. You want to experience more and in actuality, you should. But it is all up to you. There is no challenge, no obstacle, no disappointment, nothing that can keep you from being successful at whatever you put your mind to. It takes focusing on the right thing, and ensuring that your energies and efforts are channeled into what is meant for you. Remember, don't ignore your passion, because it is intimately and intricately tied to your purpose. Whatever your purpose, it will make room for you and it will expand your territory.

Your purpose is your passport to success. It gets you to the place where you are destined to be in life. It is what identifies you in the midst of counterfeits and what qualifies you for your calling. Purpose alone, however, does not guarantee you success. Throughout this book, we have sought to unveil what true success is and how you can achieve what is for you. You cannot live your life off of somebody else's success. You have to create your own. You have to discover your own path and find out what works for you. But you have to commit yourself to working diligently until the end. Even when you have achieved what you have set out to accomplish, you have to keep going. The same work that you put into acquiring it is the same work you have to put in to keeping it. Work does not have to feel like a curse if you learn to create your own work ethic and focus on what bears results for you, but without the desire to work, without the commitment to fulfill the task at hand, you will never live up to your full potential and you will continue to stand at the cusp of your mountaintop, but never actually conquer it. Don't forfeit all that is yours because of your unwillingness to work for it. Work is the key that unlocks every door with your name on it. It is time to unlock your success today. No more waiting, no more wasting. Work toward your goals today, and you will be able to celebrate your successes tomorrow.

You are already successful because you are built and created to be successful. Nothing can change who you are destined to be. The question is, will you live out that destiny? Will you reach out and grab your opportunities, and turn them into your greatest success stories? There is no one to blame if you don't. There are dreamers in this world, and there are people who get up every day and make dreams come to life. You can be successful. You can achieve everything that you set out to accomplish, and more. All you have to do is make up your mind to work hard until you see your harvest. Farmers don't throw in the towel because the ground is tough. When they can't turn the soil with their strength, they invest in equipment that can. They do whatever it takes to put their seeds in the ground and nurture them until they grow.

What is the seed that you possess? What idea? What plan? What goal? Whatever your seed, plant it.

Water it. Keep the weeds and pests from devouring it. Shield it from predators that want to snuff it out. Protect it from the storms of doubt, fear, and negativity. Press on, until you see the first fruits blossom through your tireless labor. You can be successful at whatever you put your mind to. The Universe rewards the diligent. Know that once you start working, resources will find you. Strength will locate you. Help will accompany you. It is time to resurrect the buried things that were laid to rest by doubt. You mourned over abandoned dreams that you left behind because of negative words spoken over your life. It's time to dig the dirt off of your success and let it live. Be the success story that you were created to be, and let every achievement pave the way for your next one.

CONLUSION

We have all heard the adage, "Nothing good comes easy," and it is generally true. The heavier the goal, the heavier the lifting that is involved. We all have goals, yet, not everyone accomplishes them. What makes the difference is how we handle the journey, the approach, and the work needed to get it done. If we can master these three skills, and see them as necessary vehicles for our success, then we would make the valuable sacrifices they all call for. Our journey, our approach, and our work towards success, and towards anything in life, determines the outcome.

If there is one thing that we could tell you, that we were sure would encourage you, it would be simply this: Don't give up! Give yourself grace to get it wrong sometimes. Learn to laugh at the blunders along the way. Don't make your critics your counselors, unless at the end of the day, they are showing you how to make better decisions. And love yourself, because you are great, you are powerful, and you are born to succeed.

It may take some persons one year to reach their target, while it may take others five years to meet the same target. Guess what? The most important thing in both instances is that people are on the move. They aren't staying stagnant, hoping and praying that their circumstance changes. Rather, they are actively participating in creating their own success story. You can be one such person.

Do not be afraid to start your journey, whatever it might be. Yes, the distance between the start and finish lines may seem so vast from where you stand at the moment, but with each step, that distance closes in, and the vision gets clearer, and louder, and closer. Start your journey. It precedes finishing it.

Not getting the results you are hoping to achieve? Sometimes, it may mean changing your approach. Rather than abandoning the vision, adjust the lens. See what other steps you can take to get to where you're hoping to go. Instead of turning back due to the unforeseen obstacle, go around. Dig under. Climb over. Or, move it completely out of the way. The point is, keep going. Where there is a will, there is truly a way, and the diligent and committed will always find it.

Finally, don't be afraid to work. Hard, smart work leads to a more successful life, because it is the results of our work that bears fruit. You don't get to reap a harvest without first sowing seeds. You don't become an elite athlete just by loving the sport. You have to train, you have to practice, you have to eat and sleep right, and you have to work hard. Work should never be a deterrent. Instead, it should be a motivator, because it culminates with the desired reward.

By now, you are aware that there is no easy, one-size-fits-all, magical, easy, glorious road to this thing called success. It should also be noted that success is not going to look the same for everyone. Put a hearing device to the back of a child's ear who has not heard from birth, turn it on, say something, and watch that child fix their gaze in the direction of where the sound originated from. That is success. Take the drug addict who is hooked on getting a high multiple times throughout the day, who realizes they have a problem and they simply admit themselves to a rehab program. That is success. Every day, there are success stories taking place around us, and likewise, there are success stories taking place in our very lives, but because they seem insignificant compared to somebody else's story, we don't see it as much. Don't despise the little things. You must identify and celebrate the small breakthroughs, because they motivate you to take on the other challenge that comes along.

We want you to succeed. If you've reached this page, and you're still reading, then, "Congratulations. You have succeeded." Make success a habit in your life. Make embarking upon the journey, adjusting your approach, and putting in the work the principles that precede your prosperity. Your life can never remain stagnant when you live according to these three principles of success. Are you ready to redefine success, and to start meeting the mark?

REFERENCES

1. AzQuotes. (n.d.). Dr. Phil McCraw Quotes. Retrieved from https://www.azquotes.com/quote/905548

2. Barrett, W. (2019, March 29). PAUL: Persecutor, Preacher, Prisoner.

3. Buddha: "To be idle is short of death and to be diligent is a way of life; foolish people are idle, wise people are diligent." Retrieved from [BrainyQuote](https://www.brainyquote.com/quotes/buddha_118312)

4. Cummings, E. E.: "It takes courage to grow up and become who you really are." Retrieved from [Goodreads](https://www.goodreads.com/quotes/806-it-takes-courage-to-grow-up-and-become-who-you)

5. Edwards, J. (2019, February 1). Arise & Shine: It's Time To Declare Yourself Blessed.

6. Galileo: "You cannot teach a man anything, you can only help him find it within himself." Retrieved from [Goodreads](https://www.goodreads.com/quotes/15403-you-cannot-teach-a-man-anything-you-can-only-help)

7. Jain, V. (2014). 3D model of attitude. *International Journal of Advanced Research in Management and Social Sciences*, 3(3), 1-12.

8. Les Brown: "Too many of us are not living our dreams because we are living our fears." Retrieved from [Steemit](https://steemit.com/quoteoftheday/@wiseeyes/quote-of-the-day-too-many-of-us-are-not-living-our-dreams-because-we-are-living-our-fears-les-brown)

9. Maxwell, J. (Host). (n.d.). John Maxwell Leadership Podcast. [Audio podcast]. Retrieved from https://johnmaxwellleadershippodcast.com/episodes/john-maxwell-your-influence-inventory

10. Maya Angelou. Retrieved from [Your Positive Oasis](https://yourpositiveoasis.com/maya-angelou-quotes-life-love-happiness/)

11. Nicholls, D. (2009). *One Day: Soon to be a major Netflix series*. Hachette UK.

12. Onderko, P. (2015, November 4). Follow these 6 things and you will be humbler. *Success Magazine.*

13. Quoting.com: "IF your pride is bigger than your Heart and your ego is bigger than your head, grow up or you will be alone for life." Retrieved from [Quoting.com](https://www.quoting.com)

14. Roosevelt, T.: Retrieved from [AZQuotes](https://www.azquotes.com/quote/1056535)

15. Tesla, N.: "I could only achieve success in my life through self-discipline, and I applied it until my wish and my will became one." Retrieved from [AZQuotes](https://www.azquotes.com/author/14543-Nikola_Tesla)

16. Thompkins, A. (2018, December 25). The Potter's Power: A Simple Introductory Guide to Understanding the Destiny You Didn't Choose.

17. Unknown: "Blind Spots are like rowing a boat that's full of holes, but you can't find the holes."

18. Vybs Live, M. Retrieved from [OwnQuotes](https://ownquotes.com/quote/152158)

19. Wagner, K. V. (n.d.). Quotes for attitude. Retrieved November 5, 2008, from About.com: Psychology website: http://psychology.about.com/od/profilesofmajorthinkers/a/jamesquotes.htm

20. Wall, L., & Russell, K. (Eds.). (1992). *The Road to Success Is Always Under Construction*. Walrus Productions.

21. Wayne Dyer. Retrieved from [AZQuotes](https://www.azquotes.com/quote/810045)

22. Whitman, W.: Retrieved from [One Journey](https://onejourney.net/walt-whitman-quote-dismiss-whatever-insults-your-own-soul/)

ABOUT THE AUTHORS

Joshua Edwards

Joshua Emmanuel Edwards, the first of six children is happy to be the Husband of one wife Elvetta Edwards, Father of two sons Josiah and Lemuel, and Pastor of God's people. Mr. Edwards is also an Author, coach, inspirational speaker, counselor, and real estate agent. He loves the Lord Jesus and has a passion for seeing children, youth and people be successful in all areas of life.

ABOUT THE AUTHORS

Albert Thompkins

Dr. Albert Thompkins, IV is a licensed psychotherapist, public speaker, author, spiritual life coach, and mentor. Currently, he is the Director of Student Affairs and Campus Counselor at H. Lavity Stoutt Community College. He is also a psychotherapist at Therapy 2 Thrive Psychological and Developmental Services in the BVI.

In 2011, Dr. Thompkins earned a Doctorate of Philosophy (Ph.D.) at the University of Texas at Austin. His work there involved assessing the mental health policies of faith-based organizations, churches and communities and its impact on those with mental illness. He is also the author of the book entitled "The Potter's Power: Understanding the Destiny You Did Not Choose".

Dr. Albert is happily married to his wife Shanique of 28 years. They are also the proud parents of two children, Albert 5th and Naomi.

ABOUT THE AUTHORS

Walter Barrett

Walter Barrett is a husband, and a father, a pastor, and a counselor, a motivational speaker, a restorative justice officer, and a passionate author. With a heart for rehabilitation, he works at a prison where he seeks to help inmates transition from incarceration back into their communities successfully. He sees success as crucial not only for himself, but for all those around him, as you will learn as you delve into his portion of this book, "The Work to Success "

CONTACT THE AUTHORS

Email: JawsGlobal3@gmail.com

Facebook: JAWS Global

Made in the USA
Columbia, SC
02 April 2024